DANA MENTINK

DEADLY SANDS

By Harlequin Bestseller
DANA MENTINK

Copyright © 2014 by Dana Mentink
Forget-Me-Not Romances

Discover more romance novels at ForgetMeNotRomances.com, a division of Winged Publications.

This book is a work of fiction. The names, characters, places, and incidents are products of the writer's imagination or have been used fictitiously and are not to be construed as real. Any resemblance to persons, living or dead, actual events, locales or organizations is entirely coincidental.

All rights reserved. No part of this book may be reproduced, scanned, or distributed in any manner whatsoever without written permission from the author except in the case of brief quotation embodied in critical articles and reviews.

ISBN-13: 979-8-3485-4340-2

Chapter One

"Lucille. You can't just walk around a wild animal preserve with your pockets filled with meat. It's an accident waiting to happen."

Lucille continued to chew, leaning against her Moped. "Look here, Miss Martina Barr. Don't you be telling me how to do my job. You think at the ripe old age of twenty seven you're smarter than me? I been alive twice as long and I know a thing or two that you ain't even heard yet. I am the head gamekeeper at this joint, ain't I? I have a way with them animals, don't I?"

I hated to admit it, but she was right. The woman had worked for me for the past two years and she was a wildlife savant. Meat or no meat, the animals responded to her, seemingly unaware that the woman was a few eggs short of an omelet. Ficky, her fiancé, appeared equally blind to her eccentricities. "I couldn't keep this place running without you Lucille," I said, "but I still worry about you smelling like dinner to the carnivores. Couldn't you at least carry vegetables or fruit around if you need a snack?"

She didn't dignify my idiotic suggestion with an answer. As far as I knew, Lucille never ate anything but meat. Pork, turkey, hot dogs. Once I'd even seen her carry an entire leg of lamb in her cavernous pocket. How she hadn't been devoured by the mountain lion we nursed to health last year was totally beyond me. Maybe they figured she was too tough and stringy to bother with. She squinted at me, adding even more wrinkles to her already seamed face.

A wiry haired javelina trotted over in the wake of Lucille's Moped and stuck his piggy snout against my knee.

I ignored him.

He poked again, his black shaggy sides heaving with excitement.

I remained stoic.

Then the animal began to make happy grunting noises. That did it. He looked so cute, dancing there on his delicate hooves. I relented and bent over to scratch his side. "Tito, you are a poor excuse for a pig."

Javelinas are not domestic creatures. They are wild peccaries, more pig like than anything else, but Tito is confused on that subject. After we treated a wound on his side last year, Lucille and I released him into the wild. He returned to Desert Star the next day. We released him again. Same deal. I've lost count of how many times we've tried to return this creature to his God-given piggy life. Tito's just not into being a javelina. He'd rather be a Golden Retriever.

Content with his dose of affection, Tito sat in my shadow and rested his head on his hooves.

"Where'd you find him this time?"

"Sitting at the front gate, waiting. We might as well stop trying to force him back into the big wide world. It ain't his bag." Lucille laughed and reached a hand into the pocket of her pants, extracting another wad of turkey. She began to chew, rolling the meat around to avoid the spots in her mouth unfilled by teeth. "So, Marty," she said, as she eased her twiggy legs off the ancient Moped. "Did Maynard bust out again?"

"Yes." I crammed a baseball cap over my hair. "I can't figure out how he does it. The door was latched tight last night. I triple-checked it."

"He's smarter than your average fox. At least he ain't on the loose in your trailer like that squirrel. You're gonna have to let him share your toothbrush one of these days." Lucille dissolved into a gale of wheezy laughter.

With a sigh I returned to scouring the brittlebrush in search of my escape artist gray fox. You'd think such a clever Houdini wouldn't't have lost his leg to an SUV in the first place, but perhaps he missed out on the fox survival training meeting. In any case, I'd found the door of his enclosure open at the crack of early when I arrived with his grasshoppers and crayfish.

I tripped over a branch and came close to falling. It might have been my imagination, but I could swear that Bob the bobcat was laughing from his nearby sanctuary. I shot him a look and he curled up, a bundle of innocence, on his bed. Bob is deaf, so he didn't hear my steady stream of discontent as I set off again to look for the fox. As I walked, I sucked in the gorgeous panorama that continued to thrill me after eight years.

The hospital portion of Desert Star Animal Preserve is perched on a small plateau, protected by a stand of cottonwoods and nicely peppered with shrubs and wildflowers. The rest of the property is a great sprawling mass of high desert: trees, cliffs and the odd sandstone cave, all sun baked to perfection. It's the middle of Arizona's nowhere, but it's mine, all thirty acres of it. If I wear khakis, and hide my dark bob of hair under a cap, I can almost disappear into the landscape. Invisibility is on my top ten priority list. Why else would I buy a parcel of land in a town called Ferocious?

Lucille whistled as she bent to look under the bushes.

I did the same, without the whistling. Instead, I issued

ultimatums. "Listen, Maynard Fox, you naughty thing. You come here right now or it will be the end of your crayfish supply forever and I mean forever."

"Now you're just gonna offend him and he ain't never gonna come out."

A bead of sweat trickled down my cheek. "I can take care of my animals. You've got other things to worry about. Did you go in for your dress fitting?" As maid of honor for Lucille's bizarre upcoming nuptials, I felt the burden of responsibility.

"I ain't decided on a dress. All the fluff and beads give me the willies. Plus you got to wear a petticoat. Who invented that odd contraption? I'm thinking about wearing some spanking new overalls. You could wear overalls too, to do your honor maid thing. Not that you got much to fill out no overalls."

I opened my mouth to offer a snappy comeback when the missile fell out of the sky. If I hadn't been wearing my Cardinals baseball cap, I think it would have broken my nose. As it was, the thing bounced off the brim and whacked into the ground with a puff of dust.

When I recovered my senses I snatched it up. It was a rock wrapped with scruffy newspaper.

"What in the name of cheese is that?" Lucille peered at the thing.

"It's a rock."

"You don't say." She rolled her eyes. "Where did it come from?"

Then we both became aware of a noise that grew louder with each passing minute.

"Grab that pig!" Lucille shouted.

We had only a split second before the plane plummeted down from the sky.

If Tito was a Golden Retriever he would have barked his fool head off. As it was, he grunted and squealed at the rough treatment. I didn't exactly throw him, but I sort of grabbed and shoved as I rolled out of the way of the incoming plane. We both wound up in a scratchy bunch of shrubs.

I could see through the branches of my nest that the small plane had finally come to a standstill, nose furrowed into the ground. Smoke billowed from the front end. The landing gear had either snapped off or had been forced into the soil by the impact. It came to a shuddery stop in the welcome area, narrowly avoiding the rough benches where visitors to my desert paradise sit and wait for their tour or overnight experience to commence.

Tito let out one last squeal of outrage before he trotted away, curly tail stiff with indignation. I extracted myself from the foliage and looked around for Lucille.

She clambered out from under the bench and brushed herself off. "What kind of idiot is flyin' that thing? Don't he know this ain't no airport?"

The idiot chose that moment to slam open the door of the cockpit and tumble to the ground. I ran to assist him just as a plume of flame erupted from inside the cabin. The heat was intense as I grabbed his arm and we both ran away from the burning plane. Through the crackling, I thought I heard another door bang.

He looked over his shoulder as we moved.

"Lucille," I hollered as I dragged the pilot away from the vile smoke. "Is there anyone else in there? Can you see?" She waved a hand in front of her face. "Nah, too much smoke. Oh wait a spell. I think there's a…"

Her words were drowned in a horrendous pop. The windshield shattered, sending bits of glass shooting everywhere. I covered the injured man as best I could, ignoring the prickle of pain on the back of my neck. The guy wasn't too keen about my protective maneuvers. He sat up and shoved me away.

"Get off." He was a big man, skin white as tapioca

except for the purple bruises that covered his forehead and the blood pouring from his nose.

I shook the glass out of my hair. "I'm sorry. I was trying to help you. Was there a passenger in the plane?"

"No, no one but me and I don't need help." He got up, hanging onto a bench for support.

"You're bleeding. Are you hurt badly?"

"No, so just mind your business."

A hot spot of anger began to creep up my ribcage. "Listen, mister. You shouldn't take that tone with someone who's trying to help you. I was minding my business, until you crashed your plane onto my property."

He wiped the blood from his forehead with the back of his hand. "From what I've seen, there isn't much to your property. Middle of a sand pile."

The hot spot increased to manhole cover size. "Well, it looked a whole lot better before you landed this hunk of junk here."

His thick eyebrows came together. "Listen sister, I had some equipment failure. Otherwise I never would have put her down here."

"I'm not your sister, and you're lucky my sand was here to absorb the impact. You could have smashed head first into the cliffs."

He ignored me and hauled himself to his feet, casting another uneasy glance at the burning plane.

"I think I'll go make a call to the police. Maybe they can tow your plane out of here."

His eyes widened a fraction, but he didn't answer.

Ficky came puffing up to the scene, his cheeks pink with exertion, filmy eyes wide under his coke bottle lenses. "Heard somethin.' You okay Lucy?"

Lucille nodded, gracing him with one of her infrequent smiles. "Yes, Ficky. Just fine, Honey. This guy crashed his plane. Did you hear it?"

He nodded, casting a suspicious glance at the bloodied

pilot. "Flunked your landing lessons?"

The man glared at them both and took a step toward the plane. Another hiss of flame made him recoil. He let loose with a stream of obscenities. Ficky tried to strike up a conversation but the man snarled at him to keep away.

"I've had enough of this." I stalked toward my office trailer, slammed inside and threw the newspaper wrapped rock which I'd stashed in my pocket, onto the counter. Lucille joined me in a minute. Ficky stayed on the porch step to watch the bonfire.

We called the police station in Juniper, the next town over. They were excited to hear about an actual happening. Things are not prone to happening in Ferocious and the surrounding towns so anything out of the ordinary rates way high on the excitement scale. They promised to dispatch the Chief Herself.

I hung up with satisfaction. "Let him explain equipment malfunction to Chief Spotter."

Lucille followed me into the office, picking her teeth with a fingernail.

"There's nobody else in the plane that I could find. You think Fly Boy isn't coming clean?"

"I don't feel he's taking the proper tone for a man who has crashed his plane on a person's property. It wouldn't surprise me at all if he was lying through his teeth."

"Chief will get a straight story out of him, all right. She could get blood from a turnip."

A familiar sound brought us racing outside again. We were in time to see Lucille's Moped heading for the front gate, dwarfed by the large man driving it. Ficky hollered at him.

Lucille ran, waving her arms in wild circles. "Stop! You lily-livered plane-crashing stinker pilot! That's my Moped."

The man pressed the bike as fast as it would go as he raced away.

Lucille turned to stare at me, her mouth open in a

shocked circle. Then she looked at Ficky who stood immobile, dust swirling around his bald head. "Ficky, do something. I've been robbed. Defend the honor of your wife-to-be!"

Ficky's glaze darted back and forth from Lucille to me and then back again. Without a word he started sprinting down the road in hopeless pursuit of the thief.

Lucille watched him. "Poor Ficky. He ain't never going to catch that Moped. Still it was mighty nice of him to snap into action like that, wasn't it?" Then her eyes narrowed into angry slits. "That guy stole my bike. When I get hold of him, the plane crash is gonna be the blasted highlight of his day."

I didn't doubt it for a second. I'd seen what happened to the guy who tried to bilk her out of forty-seven cents at the ice cream shop.

In the distance I heard the screech of an approaching siren. More comforting than that, I saw the battered Jeep of my favorite person on the planet: Joe Hala. My heart did that old pitter-patter-thunk thing as he unrolled his tall frame from the front seat.

"Marty. What's going on?" He took in the burning plane, shading his eyes with one hand. "Are you all right? Is anybody hurt?"

I fell into his embrace, relishing the tickle of his braid on my cheek. "We're fine. The pilot stole Lucille's Moped and took off." I was sad when he pulled me to arm's length, his eyes searching my face. "You're sure you aren't hurt?"

I smiled. "Not a scratch."

He gave me a relieved nod before he grabbed a fire extinguisher from the Jeep and began to squirt out the flames.

His dark eyes flashed in his lovely mocha skin as he let loose with bursts of chemical. "Why would the guy steal her Moped?"

"I don't know. The police are on their way. I guess they'll have to figure it out."

"Are any of the animals hurt?"

"I don't think so, unless they're scared from the noise." I jumped. "Oh man, I almost forgot. Maynard got away again. I was looking for him when the plane crashed. He could have been flattened. Will you help me search?"

"Sure thing." The flames were gone, leaving only a hissing and vile smelling smoke in their wake. He put down the extinguisher.

We began the hunt but stopped after only a few minutes when the squad car rolled up.

Chief Josie Spotter eased her bulk out of the seat. "Hey, Marty, Joe. Why is Ficky running down the road like his pants are on fire?"

I sighed. "Ummm, I think he was trying to catch up with Lucille's stolen Moped. How are you feeling?"

"As good as a woman eight months pregnant can feel." She pushed the cap back on her swollen face. "I've got ankles the size of pork roasts. If George wants any more kids after this, he's going to have to raise goats. Six is my limit."

Joe laughed. "You've almost got enough for a baseball team."

"I hate baseball."

"Right," Joe said, quickly losing his grin. "I'm going to go check the animals. I'll keep an eye out for Maynard. Maybe he headed back to his enclosure."

The chief removed the cap of her pen with her mouth as she walked around the smoking plane. I trailed along behind, filling her in on the events leading up to the loss of Lucille's Moped.

"Yeah," Lucille snapped as she joined us. "I am gonna find that no good fly boy and teach him a thing or two about respectin' other people's property. The sneaky rat fink."

Chief Spotter clapped a hand to her back with a grimace. "Maybe you should let us handle things, Lucille."

"You can have what's left of him when I'm done."

She sighed. "I'm going to get my camera. I'll be right

back. Don't touch anything." She waddled off to the car.

Joe put a hand on my arm.

"Looks like all the animals are fine. I gave Bob another treatment for that tick bite, but I think it's healing up okay. No sign of the fox."

Joe is half Yavapai Indian and half veterinarian. He would be a complete vet if he hadn't run out of money for tuition. That's why he came home from college to work here in Ferocious. He runs overnight tours on the Desert Star and helps me care for my family of injured animals. We're lucky, me and the critters.

Lucille shot out a gnarled finger toward the bushes. "There. I just saw Maynard, two o'clock."

All three of us whirled to eyeball the mass of prickle poppy. Sure enough, a set of brown eyes regarded us from behind the leafy screen.

"I'll go around behind," I mouthed to Joe. He nodded and inched forward. Lucille took up the left flank position. When we were all in place, I dove. Maynard dove, too. He was much more graceful in his movements. He slipped easily between Joe's legs and headed towards the plane.

I scrambled under the wing to get him away before he touched any of the hot metal or inhaled fumes. My fingers just brushed his silky tail when he switched directions and headed back toward the office trailer.

As I straightened to move out from under the wreck, a flash of color caught my eye. On a patch of unscorched metal right under the door was a green magnet in the shape of a pickle. I bent close to squint. A message read 'In a Pickle? Call Dilly's plumbing.' Underneath was a phone number.

"Hey, Chief," I called. "Come and have a look at this. I wonder how in the world it got to be stuck on the outside of the plane."

There was no answer. "Chief?" I called again.

A low moan wafted through the air.

Joe and Lucille looked over. We dashed toward the noise. Chief Spotter's car door was open and she lay on her side, across the back seat, groaning.

"Are you okay?" Joe panted.

"Does it look like I'm okay?" Her face was covered with sweat and she gasped in pain.

"Well actually, you look a bit, um…"

She cut me off. "I told my doctor that I'm always early. George, Jr., Willa, Penny, Paul, Frankie, they've all come early, every last one. Spotters are early for everything. Would he listen to me? No. You're fine, he says. No action any time soon, he says. You can work as long as you like, he says."

My mouth fell open. "Are you in labor?"

She shot me a look which made me glad she didn't have her gun handy. "No, Marty. I'm just sitting here practicing my meditation." Another cry escaped her lips and she rolled onto her back.

I started to sputter. "Oh gosh. Oh man. Oh…"

"Oh relax," she snapped. "I've called for an ambulance. Deputy Fisk is on his way to handle the investigation." She dialed her cell phone. A ripple of muscles across her abdomen made her squeeze the phone in a death grip. "I need to speak to Dr. Rochelle, please, and if you value your life do not put me on hold."

"Do you need anything?" Joe looked from me to Lucille to the chief. "Do you want a glass of water or something?"

"No, thank you." The unfortunate doctor came on the line. "Ah, Dr. Rochelle. How nice to hear your voice. Doing well today? Glad to hear it. Guess where I am? No, no. I'm in my squad car and guess what I'm doing? That's right, oh learned man of medicine. I'm in LABOR." Her voice made the windows of the car vibrate.

We decided to take a few steps back to give the woman a bit of privacy. It didn't make any difference as her words carried clearly in the late morning air. "That's right. L-A-B-

O-R. And where are you? In the air-conditioned HOSPITAL where I would be if you had LISTENED to me."

I grimaced. Dr. Rochelle was going to need to give himself an epidural after she finished with him. There wouldn't be anything left but some fingernails and a stethoscope. Joe and I exchanged looks and tried not to smile. The ambulance and Deputy Fisk rolled up at precisely the same moment. Two paramedics rushed to the car and fought their way through the stream of angry verbiage pouring out the window.

Deputy Fisk, a twitchy man with skinny legs and an abnormally large head, pulled out a notebook and headed over to us. Though his scalp was bare as a cue ball, the mustache on his lip was full and bushy. "Hey folks. Seems like you've had some excitement today. Why don't you tell me about it?"

I recounted the bizarre morning as best I could while he scratched it down in a notebook.

"So there was only one passenger in the plane?"

The question brought back some of my earlier unease. "I did have this weird feeling that someone got out just before the fire started."

Fisk raised an eyebrow. "Did you see the person?"

"No. We checked after the flames died down."

Lucille nodded. "I checked real good, too. Nothing in there but smoke. I would have noticed a burned-up corpse for sure."

I made sure the detective got a good look at the pickle magnet. He seemed unimpressed. "All right. We'll get a crew over here to comb through the wreckage."

A cell phone flew out of the chief's open car door, causing a paramedic to duck.

"I'd better brief the chief. I'll be right back." Fisk strode purposefully along. He stuck his head through the driver's side door and then immediately pulled it out again. For a moment, his eyes widened to the size of doorknobs. The color drained from his face and he fell to his knees.

"Aaack," was all that came out of his ashen lips.

The second paramedic grunted and hooked Fisk under his armpits, dragging him over to the ambulance. He shook his head in disgust. "You're a cop. Can't you take the sight of bodily fluids? What are you, some kind of sissy? Sit here and stay out of the way."

Fisk responded with another moan and flopped backward onto the gurney where he'd been deposited. The medic sighed, helped his colleague remove Chief Spotter from the car and strap her to another gurney. She eyed her stricken deputy and muttered something under her breath. "We'll handle the investigation as soon as I can get an able-bodied officer over here. Don't touch anything. Do you understand, Marty? Don't let anybody else touch it, either."

"Yes, ma'am," I said as I retrieved her cell from the ground and handed it over. "Uh, good luck with, er, having the baby and all that."

She snorted and in a moment, they were gone.

We turned to look at the charred plane sitting in the middle of Desert Star Preserve. It lay there like a hideous dead spider. Folks were going to be hard pressed to reconcile a downed aircraft with the wilderness landscape they came to Ferocious to see. "I cannot believe this. We're a tiny spot in the middle of a huge desert and the guy has to put down here. What are we supposed to do now?"

Joe cocked his head. "I don't know, but I think we'd better find Maynard before sunset."

The dark was closing in when we found the adventurer, or more accurately, he found us.

Part of the delay was due to the drama of retrieving the heroic Ficky from his ill-fated Moped rescue mission.

Stan at the bike shop had driven over with a loaner for Lucille to use until she could find the pilot and pulverize him to get hers back. It took her an hour and a half to find Ficky and motor the exhausted man back to the office. He required several bottles of water and a cold compress before Lucille was able to take him home.

After we'd given up trying to find Maynard, Joe and I made our way to one of our favorite spots, a low bluff that looked down on the small bend of dry creek bed that filled occasionally after spring rains. It was only a half mile away from the crash site but the plane's final resting place was hidden behind a swell of ground and trees.

We made a makeshift bench there, out of a fallen log. A pocket of seep willow trees provided shade or shelter depending on the weather. The view was unparalleled, a panorama so unspoiled and pristine it almost hurt to look at. I inhaled the unique scent of dry ground and mesquite. From my log seat I could see the sun mellowing into the horizon and the crags and cliffs that dotted my piece of ferocious paradise.

And, of course, the profile of my gorgeous Joe only complimented the scene. He has that wide face and strong chin that make my eyelids flap up and down. The braid he always wears holds back the long black hair that I have seen loose only twice. On those two occasions I came close to wetting my pants at the sheer follicular drama.

Oh, I'm not in love with the man. Much.

It wouldn't be possible to love him completely because I'm not clear on how healthy love works and I like to figure a thing out before I try it. I've got the manipulative, possessive and generally poisonous kind all worked out, but that's not for me. I want to do the love thing right when I decide to give it a try.

No, it's not love with Joe, just a strong sense of belonging. We go together like macaroni and cheese. If you don't have cheese, you've just got a sad, naked pile of noodles. Joe is my cheese. That's not amore; it's just culinary common sense. I haven't explained the theory to him yet. I'm saving it for an opportune moment.

Joe put his arm around my shoulders and I snuggled in tight. The day caught up with me and I felt all my life juices slide down to my socks. Except for the warm, happy, mac-n-cheese feeling. I was content to sit there and wait for the stars to make their appearance. Joe seemed to feel the same way. The crashed plane might as well have been a million miles away.

A rustling in the bushes made us straighten. Maynard, the escape artist fox with impeccably bad timing, poked his head out of a bush. He twitched his whiskers.

I heaved myself off the log and approached slowly. "You are a naughty boy. Come here, you bad thing. I'm putting you on a time out."

The fox decided to cooperate. He must have been getting hungry. Out he hobbled on his three legs. I scooped him up and gave him a nice scratch behind the ears, enjoying the feel of his thick coat against my fingers. As I straightened, I got a good look at the thing which lay on the other side of the foliage.

My stomach clenched and my mouth went dry. "Joe?"

"Yes?"

I could feel my vocal chords begin to tense up. Prickles erupted all over my skin. "I think you'd better hold Maynard."

"Why?"

He had just enough time to grab the animal before the screaming began.

DANA MENTINK

Chapter Two

Hysteria is exhausting.
After about half a minute of screaming and twitching like a spider on a hot plate, my body decided to take a different tact. I walked a few yards away and threw up.

I felt better. A little.

Joe gave me some privacy. He murmured soothing words while he did some preliminary investigation, gently parting the foliage that partially concealed the dead man. When I was finished he handed me a handkerchief and the fox. It's so quaint that Joe carries those things around. Handkerchiefs, not foxes. Anyway, he whipped out a cell phone and dialed.

"No, the man's been dead a while from the looks of him. I checked for a pulse anyway, but he's pretty dead. Okay. I'll make sure no one disturbs any evidence." He clicked off the phone. "Deputy Fisk is on his way."

"Why don't I take comfort in that?"

We both stared at the body with morbid fascination. The

whole thing was surreal. Aside from the blood and his position on the ground, he didn't look dead at all. It wouldn't have surprised me if the bearded gentlemen stood up and said, "Boo!"

"How did a dead guy wind up here?"

Joe pointed up at the sky.

I gasped. "Of course. He was the second passenger in the plane. I knew I heard someone jump out before the thing went boom. Why did he crawl all the way over here? Why not stay where he could get help?"

Joe knelt beside the body, which was curled in a fetal position against the log. "People do funny things when they go into shock. I'm not a people doctor, but it looks to me like he bled to death. We'll have to leave that up to the coroner." He sighed. "What a bad ending for such a brilliant guy."

I double blinked. "You know him?"

Joe sighed. "As a matter of fact, yes."

My mouth fell open. "You do? I mean, you did?"

"His name is Peter Spiegel. He's a professor of earth science at a private university in Phoenix."

"Did you take classes from him?"

"No, he took classes from me."

I frowned. "Huh?"

"Last week, he went on the Tuesday overnighter after our high desert seminar. We chatted about his academic life."

I felt another wave of hysteria coming on. "Oh man. So he went on an official Desert Star-sanctioned trip and now he's dead and I've got a plane crashed on my property. Wreckage and corpses. This is what they call negative press."

Joe rubbed my neck. "It's all right, Marty. Keep breathing. Most likely no one will ever hear about these things outside of our tiny community."

It wasn't our tiny community I was worried about. Bad press had a habit of working its way up the food chain and there was a guy at the top of that chain who scared the stuffing out of me. To everyone else, I was Marty Barr, owner of a desert nowhere. But to him…I shuddered.

I cuddled Maynard under my chin, comforted by the wee hammering of his heart. I felt a sudden need to be far from the broken body. "I'm going to go put the animals away for the night. Can you stay here and keep an eye on, er, the professor?"

"Sure. Why don't we say a prayer for him before you go?"

I took one of his warm hands in my clammy one and we prayed for the cold, dead man. Praying is fairly new to me, but Joe says it's not about the spoken prayer as much as the person doing the praying. I gave that sadness up to God and hoped He could make some good out of the catastrophe

Joe gave me a hug and a kiss on the forehead. "Things will get better, don't worry."

I didn't worry all the way back to the small roundabout. That's a fenced area that houses about an acre of rocks, shrubs, trees and hidey holes. It's the place where the animal patients that won't eat each other hang out for exercise. We try to keep the animals as free and as wild as possible until they can be released. Of course, some of them can't. That was my current fear for J.R. He's a jack rabbit. A group of men playing paintball in the desert decided to have a go at a four legged target. J.R. is completely blind in one eye, but Joe and I were hoping he would regain enough vision in the other to allow him to go back home.

Though some of the critters would be fine in the roundabout at night, others would be easy pickings for night predators. Bob the bobcat was already back in his pen because he looks at J.R. like a tasty hors douevre so they don't socialize much.

The sky was a slate gray as I headed into the roundabout to corral the two inmates. "Okay all you furry and scaly types. It's time for bed." The chuckwalla lizard, sporting a set of stitches on his rough hide, scurried right into his travel cage. Such a cooperative reptile. Either that or he saw the dark expression on my face and figured I was coming to barbecue him. I closed the door and secured him for the night.

As I hunted around for J.R., I worried some more about that dead man. Was it coincidence that a guy who took a tour here last week happened to be flying over the property on a doomed plane? And what were the odds that the same guy would stagger away from the wreck only to die on Desert Star property?

I was so engrossed in my thoughts; I didn't notice J.R. hiding until he bounded out of the shrub like a jack in the box. I restarted my heart and we began a ridiculous waltz. I approached him on tiptoe, he waited until I was within arm's length and then he shot away to a far corner.

I saw him quivering, ears rigid, under the cottonwood tree. "Hey, J.R. How are you doing there buddy? You're running around pretty good for a rabbit with one working eye. Are you getting your sight back little guy?"

J.R. took that opportunity to barrel straight into my legs. The impact knocked him on his back, giving me enough time to grab him by the scruff and wrap a towel around his razor sharp claws. I gently covered his poor ruined eyes with the other side of the cloth and he went still. My heart sank even lower. A wild creature dependent on his eyes for survival, made helpless by cruel men and their toys. "You can't see a thing, can you?" I whispered.

His heart walloped a million miles an hour against my chest. The terror seeped out of the shivering bundle and into my gut. "I promise I'll always keep you safe. You'll have a home here. I know it's not what you want. I understand that, believe me. But the bad guys will never find you again. And if they ever do set foot on this property I will take them apart one piece at a time."

I eased the fence open and took J.R. back to his cage

near Bob and Maynard. I refilled their water and gave J.R. a nice bunch of kale to munch on. He cowered in the corner, a shivering wreck. On my way back, I saw Deputy Fisk talking to Joe. The man seemed much more comfortable with corpses than childbirth. He was almost chipper. An ambulance was parked nearby.

"Hello, Miss Barr. We meet again."

I was suddenly exhausted. "Hello, Deputy Fisk. I suppose you have some questions for me."

"I've gotten a lot of info from Joe already. Had you seen the dead man before he turned up, er, dead?"

"No. Joe handled the class and left on the overnighter before I got back from releasing a snake. He's a stranger to me. I don't understand any of this."

A rotund man wearing a jumpsuit and clutching a camera crunched across the gravel. "I've got everything I need. You can load up the corpse now."

I shivered. Was there an uglier word that corpse? Murder, maybe.

"What's your take, Al?" Fisk readied his pencil.

"We're gonna need a closer look, but I'd guess he bled out. There's a nice bullet hole in his side. Would've given him enough time to walk away from the crash before he passed out. I'm going for coffee. See you back at the office."

My head buzzed. Bullet hole? "He was shot? By whom? The pilot who stole Lucille's Moped. It had to be him."

Joe nodded as he joined us. "That's what I was thinking."

"Makes sense. We found a bullet lodged in the control panel of the plane. It'll probably match the one found in your dead professor," Fisk said.

I shuddered. When had he become my dead professor? "This is crazy. What is going on here?"

Fisk shrugged. "Too early to say. Is there anything else you need to tell me? Anything odd that happened after the plane crashed?"

"No. Yes! But it was before, just before." I trotted off to the office trailer, the two men behind me.

"Where are you going?" Fisk called.

"Something fell out of the sky on me, right before the plane crashed." I threw open the door and scanned the messy desk inside. I found the rock and part of the newspaper. The rest had disappeared. I suspected the ground squirrel that had been loose in my trailer for the past two days. "Here it is."

Fisk held out a hand and looked closely at the object. "It's a rock."

"That was my guess too," I said with only a hint of sarcasm.

Joe squinted at it. "It's a piece of granite. How would that fall out of the sky?"

"I have no idea, but it almost broke my nose. It landed a minute before the plane did. I barely had time to move the pig."

Fisk ignored the pig comment. He spread out the newspaper. "Arizona Weekly. Dated yesterday."

"Uh huh."

Fisk's face screwed up in confusion. "Er, okay. I'll take this in with the rest of the evidence. I'll be in touch."

"Great. Can you take the plane, too?"

"We're not quite finished with it yet." He headed toward his cruiser.

"How am I supposed to have tour groups coming through here with a smashed-up plane in the way?" I called after him.

"You're not. Nobody comes in until we clear the scene."

I squinched my eyes shut. No luck. When I opened them he was still there. "This has been a terrible day."

The officer nodded sagely. "It will be better tomorrow."

"Only if my luck changes," I groaned.

Finally things were quiet again. Joe and I sat in my trailer, eating macaroni and cheese. My taste buds called out for a hamburger, but I ignored them. I am a vegetarian like Joe. I eat nothing with a face. Not even if it's seared with lovely grill marks and succulent juices dripping from every caramelized morsel. Nope. Strictly vegetarian for a whole three months. Vegetables and cheese are my best friends. You betcha.

My thoughts bobbed around like a balloon in the wind until I noticed Joe was staring at me.

"What?"

"Marty, sometimes I get the feeling you aren't telling me something."

I coughed on a noodle. "Who me? What would I not be telling you?"

"I don't know." He stretched his muscled arms. "I had the feeling when we found the professor, this sensation that there's something you're afraid of. Besides whatever killed the professor, I mean."

"Not me. I'm not afraid of anything. Except clowns. Something about the red rubber noses."

He laughed and reached a hand to stroke my arm. It went all tingly where he touched. "It's like we do this weird dance. I feel really close to you and then you pull away."

My face felt hot. "I guess I'm afraid to let other people do things for me."

"Is that what it is?" His eyes picked up the flicker of lamplight as he stroked a finger along the line of my jaw, turning my legs to gooey marshmallow.

"Sure. Absolutely. I'm not mysterious, really. I put my camel slippers on one foot at a time like everybody else. Stubborn is a better adjective for me. Well, and breath-taking is okay if you want to throw that in."

"Do you come from stubborn stock?"

The blood pounded in my carotids. "Me? Nah. Not really. My parents are fine. Just my own problem, I guess."

Joe watched me. More than anything, I wanted to curl up in his lap and tuck my head under his chin. But I was feeling weak as though all my secrets might come spilling out. As much as I hated myself for keeping things from him, I couldn't allow that to happen, for both of our sakes. I steered us back onto safe ground. "How is your dad?"

"He's great. He wants us to come and visit."

Joe's dad lives in a trailer just off the Fort McDowell Yavapai Nation. His mom was a Christian missionary who came to Arizona to help the native people with agricultural pursuits. She died of cancer when he was small, but he's got a picture of her driving a tractor in preparation for corn planting. Joe always kids that he was born between the tipi and the tractor. This is a joke, of course, because the Yavapai don't build tipis. They used to construct these wambunias which are made of willow branches, lashed together in an oval sort of formation. Now they mostly live in trailers and houses like everybody else.

Joe speaks of his mother with reverence and his father, too. He is a modest man, but he has a fierce pride in his family.

Pride in his family.

The concept fascinates me. I tuned back into the conversation.

"Dad says he wants to teach you how to make lemon meringue pie. That's his specialty, you know."

I knew. Eating a wedge of the fluffy stuff was like having a religious experience. Tangy custard. Pillows of meringue. Crust flakier than the people at a Comic Con convention. "Don't you think a member of the Yavapai tribe would have a more exotic specialty? Like dried venison and berries or something?"

He laughed. "Who'd want to eat that?"

At this moment, even desiccated meat spoke to my taste buds. But I'm a vegetarian. No meat. Never ever. "So what do you make of the falling rock?"

Joe finished his mac and threw away the paper plate. "I was going to ask you the same thing. It's bizarre."

"Maybe the professor and the pilot were struggling for some reason. Spiegel was using the rock to defend himself and it flew out."

"I don't think anything would fly out of the plane unless someone opened the door. Besides, why would he happen to have a rock handy in the first place? And what were they fighting about in midair?"

Logic isn't my very best subject. "I have no earthly idea. All I know is my property is now the final resting place of a body and a burned-up plane."

"I think they took the body away."

"Good. There are plenty of scavengers around here who would be interested in a find like that." The thought made my stomach quiver.

Joe yawned and checked his watch. "It's almost ten. I'd better go. We've got an early start tomorrow. I'll pick you up at 5:30."

"Huh? Pick me up for what?"

"The T.V. thing."

My heart shuddered to a painful stop. The T.V. thing. How could I have forgotten the T.V. thing? It was the final blow. "I don't think I can…"

His brows knitted. "Yes, you can."

"Things around here are…"

"Going to be just fine. Lucille can run the place for one day. The cops can come and go as they please."

"But I've got to…"

"Show up because you cancelled twice before and they made you sign a contract this time."

My mouth opened for another response but my brain ran out of excuses. "Five thirty?" The words sounded weak in the night air.

"Five thirty." He kissed me gently, lips lingering on mine. "It will be fine, you'll see."

Sure.

I bet that's what the captain of the Titanic said, too.

DANA MENTINK

Chapter Three

"Green or white?"

"What?" I bleated into my cell phone. The van hit a pothole and I almost lost my grip on the tiny thing.

Lucille voice blared through the line. "Are you and Joe gonna be wantin' green or white overalls?"

I blinked. "Overalls? For what?"

"For the wedding," she snapped. "Ficky and me are gonna wear blue and I'm not gonna have you two matching. We don't want to look like the Von Trapps. Green or white? What'll it be? I ain't got all day. I've got to see to Ficky."

I inquired of the best man as he steered the van over the rough ground. "Do you want to wear green or white overalls to Lucille's wedding?"

He laughed. "I didn't even know they came in green. Whatever she wants is okay by me."

"White," I told her. We'd look like painters, but that was a tad better than green. I had visions of the guy who shared the screen with Captain Kangaroo.

Lucille cleared her throat. "Right, I'm on it. White overalls for both of ya. Say, those cops were poking around again. They said there wasn't nothing to that rock. Just a hunk of worthless granite."

"I could have told them that. Did they take the plane away?"

"Nah. It's still there."

I stifled a groan. "How is Ficky?"

"He's got a pulled muscle, poor lamb. He's soaking his feet in a bucket of hot water. I'm making him my meat stew with the chili peppers. That will cure him. Gotta go." The phone clicked off.

Cure him or kill him. Lucille cooked with peppers I'd never even heard of before. "I shouldn't have given Lucille my cell phone number."

"You wouldn't want her to pick out your outfit without your two cents, would you?"

I laughed. In spite of the early hour and my bushel of worries, I was in a cheerful mood. The sun was just visible over the ochre cliffs and the sky was so blue you just wanted to lick it. A hawk floated in lazy circles overhead. God makes really incredible mornings in the Arizona desert. Possibly He wants to provide folks with enough stamina to make it through the afternoons that can approach scorching on the Heat-O-Meter. I don't try too hard to second guess God. He made it possible for me to escape, and that's enough for me.

Then there was the chance to spend three uninterrupted hours in the car next to my Joe. He was just as gorgeous as the sunrise. Could there be a more perfect nose? Even the slight crookedness about it was lovely. And where could you find a better chin than that? Strong but not too strong, clean shaven and the perfect complement to his cheeks.

The scrabbling from the box on my lap told me Matt the side-blotched lizard was awake. He hadn't yet forgiven me for hauling his scaly self out of his enclosure and stuffing him into a travel box.

"Now you behave today, Matt. Chin up, shoulders back. Make us look good on this idiotic television show."

Joe raised an eyebrow. "Why are you so against this, Marty? I think publicity would be a good thing for the Desert Star in light of what happened and all."

"Publicity can be good and bad." *Publicity puts your face out there for everyone to see. Everyone.*

"What you do at that sanctuary deserves recognition."

"Not me. This show is all about the animals. I made that Todd guy promise to focus on them completely. I'm merely along for the ride."

"Well he's determined, all right. He's been hounding you for a good month now about this gig." His lip curled. "T.V. people."

I settled back to enjoy the ride. As the scenery changed from desert to city, my eyes were dazzled at the sight of people, cars and colors. "Ooohh, look! Starbucks. And there's a McDonald's. Man, their chicken nuggets are great. I just….."

Joe tried to hide his smile.

"I mean, I used to like them before I became a strict vegetarian. Before you cured me of my disgusting desire to eat expired animal flesh, before my system was purged and all that."

"My choices don't have to be yours, Marty. You don't have to be a vegetarian to please me. I like you, meat and all."

I blushed. "Oh. Well. Thanks. Gee." *And I like you too. Lots.* I was saved from further inane stuttering as we pulled into the parking lot of the television station. Joe grabbed a travel carrier and a cardboard box. I followed him with a cage in each hand.

A tall man met us at the door. He thrust out his hand, then reconsidered when he saw our cargo. "Hello, there. Good to finally meet you. Welcome to the studio. I'm Todd

Chin."

We nodded and introduced ourselves. He ushered us into a small space with plenty of camera equipment and two chairs. The perimeter of the room was a snarled tangle of cords and wires.

Todd led us to a corner. "So here's the deal. Barbara is the host of the show Flora and Fauna. She'll be guiding you through the questions. We'll get you into makeup and mike you, and then you'll tape for about 45 minutes. We'll edit it down to a twenty minute segment. Okay?"

"Um, okay. Just remember that we're only going to talk about the animals, right? Nothing too personal."

He consulted a clipboard. "Sure, sure. But how about a few facts for our records. Where were you born? I couldn't find anything about your vital statistics on your website."

I held Matt's cage next to my face. "My name is Matt the lizard. I was born under a rock in the desert. It was a very nice rock, central heat and everything."

Todd stared at me. Fortunately, the makeup guy trotted in and began to pancake me. You just can't chat well when your face is being spackled. Then I was whisked into a chair. Joe stood off camera with the animals, ready to step in as my hunky assistant.

The host floated onto the set. Barbara was well put together. She had a helmet of blonde hair combed into a neat pretzel twist. Her lips were perfectly peach, a nice contrast to her smart blue suit and skirt. She shot me a thousand kilowatt smile and invited me to help myself to a bottle of water. The lights came up and made us both blink as our eyes adjusted.

The cameraman gave us a cue and we were off.

"Hello, Arizona. I'm Barbara Goodfellow and this is Martina Barr, owner of Desert Star Animal Sanctuary in Ferocious. It's an amazing place to get nose to nose with some of our wild residents. She's brought a few of her animal friends to share today. Welcome Martina."

"Er, thanks."

She glanced at her teleprompter. "First can you tell us about your mission at the Desert Star?"

I unstuck my tongue from the roof of my mouth. "To preserve the native wildlife, rehabilitate injured animals and, when possible, release them back into the wild." I even impressed myself.

"Excellent. When did you get into the business, Marty?"

"A long time ago."

She arched a delicate eyebrow. "What brought you to Ferocious? It's a very out of the way place."

My eyeballs rolled around and a bead of sweat slid down my face. Was it my imagination or had everyone stopped doing their thing to stare at me? "Oh there are lots of people in Ferocious, and animals, too. And here is our first visitor, Buddy." I reached into my cardboard box. With a flourish I uncovered the baby desert cottontail. My plan worked. Barbara melted into a puddle of "oooohs" and "aahhhhs."

I handed him over, firmly wrapped in a towel, and she cuddled him against her suited bosom, mumbling to him in baby talk.

"Aren't you just a cutey wootey? Mama just wants to snugglebuggle you in a huggy wuggy."

I left her to her snuggle buggle while I went into my spiel about the fascinating world of rabbits. She stroked the silky fur and held Buddy up to the camera for a close up. He twitched his pink nose. Barbara was smitten until I removed the cutie from her hands and turned him over to Joe. He passed Matt over to me.

"Uh oh. I see scales there." Barbara giggled nervously. "I'm not a fan of scales. I'm a fur gal. No reptiles for me."

I introduced Matt and tried to point out his finer qualities. "He's small so he can heat up quickly. That lets him be active in winter when other lizards are in hibernation."

"How interesting." Barbara was scanning ahead, looking for a more attractive guest from the list of animal visitors.

"Do you want to hold him?"

Her voice was sunny. "No, thanks. I'll just admire him from here." She read from her notes. "Tell me about his skin."

"He's got small scales on his back and larger ones on the head. Do you want to feel? He's very dry, not slimy or anything."

She reached out a tentative painted fingernail.

Who knew Matt was so sensitive?

At the touch of her manicured digit he shot up her sleeve, heading north. She shot out of her chair, also heading in a northerly direction. Up onto the desk she went, hopping up and down. Her screams filled the space. One hand clutched at her armpit while the other flopped around like a hooked fish.

The noise startled the rabbit in Joe's hands.

I forgot to mention in my rabbit lecture that cottontails can run up to twenty miles per hour in a zigzag pattern to escape predators. They also do this funky "bowling over" maneuver when they feel they're cornered. They run at the predator and kick with their strong hind legs. Rabbits freeze sometimes too, but Buddy chose the kicking option. He ran like his tail was burning, zinging into chairs until he boinged into the camera man's legs and tried his bowling over trick.

The cameraman was a good two hundred twenty pounds so the kick didn't have the desired effect. Instead the poor man was so startled he leaped backward, knocking the camera off its tripod with a crash. Two bolts flew out and a metal washer rolled over and came to rest under my chair. The cameraman came to rest on top of a stack of coiled electrical cords.

Barbara was now vibrating as if she'd received an electric shock. She hurtled off the desk and continued the frantic hopping. I was afraid Matt was going to come shooting out of her sleeve and hurt himself, or that she was going to pulverize him in her terror.

"Stand still," I yelled. "You're freaking him out. Stop squirming and I'll get him out of your sleeve. He won't hurt you."

It was no use. She began running in circles, smacking at the bump in her jacket.

I'm sure there was a reasonable solution, a way to dislodge Matt without causing trauma to either one of them. I couldn't think of it at the time. A plan formed in my mind that was long on action and short on reasonable. I stuck a foot out and tripped her. Down she went, face first onto the carpet. I put my knee between her shoulder blades as gently as I could and fished around for the lump in her sleeve. I eased the lizard out and put the poor critter into my pocket. Then I helped Barbara up and tried to straighten her jacket.

Barb slapped my hands away. "Don't touch me. Get away and don't ever come back."

She stomped out of the room, rivulets of mascara pouring down her face.

Everyone seemed to be frozen on the spot for a few seconds. Joe finally retrieved Buddy and held him cupped in his long fingers. The rabbit's sides shuddered. The camera man regarded me with eyes the size of Oreos until he bent to retrieve the camera which I noticed was still recording. Todd Chin stood with the pencil suspended above his clipboard, mesmerized by the disaster. He tried to speak but nothing came out.

I cleared my throat. "Well, I guess that's what editing is for."

A half hour later I was in his office, feeling like I was going to be given a lifetime detention. "I'm sorry, Todd. I never imagined Matt had such a startle reflex. Or Barbara either, for that matter."

Todd rubbed a hand over his eyes. "You messed up our studio."

"Er, a little, yes."

"You broke the camera."

"I didn't lay a finger on it. It just sort of fell over and bits came flying out. I'm thinking it wasn't very well made in the first place."

His pencil tapped on the desktop. "Barbara is locked in the coffee room and won't come out."

"I'm sure she will sooner or later. There's no toilet in there right?"

Joe clamped his lips together as if to contain a smile.

Todd flung some papers down. "And I still don't have my twelve-minute spot."

"You know what they say. Never work with kids or animals. It's a recipe for disaster." I gave him a charming smile.

He didn't return the grin.

I bit my lip. "So, um, how can I fix this?"

Todd eased back into his chair. "I'm so glad you asked."

A gleam in his black eyes made me quiver. The door opened and a beefy man with a drooping mustache entered.

"I'm Ken Lloyd. I own the station."

I tried the charming smile again. "Nice to meet you, Mr. Lloyd. It's a real nice studio. Thanks for having us. A wonderful opportunity and we really appreciate it."

"What did you do to Barbara?" His tone wasn't angry, more curious.

"I introduced her to Matt and she didn't take to him."

"Matt's a lizard," Joe said helpfully.

Ken's expression didn't change, but his exhaled breath caused his sandy mustache to billow. "I should have gone into the family business. T.Vs. is for the birds." His eyes bored into mine. "You need to pay for the camera repair."

I swallowed. "Okay."

"And don't come again. Nothing personal, but we have enough trouble keeping this place afloat without stampedes." Ken filled a paper cup from the water cooler and drained it. "You're the people from Ferocious. Heard you had an accident on your property. Plane crash?"

At least he didn't seem to know about the dead body, I thought with small relief.

"How did you hear about that?" Joe said.

"Hard to hide bad news. Sorry about your trouble, but it'll pass. Have a safe trip back. Work out the payment details with Todd before you go." Ken left. The door closed with a thud behind him.

The taupe walls seemed to close in around me. "So, Mr. Chin. How much, exactly does it cost to repair a camera?"

Todd leaned back and laced his fingers behind his head. "Thousands."

I hoped he didn't hear my gulp. "Uh, how many thousands?" It didn't really matter. The old bank account hovered significantly under the thousand mark anyway.

I threw my brain into high gear, trying to figure a way out.

Todd leaned forward with a smile. "How about we make a deal?"

I could feel Joe stiffen beside me.

"What kind of a deal?"

"I want my story about Desert Star. You want the camera fixed. Let's make a trade. I go to the Desert Star and get my story and I arrange for my cousin to fix the camera for nothing."

Joe's brows drew together in a black line. "I still don't see how this is our fault. Stuff happens when you work with animals and Barbara just plain lost her cool. I say we just forget the whole thing and leave."

"Oh, you don't want to do that. You signed a contract and you're liable. It would be better to let me come. Better for Marty and the Desert Star."

Joe folded his arms. "That sounds a lot like blackmail. You can't do that, Mr. Chin."

He shrugged. "What do you have to lose? It will be some good publicity for your place and you get out of here without a repair bill."

Joe and I exchanged glances.

He glared at Todd. "Maybe we just walk out of here without paying for your camera at all. It's not Marty's fault that the camera fell."

Todd's smiled, catlike. He pointed to a line on the paper in front of him. "Actually, it says right here in section nine. You pay for studio damages."

Joe leaned forward and put his long arms on the desk. "I don't like being threatened, man. And I don't like anyone threatening Marty either."

Awww. My insides blushed. But it was not the time to take on any more trouble. I stood and laid a hand on Joe's arm. "It's okay. Todd, you can come and do the spot as long as you focus on the animals."

He nodded. "Excellent. I'm glad we've come to a reasonable solution. When do we leave?"

We shuffled off to pack up the animals. I could tell by the set of Joe's jaw that he wasn't pleased. When the animals were secure, we trudged in silence through the office on the way to the van.

I almost missed it.

A blur of color on the side of a file cabinet caught my eye.

The magnet stuck crookedly to the metal.

In a pickle? Call Dilly's Plumbing.

Chapter Four

It could be a giant cosmic coincidence: the same magnet appearing in both a crashed plane and a television studio. That was it. Total coincidence. Uh huh. And my real name was Lola Falana. I managed to get a picture of it with my cell phone before we hit the parking lot.

I wanted desperately to talk to Joe about it but looking at the set of his shoulders and the veins bulging out of his neck, it didn't seem like a good time. Plus we had an unwanted passenger chomping pork rinds in the back seat.

I turned on the radio to nothing but static. Then I rolled down the window and hot air billowed in. I figured it would deter conversation. Maybe even parch his vocal chords for the whole trip. No such luck.

"So what's it like to live in the middle of nowhere?" Todd shouted over the wind as we reached high desert elevation.

"It isn't exactly nowhere," I called back. "We have flush toilets and running water, you know. Electric lights even."

He laughed. "Sure, but how did you ever come to settle here anyway?"

I gave in and rolled up the window after a bug pelted the side of my face. "I er, just sort of landed in Ferocious, that's all. Joe lives here to be close to the Fort McDowell reservation. That's where his dad lives."

Joe shot me a "don't drag me into this conversation" glance.

"I thought you looked like an Indian," Todd said, studying Joe's profile. "You Apache or something?"

Joe stiffened. "No. You Japanese or something?"

Todd snorted. "No way. My mom is Korean. Not all Asian people are Japanese."

"You don't say? Well here's a news flash. Not all Native Americans are Apache."

They settled into a stony silence.

In my book, silence was better than probing questions. It gave me time to formulate a plan. I wasn't going to be able to hold off Todd's inquiries forever. Best to get him in, give him his tour and send him packing.

But not until I fished a little info out of him. Turnabout and all that. "It was nice to meet Ken Lloyd. How long have you two worked together?"

"Only a couple of months. I'm new there."

"Have you worked in television long?"

"Not really."

"Have you produced other shows?"

He shrugged. "A couple. Just local small time stuff."

"Do you know any good plumbers?"

His chin came up. "Huh?"

Smooth, Marty.

Todd shot me a weird look. Joe rolled his eyes. Between the two of them I was beginning to doubt my detecting abilities. "Oh, I was just thinking about hiring a plumber. I've got a problem under my sink."

The problem was a stubborn squirrel, but Todd didn't

need to know that part. "Somebody told me Dilly's Plumbing was good."

He thought for a moment. "Why does that name sound familiar? Dilly's Plumbing."

I held my breath. "I don't know. Have you dealt with them before? Did they do some work at the station maybe?"

He chewed another pork rind while he considered. "Nah, can't remember. You'll have to let your fingers do the walking to find a plumber."

I slumped in the chair. The movement unsettled the lizard who was in his box on my lap. "It's okay, Matt," I whispered. "We're almost home."

We pulled in to find the burned plane still lounging in the welcome area. Not very welcoming. The smell of scorched metal didn't add to the ambiance either. A squad car was parked in the scant shade of a tree.

"Man." Todd whistled. "That must have been some crash. What happened?"

"An accident," Joe snarled.

"When are they going to get this hunk of junk off my property?" I grumped as we disembarked.

Deputy Fisk emerged from behind the wreck. "Soon. We've done all the forensic work. Just waiting for Hank to tow it. He's away on a fishing trip. Should be gone in a few days."

"A few days?" I stared at him. "Am I supposed to turn away visitors until then?"

"At least," he said. "Wouldn't want anyone to get hurt on this thing, would you? Who is this?"

"Oh sorry. This is Todd Chin from the T.V. station. He's doing a story on Desert Star."

"Huh." Fisk gave him a penetrating stare. "You look familiar. Have I arrested you?"

Chin flushed. "No. No, I've never been arrested."

"Are you sure?" Fisk's eyes narrowed. "I'm certain I know your face."

Joe didn't bother to hide his smirk. "Maybe it was some other Japanese guy."

I cleared my throat. "Uh, Todd? Why don't you go in the office and make yourself at home. There's a fridge in there with some sodas. I'll be right in and we'll get this tour done." I eyed the late afternoon sun. "I know you want to take your video before dark so we can get you home."

With a last glare at Joe, Todd headed toward the trailer.

Joe was deep in conversation with the deputy. "Are you sure?"

"Of course. I'm a professional."

"Sure about what?" I said.

"Professor Speigel didn't die from the fall at least not directly. The coroner was right. He was shot," Fisk said.

Disappointment swirled in my gut. I'd been hoping the bullet hole theory was a mistake, that the professor had just sort of bonked his head on the plane when he got out and wandered around in a stupor until he died. "So someone shot him and pushed him out of the plane? The someone had to be the Moped stealer. The one I helped to safety. Way to go, Marty.

Joe wrapped me in a hug. "You wouldn't have done anything else. The pilot needed help and you gave it to him. No way to know he was a killer."

A chill raced up my spine. I had been arm in arm with a real live killer. Of course, I reminded myself, you've been close to a murderer before. Very close.

I shivered. "But why would he shoot the Professor anyway? Seems a little risky to have bullets flying around when you're trying to keep a plane in the air."

Lucille slogged up to us. She was wearing a black mechanic's jumpsuit and yellow high top sneakers. "What happened? The cottontail looks like someone tried to skin him."

"Barbara and Matt had a confrontation."

She took a hot dog out of her pocket and ripped off a

hunk with her teeth. "Who's Barbara?"

"I'll tell you all about it later. How's Ficky?"

Her wrinkled face softened. "He's right as rain. A smidge of indigestion but that's it. He's quite a man, my Ficky." She eyed the deputy. "So where's my motorbike? Did you catch the filthy thief yet?"

Deputy Fisk put away his pencil. "Not yet, Lucille. We will."

"You'd better do it soon." She rammed the last of the hot dog in her mouth.

"I've gotta go. I have to stop by the hospital and give the Chief a report."

"Did she have the baby then? Is everything okay?"

He nodded. "Fine, fine."

"Boy or girl?" I asked.

"Forgot to ask." Fisk walked back behind the plane and got into his truck. We watched him drive away in a cloud of dust.

"Okay, Lucille. Go tell the animals to put on their best smiles. Mr. Chin from the T.V. studio is in my trailer and he wants to get some pictures."

"Man," she said. "Why didn't ya tell me we was going to be on T.V.? I'd have worn my new overalls. You could keep a body informed around here." She stamped off.

I left Joe and Lucille to their animal cheerleading and went to the office.

Todd looked up from his PDA when I entered.

"Are you ready to go meet the critters?"

He grinned. It might have been a charming grin if he wasn't such a nosey parker.

"Okay. But let me jot a few notes first to get my thoughts together." He sat down with a spiral notepad and pencil.

He jotted.
I waited.
He jotted.

I got a drink of orange juice.

He jotted.

I ate two granola bars and a handful of jelly beans.

He jotted. Finally he looked up. "I thought I heard something crawling under your sink."

"Loose squirrel, answers to the name of Byron. He likes my trailer better than his enclosure. He's harmless unless you're a newspaper or a piece of fruit."

Todd nodded and resumed his jotting.

I couldn't take anymore. I grabbed him by the elbow and propelled him to the door. "All right then, it's tour time. Here we go!"

He barely had time to grab his video camera before the door closed.

I noticed something out of place as I exited the space, but I couldn't put my mental finger on it. I made a note to self to check it after I unloaded the pesky reporter.

We headed to the enclosure where Joe was sitting close to J.R. He murmured quiet words to the quivering rabbit.

"What's he doing?" Todd asked.

"Trying to get the him used to people because he's going to have to live here permanently. The rabbit I mean."

"Why?"

"Paintball victim."

"Paintball?" His eyes flashed. "I love that game. I'm a champ in my neighborhood back home. I can take out a whole team before they know I'm there. They call me Phantom."

The tension of the day caught up with me and funneled up my backbone until it collected in my mouth. I could hear my self-control snap like a Pringle and then the tirade commenced. "So you enjoy it, do you Phantom? Well let me tell you what I know about paintball and the idiots who play it," I snarled. And I did. For a good five minutes. When I ran out of breath, Todd's eyes were wide. "Oh man. That's bad. I didn't know people could be irresponsible about it. I just thought it was fun."

"Fun is not a word I would use to describe maiming wild animals."

He held up two fingers in a Scout salute. "I never maimed anything. Honest."

Joe hadn't moved since the beginning of my verbal barrage. Only his smile had widened, that broad, wonderful grin that lighted his face and made my heart go pitty patty. J.R. finally inched his way over to Joe and snatched the kale leaf from his hand.

Tears filled the corner of my eyes. That poor frightened creature trusted Joe. I wasn't so much different from that scared rodent. Even with the current set of downed planes, bodies and potential P.R. disasters, I knew with Joe by my side, I would get through it. Ah Joe. My Joe.

Todd pulled me out of my gushy moment. "Does the property belong to you?"

"Ummm, yes."

"You bought it."

"Yes."

"How many acres?"

"Enough for an animal sanctuary," I said, keeping my tone light.

"Must have cost a bundle. Where'd you get the cash?"

Joe opened his mouth, but I cut him off. "Land in the high desert isn't all that expensive. Most people don't want to live quite this far out in the middle of nowhere, as you put it. But I thought you came to get some footage of the animals. Don't you want to start filming? Let me introduce you to Bob the bobcat. He's real photogenic."

Todd squinted up at the sky. "Oh man. I guess I've miscalculated. We've lost the light for today. I'll have to start tomorrow morning."

His smile reminded me of the Cheshire Cat's.

"Tomorrow?" I echoed. "But it's a three hour drive back to the studio."

"Yeah. Bummer, huh? I'll just have to crash here. Where can I sleep?"

Joe snorted. "How about I drive you back? I don't mind and you can return in the morning."

"Oh that's not necessary. It'll waste too much time. I don't need luxuries. I can sleep in the van if necessary. I'm easy."

But not easily fooled. If there was a way out of the situation, I couldn't find it. "There's a small tent trailer out back. You can sleep there," I growled, "but tomorrow is it. You've got to go after that."

"Why? Something going on you don't want me to see?"

"June is tourist season. Everyone wants to come to the desert before the real heat sets in."

He looked over at the plane skeleton. "I don't think you'll have visitors clamoring to come with a wreck right outside your front door."

I ignored this remark and marched him back to the trailer. With a few turns of the crank, the old thing unfurled into a miniscule bunker. A smell of must and old canvas wafted out.

"Fine," he said.

I poked my head inside. "Just checking for snakes. Or scorpions."

He remained unfazed, clambering in and testing the mattress.

I sighed. Not to be inhospitable, I tossed him an old Beacon blanket and a bottle of water.

"See you in the morning," he said, cheerfully.

"Right. First thing." I walked back to my office trailer which conveniently doubled as my home. Joe stood outside waiting. "Come in for some mac and cheese?"

He shook his head. "No. I've got to get up early tomorrow to help my dad clear some brush."

I tried to hide my disappointment. "So you won't be here for Todd's photo escapades?"

"No, but I'll be back by lunch time." He put a finger under my chin and lifted my face to his. "Everything will be okay, Marty. I promise. He's a jerk, but he'll be gone tomorrow. Call me if you need anything or if he gets out of hand."

His kiss was warm and wonderful, like hot cocoa on a stormy evening.

"Good night, Joe."

I trudged up the steps, suddenly exhausted. My tiny sleeping area beckoned, ground squirrel and all. When my head touched the pillow, I remembered the detail I'd noticed before I'd dragged Todd out of the office. I got up and grabbed the phone book. It was not where I'd left it. After Byron had removed the first ten pages for nesting material, I'd stowed it on a high bookshelf. It was now on the kitchen table. I thumbed through the pages until I noticed one with part torn away. It was the P-section.

The Printers through Plumbers page.

Plumbers.

What did Todd Chin need with a plumber?

Another coincidence? I visualized Todd's shrewd dark eyes. He was like the snakes we'd cared for. When it was feeding time, they never missed the slightest movement, no matter how quietly I snuck up on them. They recorded it all with flickering tongues and cunning eyes.

On the heels of that prickly thought, I lay down again, snuggling into the blankets to ward off the high desert chill. "Lord, thank you for getting me through this day. Please watch over Joe and the animals and help me keep them all safe. Oh, and Byron too. Amen." The worries of the day faded into one exhausted blur.

I slept.

Until an hour later when the cell phone shrilled. I banged around on the bedside table before I finally punched the talk button. "Marty Barr."

There was a moment of silence before the voice on the

other end answered. "Don't you mean Martina Escobar?"

Chapter Five

Every nerve in my body was instantly awake. I tried to speak but nothing came out. The accented voice on the other end was deep, musical, terrifying. How hard I'd had to work over the years to erase my own accent. Though I hadn't heard the voice in years, it came back with painful clarity.

"Martina? I know you're there. I can hear you breathing."

"I…I…"

"It is good to hear your voice. It has been such a long time. Where are you?"

"How did you get this number?"

He laughed. "You'd be surprised what I can get."

I swallowed the lump of ice cold fear lodged in my throat. "What, what do you want, Ramon?"

"I'm your brother, hermanita. Do I have to have a reason for calling? Families talk, don't they?"

"What do you want?"

"It's not what I want, Martina. It's what Papa wants."

Sweat collected on my forehead. "I don't care what Papa wants."

"We hear things, even in Mexico. We've been looking for you for a long time and we heard rumblings the past week from our sources. Nothing more than rumors, you understand, but they led me here, to Arizona."

Her heart squeezed. "You're in Arizona?"

"It's a lot like Mexico. Hot and plenty of view, wide open spaces. A man has room to stretch out here. I can see why it appealed to you."

I was locked in a nightmare. "Ramon, what do you want?"

"You already know, Martina. Papa wants you to come home, to take your place in the family again. It's been too long since you left. This country is dangerous, too dangerous for you."

"I'm not coming back. Not ever. He killed Mama, Ramon. How can you stay there and be his lapdog?"

He sighed. "Martina, you don't understand. You never did. Papa loved Mama as much as you. He tried to do what was best for her. If you'll just be reasonable."

"He kept her prisoner, until she couldn't take it anymore." The words rang out in the small space. "She hated living in the compound. That was the reason for the accident, Ramon. He killed her as sure as if he'd held a gun to her head."

"As always you are too emotional to see the truth."

My voice trembled with unshed tears. "Didn't you love Mama?"

His voice grew soft. "Of course I loved her. I love you too, you are my sister. But Papa is right. You need to come home where you belong. He's been patient long enough."

Not patient. He hadn't been able to find me and it infuriated him, I was sure. I tried to breathe calmly, to quiet the words that screamed to get out. "Ramon, if you love me, you'll leave me alone."

"I can't do that. It's for your own good. Someday you'll see that. Tell me where you are and I'll come and get you."

"No."

"I will come anyway. You know it."

"Good-bye, Ramon." I turned off the phone. "I love you too," I said to no one.

It was six o'clock in the morning when I finally rolled out of bed. Not that I had spent much time sleeping. Fear is a great stimulant. I tossed. I turned. I drank warm milk to no avail. Nothing could dislodge the truth.

Ramon was closing in.

My brother would find me and take me back by force, if necessary, to Papa. I didn't have any delusions about that. Papa was Patróne of a powerful drug cartel. He could and had made people disappear without a second thought. He had given Ramon a job to do and my brother wouldn't rest until he'd done it. I had no uncertainty about that either.

I'd be a prisoner like my mother had been.

I felt sick.

The face in the bathroom mirror wasn't mine. It belonged to a scared little girl with hollow eyes and fear radiating from every pore. Ghosts of the past flitted in my brown eyes. Ramon was coming for me. "Lord, help me. Please save me. Don't let them take me back. Please help me find a way," I whispered to my reflection.

Movement registered in my peripheral vision. Byron poked his head out from under the kitchen sink. He cocked his head at me and twitched his long whiskers before he disappeared again. His visit pulled me momentarily out of my malaise of fear. I put out a pile of pinecones with a side of apple slices in the corner of the linoleum. It made me feel a tiny bit better to know Byron was provided for.

Though I didn't want to leave my office, the animals wouldn't feed themselves. And sooner or later I'd have to face Todd and get him away as soon as possible. I made sure my cell phone was off before I crept out the door.

The semi-cool morning air washed over me. I inhaled and set off down the step. I fell over the stiff body and let out a shriek on my way down to the ground.

Lucille looked up from her seat on the bench and waved a chicken leg at me. "It's nice, ain't it?"

The huge block of wood that I'd fallen over, lay on its side in the sand. I made it to my feet, brushing the grit from my scraped elbows. "I almost killed myself on that thing. What is it?"

"It's for the wedding. Ficky carved it. Ain't it sweet?"

I cocked my head and looked at the grooved head and scalloped sides. I tried looking at it upside down. "Is it a bird?"

"'Course it's a bird. What else? Weddings is all about bells and doves and rice and stuff like that. We needed a bird."

I peered closer. "That's not a dove, it's a pelican."

"Yeah. Ficky was going for dove but somewhere in the middle it turned into a pelican." She put the naked chicken bone back into her pocket and gave her fingers a final lick. "I called your cell. How come you didn't answer?"

"Oh, I uh, I turned it off."

"Hmmm. 'Bout time. Phones is nothing but trouble. Like a techno umbilical cord. You okay? You look like you been ridden hard and hung up muddy. That Todd fella buggin' you?"

"Todd?" I'd forgotten all about him when I encountered the pelican. "Uh, no. He slept in the tent trailer so he can photograph today, but then he's leaving. Soon."

She nodded. "Okay. You ready then?"

"Ready for what?"

"To go into town. To help me pick out a cake. You said Saturday would be a fine day for cake pickin'."

I sighed. The last thing I needed was to go on a cake eating mission, but a promise was a promise. "Yes, I did, didn't I?" In the distance the tent trailer was quiet, flaps still drawn over the windows. "Let me feed the animals and we'll go. It'll have to be a quick trip, Lucille."

She nodded, grabbed a bucket and followed me over to the enclosure. "I believe we can power down some cake pretty quick."

I let the first group out, Bob the bobcat and Matt, and behind a sheltering fence, the baby cotton tail and J.R. Outside the fenced area, Lucille fed Tito from the bucket of vegetables she carried. He grunted, tail dancing in happy arcs as he gobbled. Maynard would have the second exercise shift in the afternoon.

I hunkered down in the small area, sandwiched between a large mesquite and an overturned crate that provided shade for fuzzy patients. J.R. hopped tentatively, snatching up the bits of kale and carrots that I'd sprinkled around. I held Buddy the cottontail on his back in a towel and fed him from a bottle. His fur was soft as sable, his eyes half closed in milky bliss as he snuggled against my tee shirt.

The sun rose in glorious June splendor, a swirl of sherbet colors. It was only slightly warm, a delicious period before the temperature moved into hotter zones. Spring in the desert. You go, God.

J.R. finished breakfast, hopped over and flopped down next to the nearby bale of alfalfa hay. I stayed as still as possible. His movements were jittery, as if was trying to escape his own shadow. With Ramon on the loose, I was just as fenced in as these poor guys. The only way to escape was to drop everything and run.

The cottontail finished the bottle and turned over, hunkering down on my lap for gentle stroking. What would happen to the animals if I left? Lucille could care for them, but she didn't have the money or business knowledge to keep the place going. They would be hurt again, left vulnerable and homeless, probably wind up in some animal shelter somewhere or be put down. I blinked back tears.

I could go to the police, but I knew full well that U.S. law enforcement had to work within the confines of the justice system. My brother and father did not. They knew how to cover their tracks and they knew how to operate outside the rules. They would get me, eventually, police or no police.

And Joe? Would he try to find me? Or would he move on with his own life? My heart ached. I'd worked so hard to get here, so hard to carve this desert niche for myself and, much as I didn't want to admit it, the thing between Joe and I was turning into a lot more than macaroni and cheese, at least in my mind. The desperation ballooned through my body.

"Come on, Marty. Get yourself together." A harder feeling spiraled up from my stomach and filled me, overriding my bout of self-pity. My mother knew I'd escape someday. She'd done everything she could to make it happen before her death. I'd risked everything to flee from my father and God helped me do it. He would help me escape this time too.

"You are safe with me," I whispered fiercely to my lap full of rabbit. "I will not let anybody take you away."

My bravado swelled. All I had to do was lay low and be careful. Arizona was a big place. Ramon wouldn't find me unless I let him. He might not even be in the state. It could be a big fat bluff. He'd discovered my cell phone number, that was all. If I could just keep away from any more publicity, good or bad, I would blend in with the neutral desert landscape. Invisible.

That brought me back to Todd and his efforts to drag me into the limelight. The man was going to leave if it was the last thing I did. I put Buddy in a shady spot, tiptoed out of the rabbit den and made my way to the tent trailer.

I knocked. "Hey Todd? Come out and take your pictures now. I've got an appointment and then I'll drive you home after lunch. Okay?"

No answer.

"You know I've got things to do today. I don't have a lot of time to show you around. You can understand that, right?" Still no answer.

"Todd?" I tried the door which swung open at my touch. No sign of him in the stuffy trailer.

Where was that obnoxious man?

I hastened back to the office.

No Todd there either.

Lucille met me as I stood in the rapidly warming sun next to the wooden pelican. "Lookin' for the T.V. man?"

"Yes. Have you seen him?"

"Uh huh. Met up with him after I finished the feeding while you was in with the rabbits. He borrowed my Moped to go for a drive. Said he'd be back by lunchtime."

A drive? Mr. Nosey Parker was roaming around the property unattended? "He's driving around the desert alone? Maybe I should go find him." I grabbed my keys.

"Nah. He said he'd spent a lot of time in the desert. A regular survivalist or somethin'. If he goes belly up somewhere he can always call for help. Besides, I told him what would happen if he didn't return my bike in good shape. Now come on. We've got an appointment with cake."

I took a moment to lock the office door before we loaded up in the van.

"Whatcha' lockin the door for? You never done that before."

"I don't want Byron to get away."

She shot me an odd glance as she extracted a wad of turkey jerky from her pocket. "That squirrel ain't leaving until he's good and ready."

I only looked in the rear view twice before I fired up the engine and took off.

Arnie was up to his elbows in doughnuts. The teensy bakery was so filled with pastry fumes that my eyes teared up. Oh the supreme joy and comfort of carbohydrates. I pressed my hands on the glass and surveyed the treasure. I was a woman in desperate need of some of those carbs. I'd spent the whole trip straining to catch sight of Todd Chin or Lucille's loaner Moped. The headache behind my temples was ready to blow holes in the sides of my head.

Arnie looked up from his rack, his massive girth dwarfing everything around him. "Morning, Marty. Lucille. What can I get for you? The usual? Old fashioned glazed?"

I opened my salivating mouth to respond, but Lucille cut me off.

"We ain't here for doughnuts, Arn. We're here to taste them wedding cakes."

"Oh that's right. I've got the samples in the back. Sit down and I'll get them. Help yourself to coffee." He waddled off.

Lucille and I fixed a cup. Mine black, hers with cream and six sugars. We sat down at a table. She wore her rainbow knit cap in honor of the occasion and even braided her puff of hair. I felt a stab of guilt. I'd been so preoccupied with my problems, I hadn't been giving her special day the attention it deserved. Ramon or no Ramon, I resolved to do better. Wedding details. Bring 'em on.

"So what types of cake were you thinking of? What kind does Ficky like?'

She looked up from shuffling the sugar packets. "Ficky said he will make sure to like anything I do." Her round cheeks pinked. "Ain't that nice? Ficky's a good fella."

"Yes he is. And you really love him, don't you?"

She stuck her tongue out of the hole from her missing front tooth. "Sure enough do. Ficky's a gem. Not many around no more. And how about you and Joe, huh? You fixin' to marry him?"

I choked on my coffee. "Marry him? Oh boy. We're not there yet, Lucille."

"Well I don't see what yer waiting for. He loves you and

all."

Now it was my cheeks that flushed. "Really? Do you think so?"

"'Course."

I filled up with a warm happy feeling. Then it abruptly drained away. Would he love me when he knew that I was an Escobar?

Arnie arrived with a platter of square cake bits, stabbed with toothpicks. Lucille whipped out a notebook and a stub of pencil. Then she popped a brown square of cake into her mouth. "What's the flavor?"

"Chocolate fudge."

"Good. Real fudgy." She scribbled on her paper. "What do you think, Marty?"

I munched a square. "Good," I agreed.

"How about that pink one?" Lucille asked, poking her pencil at another sample.

"Strawberries and cream," Arnie said.

"Hmmm. I don't like pink. I aint' gonna try it."

I didn't have any reservations about color. I ate both pink ones and declared them excellent. We munched our way through vanilla, almond and lemon cake before Lucille declared a winner.

"I want vanilla. With lots of white frosting bumps and twirls. Can you do bumps and twirls?"

Arnie nodded, chins wobbling. "No problem. Bumps and twirls it is. How many tiers?"

"How many in the Empire State Building?"

He frowned. "What?"

"Ficky and me, we want you to make it in the shape of the Empire State Building. Would that be three tiers you think, or four?"

I tried to hide my smile. Lucille had been fascinated with the Empire State Building since she got a postcard from her cousin a couple years back. She and Ficky were planning a honeymoon trip just to see it.

Arnie still stared at Lucille. "You want a wedding cake in the shape of the Empire State Building?"

"Uh huh. You can do it, cantcha? You made that cake that looked like the library last year. The spitting image, I'd say."

"Well yes but…"

"And Ginger said at the church meeting that you're the best baker this side of the Rockies. The best."

His full cheeks colored. "Well that may be true but…"

Lucille whacked her hand on the table. "It's settled then. Thanks a heap, Arnie. It's gonna be a real conversation piece."

The poor man was completely befuddled.

I eased his pain by ordering a dozen glazed doughnuts. Not all for me, mind you. I intended to share with my Joe and maybe give some to Todd on his way out of town. It never hurt to be nice to people, even those you didn't trust. Besides, if he was eating, he couldn't be asking questions.

Arnie boxed up my plunder. "By the by Marty, I told that fella to mind his business."

My hand froze on the way to pilfer a doughnut from the box. "What…what fella?"

Arnie wiped down the counter with a cloth. "Young guy. Came in just before you did, asking about you. Wanted to know about your family and such, where you came from. Mighty curious, if you ask me."

"What did you tell him?"

He winked. "I told him he shouldn't be poking around in other people's business. It isn't polite."

I was finally able to exhale. "Thank you, Arnie. What did he look like?"

"Dark hair, dark eyes."

I forced out the words. "Was he Asian or Hispanic?"

Arnie laughed. "Well of course, I could be wrong, but he looked Asian to me. Korean maybe. Are you okay? You look whiter than angel cake."

I managed a nod. "I'm okay. Thanks Arnie."

On shaky knees I made my way to the van, Lucille at my heels. She continued to jot notes on her pad of paper, oblivious to my emotional chaos.

What was Todd doing asking questions about me?

And what would I have done if it was Ramon doing the asking?

Chapter Six

Dark clouds massed on the horizon as we sped across the highway. On either side stretched endless acres of flat, dotted with mesquite and prickly pear. Distant cliffs jutted against the now gray sky. The hot air felt still and tense, like someone waiting to exhale.

Lucille dozed off. Her snores rattled the window.

I watched the wall of clouds roll in and used the time to try to figure out how to deal with Todd Chin. Relieved as I was that Ramon hadn't found his way to Ferocious, I had to admit the possibility that Todd was one of my father's henchmen. Perhaps he'd been hired to find me and the whole T.V. gig was just a ruse. There must be some reason why he was so determined to find out my secrets.

A bug splatted the windshield. Should I confront Todd? That seemed risky. If he really was a journalist and I came across too worried, it might set him into full blown investigation mode. A Geraldo Rivera quest for truth thing. Better to assume he was a dangerous nosey parker and get him out of my life pronto. It was as good a plan as any.

The Moped was parked by the wreck when we arrived. Better still, Joe's Jeep was on the scene. Lucille left to share the cake victory with Ficky and I found Joe and Todd sitting under a shade structure in the picnic area. Joe's arms were folded, but at least he didn't have Todd's neck between his fingers. Things were looking up.

"Hi, Joe. Hello, Todd." Joe rose, and I stood on tiptoe to kiss him on the cheek. He smelled of spicy musk. "How'd it go with your dad?"

"Fine. He said to give you a hug for him. I told him we'd come and visit on Sunday after church maybe. I figured we'd still be waiting for Desert Star to reopen so might as well take advantage of the down time."

I looked gloomily at the wrecked plane. "Probably. Hey, maybe Hank will come back from his fishing trip early on account of the weather and tow it."

"I doubt it." Joe laughed. "Hank is like the postal service of fishermen."

Todd yawned. "Yeah, I read about the crash in the paper. Weird that they haven't found the pilot. And there a dead body too, wasn't there? The professor guy?"

"Uh huh. So how about those pictures? You probably want to get cracking." I took two steps out from under the shade just as the skies let loose. Rain poured down in violent sheets. That's the way storms come in the desert; loud and fast. No messing around with wimpy drizzle and such.

Todd settled down lower on the bench. "Would you look at that rain? I can't take my camera out in this mess. I'll have to wait out the storm."

"It won't last long." I eyed the time. It was almost two. If he didn't get those pictures taken soon, we'd be stuck with him for another night. "I've got to take care of something in the office. When the storm clears in a few minutes, you can shoot the pictures."

"Sure thing." He crossed one denim covered ankle over the other. "I'll just wait it out here. I could use a nap anyway."

"I'll bet. You were up early this morning. Where did you go on your ride?"

His eyes were expressionless. "I toured your property for a while and then I checked out the town. Ferocious is a good name for it. It was hot by nine a.m." He laid down on his back across a picnic bench and pulled the baseball cap over his eyes.

That was it for information. I bit back a rude comment. "Okay Todd. See you later then."

I dashed out into the pouring rain and thunder. Joe ran behind me.

We startled Byron who was mid apple slice when we barreled in the office. He jumped and retreated to his under sink oasis.

"You're going to have to catch that squirrel one of these days," Joe said, shaking the rain from his braid. "A trailer is not a squirrel's natural habitat."

"That's what Lucille keeps telling me. I tried to trap him three times but he's smarter than the average squirrel."

"He does seem to know a good thing when he's living in one." Joe slid onto a kitchen chair and watched me.

I turned on my cell phone and dialed the information number. "Dilly's Plumbing. I don't know what city," I said to the perky phone helper.

"Doing a little investigation work?" Joe said.

I covered the mouthpiece. "Todd tore the page with Dilly's number out of my phone book. I doubt he was using it for nesting material." I wrote down the number and hung up. "Dilly's is about an hour from here." Then I dialed again.

Joe raised an eyebrow when I slammed the phone down.

"Not a good number?"

"The number is fine. Dilly is gone on a vacation and won't be back until next week. If I need a plumber immediately, his voice mail suggested doing a lot of baling and trying my luck with the yellow pages."

"A plumber with a sense of humor. Funny."

"Yeah, funny. For what they charge they ought to at least give you a laugh." I went to the window. "It's still raining. That's a record for a June storm."

He came up behind me and circled my waist in his strong arms. "It's not all bad. We can cuddle up and get acquainted again." He kissed the back of my neck. "I've missed you."

I relaxed against his wide chest breathing in the wonder of Joe. "I've been right here all the time, except for cake tasting."

He turned me around in the circle of his arms. "No you haven't. Since the crash your head has been someplace else. What's going on?"

I started to answer when my phone rang. I snatched it up and turned off the power.

"Why did you do that?"

"Um, I don't want to be interrupted."

His gaze never left my face. "Marty, you're afraid, I can see it in your eyes. I can hear it in your voice. Tell me what's wrong and I can help you."

Oh that it was so. I would love more than anything to lay my burden down in Joe's loving arms, to give my heart and soul into his care. But that might mean I'd lose him forever. At the very least, it would put Joe in harm's way. I could never do that. Never.

"It's nothing Joe, really. I'm fine except for the fact that my business has been sidelined on account of murderous pilots and wreckage and such. It's enough to make a vegetarian run for the pot roast."

He looked unconvinced. I traced a finger over the almost dimple in his cheek. We sat down on the saggy couch and watched the rain fall, and talked about happy nothings. The time flew away like butterflies in the sunshine.

They say every moment is precious, but some are just sweeter than others. I said a silent thank you to God for time with my Joe.

I finally tore my gaze away from him an hour later. "It's got to stop raining," I wailed. "Or I'll be stuck with Todd for yet another night."

Joe laughed. "I don't like that idea any more than you do, but it doesn't look like it's going to clear up." He checked his watch. "I really need to check on the trail at Siesta Bluff. If it washes out we'll need to put up a roadblock. Want to drive out there with me?"

"I'd love to, unless you think it might stop raining any minute."

We both listened to the pounding rain.

"Somehow I don't think so," he said.

"I've got to check the animals before we go and see if Bob's roof is still water tight. I'll meet you at the Jeep." I slipped on a jacket and followed Joe into the rain.

The animals were fine. The rabbits huddled in their shelter, snuggled down in a pile of hay. Maynard seemed to be enjoying the rain. He hopped around in a most un-foxlike fashion. I gave him an afternoon snack of grasshoppers and told him to mind his manners. Bob was enjoying an afternoon siesta in his dry enclosure. He opened one eye to check me out and then went back to sleep.

Tito was not in the igloo dog house Lucille had procured for him. He wasn't in his favorite hidey hole under the porch step either. I left a treat for him anyway, a gift from the Turnip Fairy.

Joe had the car all warmed up by the time I got there. The rain eased off but it was still coming down when I loaded my backpack with essential supplies and piled into the Jeep. Todd Chin materialized at the window with his back pack.

"Going for a drive?" he said, holding the hood of his jacket against the pelting rain.

Joe rolled down the window a crack. "Gotta check a trail. Long way. Take a few hours."

"Great. I'll come along."

Before Joe had a chance to answer, Todd wrestled the rear door open and slid inside. He hadn't quite managed to close it all the way when a black, hairy thing shot in next to him.

He yelled and scooched to the far window. "Oh man. I think there's a pig in here."

"Actually, it's a javelina," I said. "So that's where he got to." And you deserve pig tracks on your pants for barging in on my Joe time.

Joe didn't say anything, but I could see a smirk on his lips as he started the engine.

This T.V. reporter or cartel informer or whatever he was, was turning out to be harder to remove than cactus prickles. Tito, bless his heart, curled up on the seat, his back against Todd's thigh and began to snore. If that pig didn't think he was a dog, I'd be jinkied. He must have been pignapped at birth and raised by a pack of Labradors.

It wasn't the distance that made it a long trip, but the terrain. Desert Star is a fabulous mixture of all kinds of wonky topography. Hills, canyons, ravines, cliffs. I still hadn't explored the whole parcel completely. The small valley made a great home to the office and animal hospital, but the property also included plenty of winding trails leading up the cliffs. There were some neat limestone caves there and Joe took groups up regularly.

The roads are dirt, gravel in some places and treacherous in others. Not a problem for my Joe. He could parallel park a 747. Nonetheless we had to move slowly to avoid getting stuck or falling into a sandy ravine.

I tried to let go of my worries long enough to appreciate the view. Often I found myself trying to see it through a Native American lens. The Yavapai believed their land was the center of the world and all the plants, animals and humans entered it by climbing up the first corn plant. The Presbyterian missionaries showed up in the early 20th century and brought Christianity, which changed things. Still though, I could understand the idea that this amazing place of contrast was the center of the world. It was certainly the center of mine.

The rain washed the ever present dust away making the cliffs glitter like gold in the setting sun. I imagined I could see the cactus swelling as I watched, gorging themselves on God's watery gift. There were flashes of color from Indian paintbrush and blackfoot daisies that would be gone in a matter of weeks. The desert was a place of mystery and magic, and until recently, a sanctuary.

I shook away the thought. I was safe here and my animals were, too. After I unloaded this Todd person and got rid of the awful plane, things would return to normal. Ramon might retreat if I kept him away long enough. Papa would need him back home sooner or later. Feeling a mite better, I fished around in my backpack for my plastic bag of doughnuts. Following good Christian principles, I shared with Joe and Todd.

The trail became steeper as it wound between two high rock walls.

Todd took out his camera. He rolled down the window and snapped some photos.

"I thought you couldn't photograph in the rain," I said.

He grinned. "I can photograph in anything, if I'm properly motivated."

I smothered a snide remark.

Joe turned the wipers up to high.

Then everything went haywire.

The Jeep inched forward between the rocks as the storm let loose, slamming rain down and causing the tires to hydroplane.

Joe struggled to keep the wheel steady, but it was no use. The car slid all over the place as water filled up the narrow gap between the walls. We all grabbed onto something to steady ourselves as the Jeep turned into a raft, spinning in ever more rapid circles.

I heard Todd gasp as we watched the water creep up to the door handle. "What's going on?" he yelled over the torrent.

"It's a flash flood," I yelled back. "Hold on to something."

The Jeep wedged itself on a boulder, pinning us in the middle of a growing lake.

Tito leaped onto Todd's lap, adding his frightened squeal to the mix.

I felt the cold water pushing through the cracks in the door, dousing my feet and ankles. Thunder crashed and the water rose to the window. There was no way to open the doors against the pressure of the flood.

I'd been so steeped in fear lately, I didn't think I could feel any more. I was wrong. As the water level rose, I felt a scream forming. I did not want to die like this, trapped as my lungs filled with frigid water. I didn't want to feel the panic of a slow and silent drowning. Joe reached out a hand for mine.

The water continued to rise until it crested the door handle.

"God help us," I murmured. "Please."

In a matter of minutes, we would be underwater.

I opened my mouth to scream

Just as suddenly as the skies opened up, they closed again. Water drained out of the canyon as if someone had pulled the plug. In two minutes the water receded, leaving a quiet only broken by the sound of our labored breathing.

We panted for a while longer before Joe said, "I'm going to check out the damage." He crawled out of the car followed by Todd.

I spent the time trying to resume normal breathing patterns and comforting Tito.

The guys heaved for a while on the sides of the car. When they returned they didn't look happy.

"It's stuck. Completely wedged on top of a rock." Joe pulled out a cell phone and tried to make a call. No signal.

Todd said, "Let me try on mine."

Nada.

The sky was a slate gray, sinking rapidly into darkness.

"Well…..what are we going to do?" Todd asked.

I turned around. "We're going to wait here until morning, I suppose, or until we can get a signal to call for help."

His brows furrowed. "Great."

"It was your idea to come along," I grumped. They men returned to their seats.

Since the rain had started up again, a gentle pattering this time, I decided a dinner break was in order. I passed around doughnuts and water for everyone except Tito. He had to settle for celery sticks. We munched in silence until the sliver of moon rose in liquid splendor. Moonlight painted everything in glittering metallics. Joe and Todd did not seem to appreciate the beauty of the night sky. Each stared out their own window in stony silence.

The rain again slowed to a trickle.

Joe pulled on a jacket. "I'm going to hike up to the plateau and try to make a call."

"I'll come too," Todd said, shoving the pig away from his leg.

"Well I'm not staying behind," I said, zipping my own jacket.

Joe eyed the backseat. "Who's going to stay with Tito?"

I looked in the back seat. Tito shot me a pitiful, pathetic, pig look. He laid his snout on top of his little pig hooves in an Oscar worthy performance. "Oh brother. Go on then. I'll babysit the pig."

Todd laughed. "Don't forget to have him in bed by eight."

I shoved his camera at him. "Why don't you take some pictures?"

"In the dark?"

"Of course. You can take pictures of anything, remember?" I said sweetly.

He took the camera and they walked up slope, the moonlight reducing them to dark shadows against the gray ground. Silence folded in around me. I peered out into the night thinking about Ramon.

I remembered our fort, the slapped together, cardboard affair we played in for months. Mama brought us cheese sandwiches and cookies. We piled up berries and leaves, imagining we were explorers in a hostile land. We'd even slept up there, admiring the moon as I admired it now. Ramon was skinny then, all arms and legs and laughter. Where had that little boy gone?

Now he was out there somewhere in the dark, hunting me, stalking me. Goosebumps prickled my back. "Snap out of it, Marty," I scolded. "You're freaking yourself out." Not hard to do, since I had a teeny weeny fear of the dark. Though I would never admit it, I still slept with a nightlight. I decided to try a little song therapy but the only song I could remember was "Jesus Loves Me." Figuring that covered all the important stuff, I began to sing. The music filled me up. Even Tito enjoyed it. His springy tail went round in circles.

I sang so loud I almost missed the first one, but the second one rang out loud and clear.

A gunshot.

And then, one more.

Chapter Seven

I couldn't move.
Through the misty window, I strained to peer through the darkness.
Two shots.
Joe could be…
I squeezed my hands together, my lungs threatening to explode. Tito grunted anxiously, his muscles taught, legs rigid.
My body told me to stay. Hide. Fold up into a tiny ball and mash myself onto the floor of the Jeep. Stay safe. Stay alive.
But the shots…
But Joe…
I wrenched open the door, shut it before Tito could get out and took off running up the slope. Joe, Joe, Joe. I slipped on wet gravel and skidded to the ground, water soaking into my jeans. Just as I made it to me feet, two figures moved fast down the trail toward me. One was staggering, trying to hold up the other.

My mouth opened in a soundless scream.

Joe's face was strained under the effort to keep Todd on his feet. I ran to them both and held up Todd's other side with my shoulder, half running, half stumbling. We hobbled down to the Jeep and pushed Todd in, out of the rain. I climbed in next to him and Joe made it into the front seat.

Tito squealed as I leaned on him.

I looked into Todd's face, pale in the moonlight. I didn't see any blood. There were no holes that I could see as I looked over his jacket and pants. "Where are you hurt? What happened? Were you shot?"

Todd was out of breath so Joe took over.

"We climbed to the plateau. I was about to make the call when we saw lights. Like flashlights. Two of them. We stayed quiet and watched until Twinkletoes here tripped over a rock and messed up his ankle. He was so loud about it whoever it was heard the noise and shot at us."

"I was not loud," Todd said through gritted teeth. "The noise carries in this thin air. And don't call me Twinkletoes."

I stared at Todd. "So you weren't shot? You twisted your ankle and that's why Joe was carrying you? No bullet holes?"

He grimaced. "Sorry to disappoint you."

I let it all sink in. "Who was it? Who would be on my property at night? And shooting at people. What kind of person shoots at people out of the blue?" A picture of Ramon flashed in my mind but it didn't make sense. Ramon would know better than to poke around the desert at night. We grew up in a desert and he knew how dangerous they could be not to mention the fact that he certainly wasn't likely to find me hiding under a cactus. Plus I was pretty sure his aim was to take me back to Papa alive, not shoot me dead on sight.

"Will they come for us? The shooters?" I said, peering into the blackness.

"After they squeezed off a few rounds, they loaded up in a truck and took off out the east entrance. I don't think they'll be back tonight." Joe opened the door again.

"Where are you going?" I said, gripping his arm.

"Back up until I can get a signal and call the police. We aren't getting out of here any time soon."

"Are you sure it's safe?"

His eyes met mine in the darkness. "Nothing's sure, Marty, but I think they've gone. Be back soon."

He kissed me and left without another word.

Todd made a face and reached around behind him.

I tried to look at his ankle, but he shook me away. "It's fine," he said. "I've just gotta get my backpack out from under me."

We pulled it off and tossed it on the floor near Tito. I yanked a first aid kit from under the seat and activated the cold pack. Todd loosened his boot and put in on his ankle.

"What a night." I felt like I'd aged a decade.

"Amen to that." He settled back onto the seat. "You sure attract trouble, Miss Barr. Plane crashes, shooters."

"Pesky photographers," I added helpfully.

He smiled and I could see a hint of charm there.

"Yes, those, too. I did manage to get some pictures before I fell." He carefully removed the camera from around his neck, replaced the lens cap and slid it back in its pouch.

"Pictures? Excellent. I'm sure you can't wait to get back to the studio and get to work."

He opened his mouth to reply when Joe slipped back into the car.

"I got through. Fisk will get over as soon as he can't but they're working a big accident so we're going to be here for a while."

I sighed and hopped over back to the passenger side. The blanket stowed under the front seat went to Todd. Joe found another which he insisted I take. I snuggled up as close as I possibly could to him and we shivered together. In a few minutes, all male occupants and the pig were snoring. I wondered how men could fall asleep after being shot at.

I was alone with my thoughts. And no nightlight.

Though I closed my eyes, sleep eluded me. Worries chased after one another in my mind like greyhounds after rabbits. Shooters. In Desert Star. Searching for something. It had to be related to the plane crash somehow.

The time ticked by in painful slow motion until Deputy Fisk finally pulled up just before sunrise with another officer who went by Petey. We piled out and Joe filled them in on the shooting.

Fisk's stub of a pencil flew across the notebook and there was a gleam of excitement in his eye. "Well, well. A shooting, huh? What kind of gun, you think?"

Joe shrugged. "Guns aren't my thing."

"I'm guessing a thirty eight, or a nine millimeter," said Todd who was propped against the side of the Jeep.

Fisk wiped the moisture from the plastic shower cap he wore over his hat. "Wonder how this all fits together." He sent Petey to take pictures of any tire tracks that might have outlasted the rain.

"Me too," I said with feeling. "And I can't wait to get that hunk of junk off my property. It seems like it's the cause of all this trouble."

"Hank said he'll be here on Monday morning first thing to tow her."

My sigh was loud in the thin desert air. "Great."

The deputy, Petey, Joe and I took another shot at moving the Jeep. Our combined muscle edged it clear of the rock and the fine old vehicle started without a hiccup. Joe's relief was palpable.

Fisk jotted down a few more notes and flipped the book closed. "I'm going up to Riverton now. Be gone until tomorrow night. I'll be in touch later with any developments."

"Riverton?" I asked, pulse pattering. "Would you mind giving Todd here a ride back to Phoenix? It's on your way."

Todd's eyebrows drew together. "But I've got more

pictures to take."

"In light of recent events, I am rescinding your photo op."

"You can't do that. What about the damage to the camera?" he said.

"Bill me." I didn't have the cash, but I'd find a way to pay for repairs. Small price to pay for unloading Mr. Twenty Questions.

Fisk eyed Todd closely. "I'll be happy to give you a ride. It'll give me a chance to remember where I know you from. I never forget a face."

I retrieved Todd's backpack and handed it to him. "Safe travels," I said with a smile.

He glared at me and hobbled away.

Deputy Fisk's voice carried over his shoulder. "You sure I never arrested you?"

For the first time in days, I felt a sense of relief.

Joe must have felt it also. He wrapped me in a tight hug and kissed my forehead before we bundled into the Jeep and headed back down the mucky road.

On the way, we finished the doughnuts.

I wiped sugar from my chin. "What time is it?"

"Five thirty in the morning."

"Acck. No wonder I'm tired."

His turn to yawn. "Yeah. I'm going to catch a few winks before church." He gave me a quick look. "Are you up for service today?"

At the word 'church' I felt the familiar twist of fear. "Ummm, well, I'm not sure. I…well…yes," I heard my mouth saying. "Yes, I'll come."

He smiled, showing his almost dimple. "Excellent. I'll pick you up at ten."

"Okay." I tried to stifle another gargantuan yawn. "If I'm not awake, have Byron fetch me," I said before I drifted off to sleep.

Byron didn't have to fetch me. My body clock did its job and woke me for the morning animal feeding. All the inmates seemed unusually chipper, rejuvenated by the rain. The smell of washed earth pepped me up, too. The daylight was brilliant enough to chase all the night time drama away. I was filled with confidence. Church. I could do it. This time, I would make it through the door.

I decided to go all out. I put on my fancy jeans, the one without the patch on the knee and pulled my dark hair back into twist which I kind of smashed up in a hair clip on top of my head. And the finishing touch? Lip gloss. Sable Sand. Whew. Complicated beauty maneuvers, but well worth the effort.

Lucille waved at us as we pulled out of the drive.

"Goin' to try it again, Marty?"

I nodded, feeling sheepish.

"Good girl," she said. "You're bound to do it sometime or another."

"Can you give Tito an extra apple when you see him? He had a rough night. I'll fill you in later."

She waved with one hand and took out a stick of Slim Jim with the other.

Joe was wearing his Sunday best. Black jeans, which made his long legs look even longer, a short sleeve plaid shirt, hair pulled back in a neat braid. He eyed me as we drove. "You look extra good this morning. Prettier than sunrise."

Score one for the Sable Sand lip gloss. I blushed. "You look pretty too. I mean, handsome. Real handsome." So handsome, my stomach went all silly on me, the darn thing.

He smiled. "I've been thinking about this shooting business. It's got to be related to the plane crash. It wouldn't surprise me if the bullets came from the same gun that killed the professor."

My eyes widened. "Man. What is going on here? I mean, I own a whole bunch of sand and some gimpy animals. Why are people so interested my property?"

"I don't know, but we're going to find out."

I'd seen that determined set to his chin before. He would find out, for sure. Maybe everything. I shivered. "Joe, how do you feel about surprises?"

"What kind? Like somebody gives you a bunch of flowers surprises?"

"Oh, I don't know. Like, um would you, you know, still like me if you found out some, er, surprises about me?"

His face was puzzled. "Sure. I've liked you since the first time I saw you and I didn't know anything about you then."

I'd never thought of that. Maybe there was a way to tell him, to come clean without losing my precious Joe.

"So what do you want to tell me?"

"It can wait," I said as we pulled into the dirt parking lot of the Rejoice in Jesus church. It was more of a cottage type deal, wood frame with maybe twenty chairs. That worked about right as the membership totaled seventeen on a good Sunday. Joe got out and opened the door for me. Darling man.

He took my arm and we headed up the crooked walkway.

I made it all the way through the threshold this time before it started.

My throat closed up.

Breathing became difficult.

Sweat prickled my forehead and the back of my neck.

Calming breaths, Marty. Calming breaths. In with the good air. Out with the bad. It's just a building.

The room began to spin.

"Joe," I whispered, "I…I've gotta go."

He squeezed my hand and led me outside to a little bench on the front porch. His black eyes were filled with compassion as he dropped a kiss on my temple. "Why don't I stay with you? I can hear the message from out here."

"No," I said, blinking against the black spots that swam in front of my eyes. "You go in. I'll be fine here. Really."

He pressed his warm palm on my cheek. "Okay. I'll be back soon. I'm proud of you for trying again."

The music swelled and wafted out the door. Pastor Enrique's rich voice filled the church. I could hear every word of his opening prayer. I had been so hopeful that this time I'd at least make it to a chair or even to a deserted corner. I tried again to understand why I was a prisoner of this fear that started the day my mother was killed.

The day she broke free from my father's grasp and stepped in front of that car.

I could still see her body pinwheeling through the air from the impact, dark hair fanned around her like the feathers of a falling bird.

"Lord," I prayed, "teach me to forgive. Help me to let go of the anger that keeps me from you. Please, God. I can't do it myself. I've tried, but I'm just not big enough."

The soft hum of voices was different than my childhood church. I remembered the great silent walk to the front pew, the expensive draperies paid for by my father, the looks he got from the congregation.

Fear.

Respect.

Reverence.

For a man who bought and sold drugs.

Respect.

For a man who would not let his wife go.

Fear.

Of a man who could snap his fingers and have any one of them executed.

I shook my head against the memory. The church folks stirred and began to sing their last few songs. I sang along. The music was simple, peaceful.

Joe and the entire congregation were used to my strange psychosis. I told them my mother was killed outside of a church and they never asked any more about it. Each one, in his or her own way, tried to ease my struggle. Ruth, a woman old enough to be my grandmother, patted me as she exited the church. "Next week, honey. I can feel it."

I gave her a brave smile. Every Sunday without fail she saved me a seat next to her. Optimistic sort, that Ruth.

After all seventeen people filed out, giving me handshakes and heading for the coffee and doughnuts, Pastor Enrique found me and caught my hands in his. "Marty. You made it through the door. Praise God." He smile was brilliant against his mocha skin.

I felt my cheeks heat. "It's so ridiculous, isn't it? I really thought I was going to do it this time, Pastor."

"You will, honey. You will. God is patient. He will be there waiting for you when you're ready." He squeezed my hand and winked. "Until then, He can reach you on the porch too, you know. He's that good."

I hugged him.

Joe brought me a coffee and doughnut. He didn't say anything about my hasty departure. He just kissed the top of my head as we headed for the Jeep.

"Are you ready to go see my dad?

"You bet." Joe opened the passenger door for me and I settled in.

Just as he fired up the ignition, I saw something on the floor of the backseat.

Something that definitely wasn't supposed to be there.

Chapter Eight

The bashed up notebook was no bigger than a calculator, spiral bound with a brown coffee stained cover. It wasn't Joe's. The guy is fanatical about keeping a neat vehicle. He may drive an '84 Jeep but the thing is clean enough to eat off the floor. That, and the fact that there was a name scrawled on the front cover of the book.

Peter Speigel.

As in Professor Speigel? The recently murdered Professor Speigel?

Uh oh.

"This is Speigel's," I said.

Joe returned my look of shock. "How did it get in my Jeep?"

"I don't know. Wait a minute, yes I do. It must have fallen out of Todd's backpack when I tossed it on the floor last night." My brain fought over topics. Should it worry more that I was in possession of a dead man's notebook? Or Todd was?

With cold fingers I opened the book. The first few pages were topographical sketches of a place that looked mighty familiar. I turned it this way and that. "These are maps of the Desert Star. Vague sketches, anyway."

"Can you pick out anything in particular?"

"Not really. There are the cliffs in the background and Siesta Bluff. Not much more detail than that and the two main roads." I thumbed through the other pages and groaned.

Joe darted his eyes from the road to the journal. "Find out anything?"

"The man's handwriting was reprehensible."

"Other than that."

"It's just a lot of notes about desert life. The composition of rocks and a note to call his dentist. Did he ask about anything in particular during the overnighter you took him on?"

"No. He was pretty quiet. Spent a lot of time looking through binoculars and wandering off. I was afraid he'd run into a diamondback or something, but he seemed to like being alone."

I flipped through the back of the book which was a series of empty pages. A small slip of paper fluttered out. It was a page torn from a book.

"Listen to this. The upper air burst into life! And a hundred fire-flags sheen, To and fro they were hurried about! And to and fro, and in and out, the wan stars danced between. What in the world is that? Sounds like funky poetry."

"It is, but I can't remember the poet or the title. Do you?"

"If it doesn't have to do with green eggs or ham, I'm no help here."

He grimaced in concentration. "I know I've heard it somewhere. No use. I can't bring it up, but I happen to know someone who can."

"Who?'

"My dad is a poetry nut."

"Really?"

"Really."

"Not bad for an Apache," I said, avoiding his gentle sock to my shoulder.

Joe's father met us in the small yard in front of his doublewide trailer. The temperature was approaching the hot zone, even though it wasn't quite noon. Mack Hala knelt next to a tomato plant heavy with red fruit. He slowly stood, took off his cowboy hat and wiped the sweat from his creased forehead. His skin was as brown as the soil in his garden beds.

"Joey," he called. "And you've brought Marty with you." His face lit up as he limped over to hug Joe and kiss me on the cheek.

"Hi, Mack," I said. "What are you doing out here weeding in the heat?"

He chuckled. "Heat? This ain't heat. Hasn't even topped ninety yet. Come in. I'll rustle up some lunch. I was hoping Joey would convince you to leave the animals for an afternoon and come along today."

We followed him into the relative cool of the trailer. It was battered but spacious. A collection of violets bloomed in purple profusion on the window sill. The living area and kitchen were separated from the bedroom by a narrow corridor. A pungent smell of lemons filled the air.

Joe inhaled deeply. "Oh man, Dad. Are you by any chance making pie?"

"Yes, my dear son, I'm making pie and I hope your lovely gal Marty will help me."

"I'll try," I said, wrapping myself in the striped Wally's Diner apron he handed me. "But I make no guarantees."

We chatted as he pinched folds into the piecrust and beat the eggs while I juiced the lemons. "You know Marty," he said, "I always wanted a daughter to cook with. Mrs.

Hala--well she was a fine woman, but, God bless her, not much of a cook. Her biggest triumph was hamburger casserole and we had to get used to crunchy noodles. Remember son?"

Joe grimaced. "That's part of the reason I became a vegetarian. I knew I'd never have to eat hamburger casserole again."

Mack pointed a floury finger at Joe. "I tried to get that big lug to cook with me, but he had better things to do."

"I didn't want the neighborhood girls to catch me wearing an apron," Joe said. "Bad for my image."

I laughed. "I'll bet."

Mack bustled around the small space rounding up cornstarch and sugar. The kitchen felt comfortable like a pair of well-worn slippers. What would it have been like to be his daughter? Who would I be if I hadn't had Patróne Escobar for a father? There would have been people to talk to and play with, maybe. People who weren't afraid to come near. Would I have spent days riding bikes and living in a run-down trailer that smelled of pie and coffee? Mack would have been the kind of father that taught with love, instead of intimidation. I was overwhelmed by a great sense of longing.

A deep sigh escaped my lips.

"You okay, honey?" Mack said.

I looked up to find him eyeing me closely. "Oh, yes Mack. I'm fine. Just preoccupied with all the things that have been going on back home. Complete chaos, as I'm sure Joe's told you."

He nodded gesturing for me to add the egg yolks to the warm custard as he stirred. "Slowly now, we don't the eggs to curdle. Yes, I heard about your troubles. I'm mighty sorry, honey, but it will all clear up. What was it your mother used to say, Joey?"

"It's always darkest before the dawn," Joe said.

"That's right." He let the custard cook until little bubbles exploded to the surface. "Now I'm going to show you the secret Hala meringue recipe. It'll make a pile so high it'll look like Everest."

We stood, elbow to elbow, beating egg whites within an inch of their lives. A pinch of sugar and cornstarch and the stuff turned glossy and stiff. I plopped mounds of it on top of the warm custard. Soon the pie was adorned with a mountain of pearly white. Mack popped it into the oven and set the timer for five minutes. Joe and I made cheese sandwiches and put iced tea and potato chips on the scratched Formica table. We settled down to eat while the pie cooled, scenting the place with a heavenly cloud of aroma.

While we munched, Joe pulled out the scrap of paper from the journal. "What do you make of this, Dad?"

Mack put on a pair of glasses and held the paper close to his nose. "Coleridge." He looked over the paper at Joe, eyebrows raised. "You reading Coleridge, son? I wouldn't have guessed."

"No, Dad. It's not mine. We found it in the professor's journal."

Mack's eyes widened behind the think lenses. "The murdered professor's journal? Really? Well who would imagine that? It's the Rime of the Ancient Mariner, I think. Mrs. Hala was a real poetry gal. She taught me a few things. I couldn't abide the stuff at first but it's a wonder what a body will do when they love someone."

I saw the wistful look steal into his eyes again. He missed her. After all these years, his heart still yearned for his dead wife. A strange thought burst into my head. Did my father miss my mother? True, he'd treated her like property, owned her body and soul. Still, he'd never remarried and I'd seen him, every Sunday, put a white daisy on her grave.

I hardened my heart against the ridiculous notion. He couldn't have loved her. If he had, he would have let her go.

Mack extracted a battered book from an equally battered bookshelf. He thumbed through the pages. "Here it is. I was right. Samuel Taylor Coleridge." He smiled proudly. "Not bad for an ancient mariner like myself, eh?"

I laughed. "Very impressive. What does it mean?"

"I'm not much of a Coleridge scholar. I'm more the Robert Frost sort of guy. As I recall it's a very long poem about a sailor who goes on an epic journey and confronts a lot of horrendous dangers. I remember he shoots an albatross at one point and the crew hangs it around his neck because they believe he's brought disaster down on them. Lots of weird supernatural stuff going on in it."

My head whirled. Albatross? Sailors? "But what does this passage mean?"

He peered at the paper. "Talks about the sky and the sea. Descriptive, some sort of celestial event. That's about all I can tell you without doing some research. Was the man an English professor?"

"No, geology." Joe looked at me and shrugged. "Maybe the guy just loved poetry."

I frowned. "I guess we'll never know." It made me sad to think of the man who admired such beautiful words, dying such an ugly death.

Joe and his father went outside to spread mulch and I watched through the window while I tidied up. Joe's strong arms shoveled the piles of bark under the shrubs and Mack slowly raked it flat. Joe stopped to laugh, throwing his head back in the sunlight, the sweat darkening his face to a deep bronze.

My breath caught. Two good men, two fine men, two men I could love forever.

But only if I took the chance and came clean. My path was suddenly clear to me. I had to tell Joe the truth, even it if meant losing him.

I'd lived a lie for much too long.

Would they still love me?

Would they run?

Could they forgive?

I had no idea but I knew that I needed to tell Joe.
And soon.

We stayed for a spaghetti dinner and obscenely large pieces of lemon meringue pie. The tangy wedges of custard along with that sweet billow of meringue made my head swim with pleasure. It was so improbable that a person could concoct something so fantastic using only eggs, sugar and lemon. A culinary mystery.

Mack wrapped up a piece for me and Joe to take home.

"You might need a little extra something to get you through the chaos," he said with a wink.

He had no idea.

An hour after dusk we headed home. I waved at Mack until he was a tiny dot in distance.

The swell of longing returned. "I love your dad."

"Me too." He gave me a sidelong glance. "He's pretty fond of you, I know. He always asks me to bring you along when I visit. Sometimes I think he likes you better than me."

The moon rose over the cliffs, a curve of silver in dark velvet. Silence filled up the space between us.

I opened my mouth to tell him and then thought better of it. Probably not a good idea to spring "cartel connections" on a guy while he was driving. Instead I asked him what he thought about the whole poem thing.

"I don't know Marty, but I'm more curious about why Todd is hanging onto this notebook. No matter where he got it, it's connected to a murder case. Isn't it police evidence?"

That shocked me. "Oh man. Of course it is. We'd better get it to Deputy Fisk."

"You said he's coming tomorrow to supervise plane removal. We can give it to him then, but I wonder how Todd got hold of it in the first place. If it was logged in as evidence, he wouldn't have access so he must have gotten hold of it another way. Do you think he knew Speigel?"

I had no idea. The whole matter was taxing my neural

network to the limit.

Joe's cell phone rang. He pulled over. I love that about Joe. He's a careful person. He would never change his pants while driving or something dumb like that. "It's for you," he said.

For me? I suppressed a shudder. It couldn't be Ramon. That was just too horrible to contemplate. I cleared my throat. "Hello?"

"Would marshmallows work?"

I finally managed an efficient exhale. "What?"

Lucille's heavy breathing filled the line. "Marshmallows. They wouldn't hurt when you throw them. 'Course we'd have to get them miniature kind."

"Lucille?"

"Yeah?"

"Why are we talking about throwing marshmallows?"

She thought for a minute. "I was talking to Preacher and he said ya can't throw rice on account of the fact that it sprouts all over and it ain't good for the birds. I don't want no sick birds at my wedding, so I says, 'How about the birdseed?'"

I've known Lucille a long time. It's best not to derail her mental train once it's left the station. I waited patiently for her to continue.

"So he tells me people slip on the birdseed and it falls in the cracks of the pavement and sprouts and grows weeds and stuff, so no birdseed. I read about folks tossing butterflies but that's plain ridiculous. Who in their right mind would want to be showered with bugs?"

"How about bubbles?"

"Who's Bubbles?"

I noticed Joe was trying to hold back laughter. "Never mind about that, Lucille. What do you want to do?"

"Well Ficky and me was thinking about marshmallows. They don't sprout and ain't gonna hurt anyone or put an eye out or nothing. Plus when we're gone Preacher can let Dino out to eat up all the leftovers. Don't that sound nice?"

Dino was the pastor's ninety pound Labrador who would eat anything from table scraps to license plates. "I think it's a great idea. Wedding marshmallows. Perfect."

"Yeah? You really think so?" She sounded pleased. "Okay then. I'll put it on the list. Fifteen bags of marshmallows. Or maybe sixteen so everyone can fill up their pockets to snack on later. Thanks, Marty. I been wondering about some other stuff but we can talk about that when you get back. I gotta go tell Ficky the good news."

She clicked off.

"Lucille is going to have people throw mini marshmallows as they leave the church. How does that grab you?"

"I've never heard that done before, but it sounds about right for Lucille. What does Ficky think?"

"I gather he thinks whatever she thinks is inspired."

"Ahh. The perfect couple."

For the rest of the journey we admired the ink dark sky and tried to pick out constellations. The cool air whipped in through the open windows, bringing in the smell of the night blooming cactus. My heart filled with the volume of so many blessings. A pristine landscape, a wonderful man, going home to my safe haven. But the niggle of responsibility resurfaced as I admired Joe's moonlit profile.

I had to tell him tonight.

Would this be the last night he would love me? The thought took my breath away. I leaned my head against the door and closed my eyes as we glided back to Desert Star.

Chapter Nine

It was after midnight when we got back and I was wide awake. I sucked in a deep breath and offered up a prayer for courage.

"Joe," I said as we piled out of the Jeep, "can you come in for a minute? There's something I need to talk to you about." A bead of sweat trickled down my back in spite of the cool air.

"Sure. I'll grab my cell phone." He turned back to the Jeep while I fished out the keys to my office.

I didn't need them.

As I reached for the door, it crashed open and a figure hurtled out.

A heavy weight plowed over me. I fell backward down the steps and the intruder used me for a doormat. I screamed as hit the ground but it came out as more of a gasp when the air was steamrolled out of me.

I heard the sound of Joe's keys falling on the ground and running feet.

"Stop!" Joe shouted.

There was the noise of more running feet and Joe appeared on his knees beside me. His eyes were wide with fear. "Marty, Marty. Are you okay? How badly are you hurt?"

I was too winded to reply. Pain coursed up and down my ribcage.

He fumbled for his phone. "Lie still. I'll call 911."

I reached out a hand to his wrist. "No," I croaked. With great effort I reinflated my speaking machinery. "I think I'm okay."

He helped me to sit up. It was a slow and painful process. The night whirled around me in brilliant swirls of light and dark. My stomach throbbed and the rest of me was numb.

Joe rested his hands on my clavicle. He gently poked and prodded my head and neck. "Sit there for a while. Don't hurry to get up."

No worries there. I couldn't figure out which direction was up anyway. I was sure my eyeballs were rolling around like the fruits in a slot machine.

He pushed the hair out of my face and looked into my pupils. Gosh that guy was gorgeous. Those dark eyes sucked me in every time, even after I'd been mashed like a potato. I squeezed my eyes shut and waited until everything stopped spinning.

"No blood, but you might have a concussion. Can you get up?"

I nodded.

Joe hooked a shoulder under my armpit and heaved me to my feet and into the trailer.

Or what was left of it.

Even with my eyes still doing loop de loops I could see the place had been ransacked. The file cabinet was open and papers were strewn all over the floor. My dresser drawers were dumped out on top of the bed and the contents of my clothes closet were flung all over the place. I took it all in.

And then it all came out. I began to cry. Tears gushing, nose running, chest heaving, the whole enchilada kind of bawling.

"What…" I blubbered. "What is going on here?" More wailing. "Who is doing this to me?" Streams of salt water streaming down my face. "I can't stand….any….more."

Poor Joe.

He tried to take in the devastation in the room and assess the extent of my hysteria the same time. Then he said something soothing, I don't remember the words exactly, before he put the kitchen chair upright and plopped me into it. He turned all of the lights on and filled a towel with ice.

"First things first. Put this on your forehead."

"Why?" I wheezed. "It doesn't hurt."

He looked at me. "It will. Looks like the door hit you in the head."

"Swell. The trampling must have distracted me from my forehead."

Joe gingerly tilted my face toward the lamp and checked my pupils. "I don't think it's a concussion, but we should go to the hospital anyway. You need a CAT scan to be sure."

All of my sore muscles tensed. "I am not going anywhere," I said through gritted teeth.

"Why did I guess that would be your answer? I'm calling the police though. We're going to have to get them on speed dial if things don't settle down around here."

Joe repeated the whole sad saga for the cops. "They thought it was a crank call for a minute there. Haven't seen this much action in decades."

A thought struck me so hard I jumped. "Byron. Where's Byron? Do you think he's hurt?" I tried to stand but the pain folded me up again.

"Sit. I'll find him." Joe hunkered down like a bloodhound tracking a scent.

"Look under the kitchen sink, way in the back."

I watched with pulse pounding as he picked his way to the sink. The majority of the kitchen equipment was dumped all over the floor. Had poor Byron met the business end of a cheese grater? Was he lying dead under an omelet pan somewhere?

Joe extracted a pen light from his pocket and shone it into the dark space.

"It's okay. Byron looks fine. He's crammed so far back in the corner the guy probably didn't even see him. Plus he's half buried in a pile of papers he's shredded."

I relaxed in the chair but that put a strain on my bruised ribs so I sat up again. "What could anyone possibly want in my office? I have all of five bucks in change and no credit cards lying around. There's not even anything worth taking in the refrigerator unless you count Gouda cheese and a Ding Dong I was saving." Tears welled up again.

"It's probably the same guy who shot at us last night. Did you get a look at him when he knocked you over?"

"Only at his shoes. Sneakers, very dirty. How about you?"

He sighed. "I was facing the Jeep. By the time I turned around he was practically gone. I only know he was wearing a jacket and he looked pretty solid. I heard an engine so he left a car somewhere close by."

"It's just crazy. None of this makes any sense." Now I could feel the goose egg on my forehead where the door slammed into my head. Joe came over to peek at my pupils again. He must have been satisfied because he began to clean up, righting furniture and stacking papers.

"I'll help," I said but he gave me a firm shake of the head.

"Nope. You're going to sit there. No arguments."

I sat there admiring my Joe. What other guy would clean up a gal's trailer? Pick up her socks and underwear. My cheeks warmed at this part.

He continued around until everything was either put away or stacked in piles for later. Then he fixed me a cup of hot tea and put fresh ice on my head. I tried to hold the ice pack in place and drink at the same time.

We pondered while we sipped tea. The object wasn't robbery unless the perpetrator was an idiot who couldn't see that I was living an iota above the poverty line. No. Scary Man was looking for something.

I put my cup down. "Joe, the only thing valuable on this property is the animals and you wouldn't get a dime for them on the black market. None of them are close to being perfect specimens."

He nodded in agreement. "Yup."

"Then what do I have that would make people crash planes, carry out armed searches and destroy my office?" Okay, I knew my brother was looking for me and he no doubt was armed, but his goal was to take me in alive and kicking. Papa wouldn't want his property damaged.

He stifled a yawn and checked his watch. "I don't know, Marty. I do know, however, that we're not going to figure it out tonight. It's almost one thirty in the morning and we both need sleep. Come on, let's get you tucked in."

Joe helped me ease onto the mattress and pulled off my shoes. The old raggedy comforter settled across me like Joe's gentle good night kiss. He cracked the window slats next to my bed.

"I'm going to sleep in the tent trailer and come check on you every few hours. I'll just whisper through the window slats and if you answer me I'll know you're fine. If you don't answer I'm going to have to come in here and roust you to check for altered consciousness. How does that sound?"

I nodded, throat suddenly clogged. "You are so good to me. I, I wanted to tell you something."

He pushed my bangs gently away from the bump. "You can tell me later, Marty. Right now, you need to rest."

My voice sounded very small. "I don't deserve you, Joe."

"Hope you still feel that way when I wake you up in two hours." He turned on my nightlight.

How did he know that my nightlight would banish all varieties of scary monsters? Darling man.

One more kiss and he was gone.

I'd been battered and bashed but at least I still had Joe.

For one more night, anyway.

Some diabolical hand pounded on my door the next morning shortly after sunrise. I had to open my eyelids with my fingers. When I moved my head it felt like there was an axe stuck between my brain hemispheres. The rest of my parts put in their two cents worth as I stood and waited for my head to catch up with the rest of me.

I moved at a snail's pace toward the door. I hadn't had much recuperative rest because true to his word, Joe had whispered through the slats every two hours or so. "Marty, can you hear me?"

I must have managed to mumble a coherent response each time as I'd made it through the night without being carted off to the hospital. This knock wasn't Joe's. It was too loud and too low down on the door.

Could it be Intruder Man come back? I didn't think he would bother knocking and Joe would have stopped him for questioning before he reached the porch. Several minutes later I was still making my painful way to the door. Any self-respecting tortoise would have left me in the dust.

I almost reached the handle when it opened without my help.

Lucille wore her tie dyed overalls and an orange bandana around her hair. "Man you took a long time to answer the door. Maybe you ought to think about some vitamins. My great aunt Alice moves faster than you and she's eighty five." She stepped over a pile of papers on her way to the refrigerator for some orange juice.

"Good morning, Lucille," I said as I freed the coffeepot from under a stack of dishes and plugged it in. Then I lobbed an apple into the open door under the sink. It would have to suffice for Byron until I could bend over without serious repercussions.

"Morning. I'll have you know I been busy while you're here lollygagging in bed. Things are all set for Friday."

I watched the coffee squirt out drip by heavenly drip. The bottle of Advil on the kitchen table must have been left by my sweet man sometime in the wee hours. There was a note too.

Marty, went to help Jeff. His cow's breach. Be back as soon as I can. Stay in bed and take it easy. Call my cell if you need ANYTHING. J

That silly cow had been nothing but trouble for Jeff since the day he got her. We'd spent plenty of hours trying to find that rascal and bring her home. Didn't surprise me at all that she'd find a difficult way to deliver her calf. There was a good reason she was named Calamity. I swallowed two Advil without any water and poured myself some coffee. Then I sat. Carefully.

Lucille refilled her cup with more orange juice. She scanned the stacks of kitchenware that Joe had picked up off the floor and laid on the sofa. "You know, I don't mean to be critical, Marty, but your housekeeping could use some sprucing up. Sakes alive. Ain't you got cabinets for these pots?"

I stopped between sips. "I had an uninvited visitor last night and he was much bigger than a squirrel. He messed up the place."

"You don't say?" She sat down on the kitchen chair so hard the floor shuddered. "An intruder? Was he driving my Moped? Was it that stinker pilot?"

"Not that I could see. I was pretty much lying at the bottom of the porch steps the whole time. Joe couldn't identify him either."

She peered closely into my face. Her face creased into a web of concerned wrinkles. "Well honey. Look at you. Your face is all black and blue. Did that guy hurt you?"

I gave her a Reader's Digest version.

Her eyes widened until her eyebrows disappeared under the bandana. "I'll just bet it was that good for nothing pilot. When I get my hands on him I'll fricassee his goose all right. There won't be anything left of him but his shadow."

My heart warmed. Lucille really did think of me as family. My brain replayed her earlier conversation. "What were you talking about before? What is all set for Friday?"

She whipped out some cocktail wieners from her pocket and munched, eyes sparkling. "The rehearsal."

"The rehearsal for what?"

"For the weddin', of course. And Ficky got the most perfect spot for the after party and it ain't gonna cost a dime. Well, except for the food. Maxine said she's goin' to make her chicken pot pies and Diane's bringing chipped beef on toast. That's not my favorite, but I didn't want to hurt her feelings. She's sensitive." She dug some meat from between her teeth. "'Course we'll have to have somethin' there for Joe, bein' as how he don't eat meat. Maybe some broccoli or something. I'm gonna have a humongous ham for everyone else. Nothin' better than a big wad of ham to put a person in the party mood."

I gulped more coffee. It didn't help. I was still drowning in incoherent conversation. "Lucille, did I hear you say you're having the wedding rehearsal on Friday? This Friday?"

"You bet. I mean I think it's plumb silly anyway to have to practice gettin' married. You ain't gotta do much but show up and say two words. Why you need to practice? Anyway Ficky says it's tradition and what are you gonna do about that?"

"But you haven't even decided on your wedding date yet."

"Oh yes we have. Next Saturday."

My mouth fell open. "Next Saturday? I thought we were talking the end of June, maybe July."

"Can't, on account of the bowling tournament."

I could understand each of her words but somehow when put together, they made no sense whatsoever. "Lucille, what are you talking about?"

She swallowed the last cocktail wiener and sat back. "Ficky scored us a reception hall. It's the bowling alley. Took a lot of convincing on his part but he done it. Ain't he just the skin on the cream?"

I blinked. "Wow, the bowling alley. That's er, unique."

"Yup. It's air conditioned and carpeted and Greg, he's the owner, even said we could have the cake and vittles inside, so long as we come back later to shampoo the carpet if somethin' gets spilled." She tapped her chin. "The carpet is mostly purple. You think we can find a punch recipe that's purple so's if somethin' spills it won't show?"

"Um, probably. So....we're rehearsing this Friday and you're getting married next Saturday? As in a little over a week from now?"

"You betcha."

Oh man. I just had to get my brain invited to my life again. I was so far gone I hardly knew where to begin. Wedding, Marty. Focus on Lucille's wedding for five minutes. "That's wonderful. I'm so happy you picked a date. What can I help with?"

Lucille patted my hand. "Nothin' right now, hon. You just rest and heal up." She looked at my wall clock which now sat on the floor near the oven. "So's I better get my chores done around here. I gotta go buy my wedding overalls and get me some bows and stuff to decorate. Maybe some of them tissue paper bells. You wanna help with the decorating when the time comes?"

How did one go about decorating a bowling alley? "Oh, uh, sure, yes, absolutely."

She reached over and patted my hand. "You know what, Marty? You've been such a help to me, I'm gonna order your overalls today when I go to town and then I'm gonna fix you some of my six pepper stew. It'll just cook all those bruises right off of you."

"Oh, you don't need to do that," I started. It did no good.

"I insist. I'm gonna throw in one of them habaneros. Whooeee. If that don't slam you into wellness I reckon' nothing will. You'll be dancing the Macarena in no time." Lucille tightened her bandana until there were no more wrinkles on her forehead and headed out the door. When she got to the threshold she stopped and fished around her pocket. "One more thing I forgot to tell you."

Was there any other wedding topic we hadn't covered? I pressed a hand to the top of my head so it wouldn't fall off. "What is it?"

"Somebody called yesterday while you was out. I wrote down the message but I accidentally left it in my pants." She handed me a greasy slip of paper.

My heart began to pound against my bruised ribs. "Who...who was it?"

"Dunno. Some guy. He'll be here tomorrow. It's all on the note. Bye."

Chapter Ten

I unfolded the paper with clammy fingers. Lucille's spelling was unorthodox but the message was clear.

    Bento familee wants overnite tour. Three peple. Be here noon.

The relief flooded through me.

It wasn't my brother, it was a message from an actual visitor. Better still, it was from a real live family of visitors wanted to take our overnight tour. A bonafide paying bunch of tourists. I would have jumped up and down. Instead I poured myself another cup of coffee to celebrate. If only I had a doughnut chaser.

The angry throbbing in my head increased. Then it became more of a rumbling that filled the trailer and rattled the windows. When the kitchen table began to vibrate I went to the window. It was an enormous tractor trailer crunching toward the downed plane. Deputy Fisk followed in his cruiser.

Oh joy. The awful plane, the symbol of all that had gone wrong in my life since the rock fell out of the sky, was going to be removed from the Desert Star. The blackened thing had practically become a fixture. I'd had to shoo away a number of local rubberneckers who wanted to get a look at the wreck.

Hank was hooking up chains to the rear of the plane. Too bad all my other problems couldn't be dragged away too. There were still sturdy assailants and my crazy brother on the loose. My head began to pound again.

"One thing at a time, Marty." I held on to the railing and inched my way down the porch steps, muscles complaining all the while. Deputy Fisk met me at the bottom.

"You look like a train ran over your face."

"Thanks for pointing that out. We had an intruder last night. Joe called you, remember?"

The Deputy's eyebrows shot up and out came his little notebook and pencil. He blew out his mustache. "It was a busy night. Okay. Tell me everything."

I rambled my way through the story. Joe showed up at the tail end. His face was still etched with the same concern I'd seen the night before. "Marty. What are you doing up? You should be in bed."

"I was, but Lucille came and then this lovely tractor trailer rolled in and here I am."

He eyed me closely. "Do you want to sit down? You look…"

"Like a train ran over my face? No. I'm upright so I'd better stay that way."

Fisk finished scribbling. "Did you have anything to add, Joe? Can you give me a description at least? Height? Build? Race? Anything?"

"Not really. He was beefy that's about all I can tell you. Wearing dark clothes and a cap."

"And I'm guessing he wears a size 12 shoe."

Fisk looked impressed. "How'd you come up with that?"

"I've got a size 12 bruise on my belly."

"Ah." He jotted a note. "I'm going to drive by every few hours to keep an eye on the place."

"Thank you. Did you get Todd Chin safely delivered?"

"Uh huh. Not much of a talker. Still think I know him from somewhere. It's been driving me crazy. Doesn't matter. It'll come to me sooner or later."

Hank hooked up another set of cables to the plane and made sure the area was free of people and critters. Then he tilted the bed of the truck and pulled that big bad boy right up onto the trailer.

I applauded, tears crowding my eyes. "Thanks so much, Hank," I yelled, over the roar of the engine. "You are a wonderful man."

He doffed his cap and bowed before he drove away.

The plane left a weird, imprint in the sand, as if a giant had dragged his feet sliding into home plate. We admired the wide open space, sans wreckage.

I was back in business. Business. With a jerk I remembered Lucille's greasy note. "Joe. We've got some customers coming." I grabbed his wrist and turned his watch to face me. "They'll be here in an hour and a half. I'd better get the animals fed."

"What are they signed up for?"

"An overnighter," I yelled over my shoulder, ignoring his protective clucking and the pain in my head.

I scurried through the animal feeding, most of which Lucille had already seen to. The rabbits got clean hay and a new salt lick. "Tito, where are you?" I whistled and jangled his feed cup. No pig. "Well wherever you are, be nice to the visitors. They're the paying kind."

I scrunched on a baseball cap, hoping the brim would hide my purple goose egg as I dialed the cell phone. Ficky answered on the first ring.

"Hello, Ficky. It's Marty."

"'Lo, Marty. It's Ficky."

"Yes, er, I know. Listen would you please give Lucille a

message for me when she comes over for lunch?" I waited. "Uh, Ficky? Are you there?"

"Yes, Marty. It's Ficky here. Is it a long message?"

"I don't think so, why?"

"I wondered whether to write it on a Post-it or a piece of paper."

"Ummm, I'd go for the piece of paper."

"Okay. Go ahead."

"Please tell Lucille I'm going with Joe on that overnighter with the Bentos and could she please feed all the animals tomorrow. Did you get that, Ficky?"

"No. I couldn't find a piece of paper."

I sighed. "Do you have a Post-it?"

"Yes, I do."

"Okay. Then write the message on the Post-it."

"Sure. What was the message?"

I took two deep breaths before I repeated my list very slowly for him. "So can you give the message to Lucille today?"

"Yes, ma'am. I'll deliver the message."

"Excellent. Good-bye."

"Good-bye Marty. This is Ficky, signing off."

I marveled as I hung up that God had managed to create a person who was the perfect match for Lucille.

"Our God is an awesome God," I said, as I jotted a quick grocery list.

Joe was already packing up the first aid kit and washing out the cooler. "Marty, I really don't think you should be going on an overnighter after you got clobbered. It's not a smart idea."

I smiled. "You are so sweet. And I'm going. And you know there's no point in arguing."

He sighed. "Yes, I do. I figured I throw it out there anyway. So I won't waste my time telling you that you shouldn't drive after a head trauma?"

"Right. I have a hard head."

"That's the truth."

I shot him a sharp look before I drove to the Shop 'N' Go, my brain running like a squirrel on a candy high. Three men for the tour, plus me and Joe. That meant dinner and breakfast the next morning. Normally I'd have given them a survey via the phone about their eating preferences, but there was no time to stand on formality. We'd grill vegetables and add them to sliced sourdough with slabs of cheese. Throw them on the portable barbie for a minute with a foil-covered brick on top and voila! Instant paninis. If they complained at the lack of meat, we'd distract them with s'mores. There is not one soul on the planet who can resist a nicely browned ooey gooey marshmallow. At least, not one that I'd ever met.

In a matter of fifteen minutes the shopping was done and I raced back to the Desert Star. On the way, a dark thought wormed its way into my bubble of happy productivity. Joe. I hadn't had a chance to tell him yet.

Funny. Last night I'd been bashed by a guy who could be a murderer for all I knew but that fact didn't scare me half as much as telling Joe the truth about Martina Isabella Escobar. I squirmed in the seat. Didn't he know the important truths already? He knew my heart and soul. He knew the fact that I can't stand pimentos or watching an animal suffer. He knew I loved him more than my own life. Okay, I hadn't exactly told him in so many words, but he knew.

Didn't he?

Surely that would all turn out to be more important than my family tree.

Wouldn't it?

The thoughts were just too prickly to hang onto. I turned on the only music station I could get in mid-nowhere and hummed along. It was 12:30. I had half an hour to help Joe load up the sleeping bags, tents, wood for the camp fire and other overnight necessities.

We heaved the last cooler into the back of the van as the

Bentos pulled up. The door of their Pontiac flew open and a young boy, maybe ten or so, hopped from the car like he was spring loaded. He raced over to the weird tracks left by the plane removal and began to take pictures, nose close to the ground.

"Uh, hi. I'm Marty Barr."

He didn't answer.

Another man emerged from the car, his bald head gleaming in the sun, shirt struggling to hold his wide expanse of belly. He extended his hand. "Hello. I'm Allen Bento. You can call me Al. The shutterbug over there is Allen, Jr. We call him A.J. And the other guy…" he looked behind him. "Come out of the car, dad," he called.

A slender silver haired man emerged from the car. He had a thin, well-trimmed mustache and a pencil tucked behind his ear. He shook our hands as Allen introduced him.

"This is my father, Allen, Sr. We call him Big Al."

I introduced Joe and myself to all three Als.

"We're keen to get started. When do we leave?" Bald Al said.

Joe explained our itinerary and a few important details about the desert experience, namely, it's a wild place, not a Disneyland adventure. "What are you looking to get out of the trip?" he said.

Al chuckled. "We want to experience nature, I'm a big outdoorsman, myself but my job keeps me in the office too much. I'm in the shoe business. Anyway, my son A.J. hasn't much gotten into camping so his mother suggested I take him on an adventure."

The kid was now on the ground, poking a finger in the sand.

"He could use a dose of adventure," Big Al said. "Spends his days in front of the iPad. Surprised he hasn't grown a plug out of his ear."

The boy ignored the conversation and continued to take pictures of the tracks.

"You'll have lots of opportunity for great photos," I called to A.J. "Would you like to come to the animal hospital and meet our patients?"

Bald Al nodded. "Oh that would be great. How about it, son?"

The kid straightened. "I guess so, but I'm going to photograph all of this. This could be a spaceship signature."

I did a double take. "Er, a what?"

A.J. snorted. "The imprint from a spaceship landing. Don't you know that?"

"I'm sorry to disappoint, but it was a plane crash."

"Really?" Bald Al wiped the sweat from his forehead. "You had a plane crash here?"

"Yes, but that's all taken care of now." I led the way to the hospital. The two oldest Als followed me. "So you son is into spaceships?"

Big Al sighed. "He's the biggest conspiracy theorist you'd ever want to meet. It's unnatural for a kid. That's what I tell his mother, anyway. He should be listening to obnoxious music and taking selfies, not monitoring Roswell chat groups."

"Now we're all going to enjoy a wonderful outdoor experience," Al said, hitching up his pants. "No technology or modern comforts, just men and nature."

"Right," I said pointing out the charming attributes of J.R. and Matt.

Bob played along, slinking across his enclosure at just the right moment. He has a flare for the dramatic, that bobcat.

"Uh huh. Nice animals," A.J. said, finally making eye contact. "Man, what happened? It looks like someone punched you in the face."

"Er, door injury."

"Too bad. When can we get out of here?"

"Now. Right this way," I said.

We collected again at the welcome area and loaded up

the van. Joe drove and I sat in the passenger seat. The two oldest Als sat in the next seat and A.J. in the way back with the tents.

"Tents, eh?" Bald Al said with a sniff. "I thought we'd be sleeping under the stars."

"No problem," I said. "Whatever you want is fine." We aimed to please our two legged clients. If the guy wanted to sleep on the rocky ground with all the critters, he was welcome to it. As for me? I liked walls, even if they were only made of nylon.

Just before I closed the last door, Tito did his Golden Retriever trick. He leaped into the back and hunkered down on top of the sleeping bags with a happy grunt.

"What is it?" A.J. said, scooting as far away as he could get. "Get it away from me."

I groaned. "He's a javelina or peccary or pig, whatever you prefer. Tito, out!" I commanded. "This is a people only trip."

He twitched his ears. That was pig for "Not by the hair of my chinny-chin-chin."

I was faced with a choice. Drag him out and let the Bentos witness an all-out piggy fit, or let him tag along. "Is it okay if we let Tito come? He's pretty well behaved. You won't even know he's there. Actually, he could be the night sentry. He's very brave." This was stretching it a bit, though I had seen Tito scare a toad away. Then again, he hadn't exactly frightened the amphibian into a quivering pile of flippers either. I recalled the toad sauntering away rather than fleeing and I suspected at the time he was probably laughing.

Anyway, the three nodded, more out of shock than agreement, but it was enough for me. We hit the road, three Als, two guides and a stowaway pig.

"I'm hot," A.J. piped up from the back a few miles later.

I set the air conditioner to low.

"I'm still hot," he said again.

"It will take a minute for the air to cool off."

"Why is it so hot here?" the boy whined.

I tried to monitor my sarcasm level. "That's because it's the desert." Joe poked me with his elbow. "What are you hoping to see during your visit?"

The boy did not look at me as he answered. "Aliens."

"We're not that close to the border," Joe said, with a hint of a smile.

"Not that kind of alien," A.J. said. "The kind from outer space. Like the kind that landed in Roswell."

Big Al huffed. "Ridiculous. The kid is cracked."

"Roswell is in New Mexico," I pointed out. "This is Arizona."

"No, duh. It doesn't matter. Aliens need a wide open area in the middle of nowhere to land. This is the perfect place."

I kept my voice light. "I thought that whole Roswell business turned out to be a weather balloon or something."

A.J.'s eyes rolled around in his head. "Of course, that's what the government wants you to think. How gullible can you be?"

Joe gave me another subtle nudge which curtailed what was about to come out of my mouth. "Well let me know if you spot any aliens."

"Hey, I've got an idea. Let's stop at the creek." Joe said. "There's enough water to get your feet wet and I'll break out some cold sodas."

Good old Joe. Sheer genius.

We drove up to Thornapple Creek. Thanks to the recent downpour it was still a creek. Not a very big one, but it bubbled and meandered in a respectable fashion. Father Al and his son took off their socks and waded around in the water. Tito set off to look for roots. Big Al sat on a rock and scribbled page after page in his journal.

Journal! "Oh man," I whispered to Joe. "I forgot to hand over the professor's journal to Deputy Fisk."

Joe patted me on my shoulder. "It's okay. We'll drop it off as soon as we get back."

I relaxed again, my pores drinking in the brilliant sunlight which eased my aching muscles. Spring in the desert is awesome. Sure you've got your crazy storms, but the temperatures are still in the moderately hot zone and the rain paints the desert with color. From my seat on the rock next to Joe I saw the lavender flowers of the feather dalea and the muddy purple range ratany blooms. Miracles, every one of them.

I noticed Big Al looking at me as I fingered a branch of yucca. "It's a soaptree, named for the squishy goo in its roots. Indians used it to make shampoo and soap. Cattle eat the flowers and you can even eat the palms in an emergency. All that in one plant. Amazing, don't you think?"

Big Al did not look impressed with my ecological dissertation. He turned back to his journal without a word.

"And Grandpa says the kid is fixated. I wonder what the old guy is writing about over there," I said into Joe's ear. "He's got the beginnings of a novel, by now."

"Probably writes haiku," he whispered back.

Somehow I didn't think so. "Hey A.J," I called to the boy. "Come back down here, okay? It's not a good idea to climb around the rocks, barefoot."

A.J. gave me a sassy look. Then his expression changed. A sort of glaze came over his face and his mouth opened in a wide circle. He didn't scream, but his face told me he was having a close encounter with something.

And it wasn't aliens.

Chapter Eleven

Joe made it to A.J. a step before me. Big Al remained on his rock, oblivious. Bald Al huffed up the rocky pile after us.

"It's a rattlesnake," A.J. said, his voice a whisper. He pointed at his feet. "It's going to bite me."

Joe peered into a rocky crevice.

"What is it?" Al huffed.

"A rattlesnake," A.J. whispered again, his eyes huge, face white as Elmer's glue.

Bald Al jumped as if he'd received an electric shock.

"No, hold on there." Joe shined his penlight into the gap. "It's not a rattlesnake. It's a glossy snake. They're totally harmless. A good four footer, too." He slapped A.J. on the back. "Way to spot, 'em. You're the first person to find a glossy snake specimen so far this year."

A dash of color returned to A.J's face. "I…I am?"

"You betcha. Let's go get your iPhone and take a picture." Joe led us all down the pile. By the time they got the camera, A.J. was actually smiling. Did I mention that Joe is a genius?

Bald Al looked a bit peaked, I noticed. "Are you okay, Mr. Bento?"

"Oh sure, sure. Poor A.J. hasn't seen too many snakes. Easy to mistake the flossy snake for a rattler."

"It's glossy, not flossy," Big Al said from his spot on the rock. "If it was a rattler, we would be in a heap of trouble right about now."

The crabby man was right. Western Diamondback Rattlers are aggressive and highly excitable. Not to mention their heat seeking pits and potent venom. We'd dodged a land mine to be sure. Glossy snake or not, I was determined to keep a tighter leash on these happy campers until I'd delivered them safely back. I whistled for Tito and we piled in the van.

The sun was low in the sky when we made it to camp, an open plateau with spectacular views and a handy outhouse tucked behind a screen of mesquite. I hadn't wanted to put in the outhouse, but it seemed that even the staunchest nature lovers appreciated one tiny bit of civilization in their wilderness. Anything to oblige.

Joe and A.J. set to work pitching the tent while I started the portable grill for dinner and stacked the wood for the campfire. Since I had to work with pain from my stomped ribs, it took me a while.

Al laid out his sleeping bag on a mat, prepared for an evening of star watching. Soon there were two tents standing at attention. One was for Joe and one for Big Al and A.J. I opted to sleep in the van, since my bruised body required the comfort of padded upholstery. Besides, I knew what sort of creatures enjoyed a nighttime stroll.

The campfire blazed under my attention. Bald Al asked me about my fire starters. I held one up for him to see. "Just a crayon wrapped in wax paper. Much better for the environment than lighter fluid. I learned it from a Girl Scout leader."

He helped me cut up the red peppers and zucchini. After a few minutes on the fire they had lovely grill marks and a divine smoky fragrance. We took them off and layered them with slabs of Havarti on thick slices of sturdy bread. Onto the grill and then a foil wrapped brick went on top.

Soon it was time to enjoy our sandwiches and store bought potato salad. We gathered around the fire. Tito too, until I gave him some sliced red pepper and a wedge of zucchini. It grew silent, except for the sound of munching. The sun continued to slip toward the horizon in a pool of molten color.

I had a frightening image of the last time I'd watched a sunset out on my land. Surely there was no way an armed assailant would attack again? The skin on my neck prickled as I imagined a gunman hunkered down behind a rock, scoping out a target on the back of my head.

Stop it, Marty. Fisk said he'd keep an eye on the place. A felon would have to be crazy to come back. Then again, someone had been crazy enough to break into my office. I forced myself to tune in on the new conversation between Joe and A.J.

"But how do you know it was aliens?" Joe asked.

A.J.'s face was eager as he leaned toward Joe and shoveled food into his mouth. "Eye witness reports, man. Some even talked about alien autopsies. Boy, I wish I'd been there to see that. Dead aliens. Sweet. Don't you believe in aliens?"

"I believe God the father made us in his image and He made all the life in the universe. That's pretty much all I need to know."

"But there's life out there that we haven't seen yet," A.J. said between bites. "Real aliens, extraterrestrials that are way smarter than we are."

I didn't think that was saying much.

Joe finished his sandwich. "You know A.J, the Indians were here a long time ago. They saw white ghosts come onto their lands bringing some good things and some not so good things. They were strange ghosts who arrived unannounced and uninvited."

"Really? Ghosts? Oh wait a minute. You mean white people."

"Exactly, but to the Yavapai they might just as well have come from outer space."

A.J. was silent for a minute. "Yeah, but outer space aliens are neater. I read in a book they have these big pointy heads and only two fingers on each hand. Isn't that cool? I'm on a bunch of message boards and we talk all the time."

Joe laughed. "Well, I guess everyone needs a hobby." He turned to Big Al. "What's your hobby then, Mr. Bento?"

Al's silver hair glowed in the firelight. He finished his sandwich and wiped his mouth with a napkin. "I'm a people watcher."

"That certainly is more interesting than television." I spoke theoretically because I don't actually own a television. I wondered what the senior Al had been scribbling down in his journal all day. Joe was right. It was probably harmless but my ever growing sense that someone was out to get me colored everything suspicious in my eyes.

Joe and Big Al gathered up the dinner plates and piled them all into a bucket and snapped on a lid. I'm sure there's a really nifty way to wash dishes in the desert without the benefit of running water but I'm just not that energetic. We take the bucket back to the office and wash them there.

The sky was a pearly gray by the time we finished. I rallied the troops for the night hike while Joe went ahead to check the trail for anything with teeth, claws or, perhaps, bullets. When he got back and gave the thumbs up, we donned our jackets, grabbed iPhones and water bottles and followed him into the gathering dusk. Tito trotted along at my side. He heels nicely for a pig.

On the way I dazzled the visitors with my botanical knowledge.

"This month the saguaro fruits begin to ripen." I pointed to a perfect prickled specimen. "Each fruit is sweet and full of seeds, as many as 2000 in each one. It's a source of food for many desert animals."

"And native people," Joe pointed out.

"And native people," I agreed. I'd enjoyed a mean saguaro fruit jam from Mack's kitchen before. It was an old Yavapai recipe, or at least that's what he'd told me.

"What kind of animals eat the fruits?" Bald Al asked.

"Javelinas, coyotes, foxes, ants, birds and the like."

A.J. sniffed. "It's cold out here."

Oh boy. Again with the temperature complaints. I pointed to a massive armed plant, at least fifteen feet high, "Did you know that a saguaro cactus like that one can grow from a seed the size of a pinhead?"

"Fascinating," A.J. said in a most unfascinated tone. "This would be a great place for dirt biking."

"We don't allow that here. It's too destructive for the environment."

"Figures," he said. "Wouldn't want to ruin a perfectly good barren wasteland. What's the matter with that pig? How come it follows you around like a dog?"

"He's a Golden Retriever in disguise." I edged closer to the older Als and continued my nature tirade. They appeared to be a more interested audience.

Bald Al stopped suddenly. "What was that? That noise. Did you hear it?"

"Coyote," Joe answered.

We listened for a moment to the eerie call, the sound of wet fingers rubbing over glass. There was an answer from the other side of the plateau. Two short barks and a yodel.

Al clapped his son on the back. His chuckle was loud in the thin air. "Don't worry son. If any coyotes show up, we can outrun 'em."

"Not unless you can beat thirty miles per hour," Joe put in.

Al's laugh sounded shaky.

The trail emptied out at a high spot, ringed with mesquite and patches of prickly pear. We checked for bugs and sat on the wooden benches Joe and I made last year. The sky was an endless spangle of brilliant stars against black velvet. It's another God-made reward for desert dwellers: the most incredible stargazing you could imagine. The only place with a better view must be from God's side of Heaven.

"Let's see if we can identify any constellations." Joe pointed out Bootes the herdsman driving his bear across the sky. We followed his finger, trying to find Arcturus, the brightest star in that configuration.

Those distant stars always gave me a pang. "Poor Bootes," I murmured. "You'll never be with your mother again, will you?"

"Where's the mother?" Al asked.

"According to mythology, Bootes' mother was changed into a bear and Bootes almost killed her while hunting. Zeus rescued her and put her in the sky as Ursa Major, the Great Bear." I didn't share the rest of my melancholy thoughts. Bootes could roam the whole heavens, but his mother remained just out of his grasp. Close, but never quite close enough.

Joe redirected us to Scorpius, the giant bug in the sky.

"I know that one," Big Al said. "Hera sent the scorpion to kill Orion. That's why they're on opposite sides of the sky, to keep them from offing each other."

"That's one version," Joe agreed. "Kinda morbid though. I like the Chinese description. They call it the Azure Dragon who arrives to announce the coming of spring. Or the Maori legend that it's one of the posts used to hold Sky Father in place."

I liked that one too. I could picture God up in that sparkling vault, sitting there, watching over His people. Tito snuggled up against my leg, his wiry hair scuffing my jeans. Absently, I scratched behind his ears until he began to snore.

My mind wandered back seventeen years. I was a ten year old astronomer, peering into the Mexican sky with Papa.

Papa put gentle hands on my head to turn my face in the right direction. He laughed at my comical descriptions of what I saw written in the sky, and I felt a surge of pleasure. "All the stars," he said, sweeping his arm across the sky, "are for you, my Martina. They are all shining just for you."

Later that night I was out of bed, searching for some leftover posole to snitch when I heard loud voices from my father's study. I peeked through the crack in the door in time to catch the angry words, in time to see the skinny stranger fall to the floor as my father smashed a fist into his face.

"No one takes what is mine," my father hissed, his face unrecognizable. "You will be a lesson to others."

I drew back, frozen there in the darkened hallway for a long while. The man's whimper lingered in my ears as I tiptoed away. I waited until the next day when Mama and I were alone.

"Why did Papa hurt that man last night?"

My mother looked startled. She admonished me for spying.

"Pastor says violent hands are a grief to God," I said. "Papa hit him and knocked him down. I heard him cry out when they dragged him out to the car."

She pulled me into her arms and stroked my hair.

"Papa is two men, Martina. He has only given one to God, and the other makes him do bad things, very bad."

"When will he give the other one to God?"

"I don't know, mija. That is between Papa and the Lord."

I felt the beat of her heart against my cheek. A new thought rose in my head. "Mama, are you afraid of Papa?"

She pulled me to arm's length and looked into my eyes for a very long time. "Come. Let's go get your paint box and make some pictures."

Tito rolled over and nudged my leg, snapping me out of my reverie. The menfolk seemed to be done with their star gazing. A.J. was picking up rocks and stowing them in his pockets. I figured the 'take only photos, leave only footprints' thing would be wasted on him. We shouldered our gear, I woke the pig, and we headed back to camp.

The fire required a bit of stoking on my part but soon the embers were just right for marshmallow toasting. I broke out the wire hanger roasters (nobody wants to eat a perfectly clean marshmallow off a dirty stick) and we began the time honored tradition of s'more making. Big Al didn't participate. My opinion of him was not on the rise.

Joe toasted his marshmallow to the perfect golden brown stage. My impatience inevitably led to flaming mallows, which Joe found a source of endless amusement. They wound up crunchy on the outside and gooey on the inside, perfect for melting the chocolate and squelching between two graham crackers. A.J. applied himself to the task with zeal. He achieved a marshmallow record, roasting seven of the squishy things at one time.

His sticky grin was the first real smile I'd seen from him since our adventure began. Aside from his alien fixation, he must be a normal boy after all. It made me feel better toward the kid. Until he began throwing rocks while we cleaned up and extinguished the campfire.

I ignored the first two throws. When I heard the thunk of a rock bashing into the van, I stepped in before Joe had to.

"Hey, A.J. Quit throwing rocks, You're going to break something."

He let loose with one final rock. I heard the plunk as it hit the passenger door. The sound sent Tito scurrying under the van. He may think he's a dog, but he's got all the courage of a miniature hamster.

I gave the boy my most severe glare.

"Oh all right," A.J. grumbled. "I need to use the john. Where is it?"

Joe took all the Allens on a field trip to the outhouse. We had learned through experience it's best to find the biffy before bed. The trick saved us from having to send out search parties for folks at three a.m.

We saw A.J. and Big Al to their tents and made sure Bald Al was securely tucked into his bag.

"Are you sure you want to sleep out?" Joe said. "You can bunk in my tent if you want."

"I'm sure," Al said. "It's been a dog's age since I slept under the stars."

In my opinion, when you're asleep, you don't really appreciate the cosmic show anyway, but I didn't say so. Instead I wished him good night and Joe walked me to the van.

The moonlight illuminated a quarter-sized dent on my van. I picked up the rock A.J. had thrown. "That rotten kid. How can such a little rock make such a big dent?"

"Must be a heavy one," Joe said.

I dropped it into my pocket and let Tito in the van. Joe wrapped me in his warm flannel hug. He smelled like marshmallows and campfire, better than any cologne on earth. If only I could wish everything else away and just stay forever in his arms.

"You're quiet tonight. Are you feeling all right Marty?"

No. Completely petrified about losing you. "Oh sure. Sore from my trampling, but okay." Tomorrow. I'd tell him tomorrow if it was the last thing I did. I shivered.

He gave me another squeeze and rubbed his hands up and down my arms to warm me up. "All right. I'm going to check the fire one more time before bed. Whistle if you need anything. Good night, Marty."

"Good night, Joe." I swallowed and blurted it out before I could think too much about it. "You know, if I was going to love someone, I mean, in a woman/man sort of way, I'd probably pick someone who was really similar to you or maybe even could be you if that was what I was going to do and the circumstances were right and all."

I sighed. Smooth, Marty. Real smooth.

He raised my chin to look in my eyes. "I love you too, Marty," he said before he kissed me again.

Chapter Twelve

In my dream Ramon was flying a plane above Desert Star property and I was standing on the wing, holding on for dear life. He was cheerful, whistling, like he used to do when he was a boy. I begged him to stop and land the plane. He shouted something through the open window which I couldn't hear. Then he took out a gun and fired a shot.

The scream was loud enough to wake Tito. Cold sweat prickled my forehead as the screams continued. Hang on. I became aware of an important fact. The screaming wasn't coming from my mouth or even inside the van.

I sat up so quickly, my vision blurred. Tito, his ears plastered back on his head, dove under the back seat. It was still dark, hours before dawn. The terrible racket continued. I pulled on my boots and leaped out of the van, trying to pinpoint the source of the hysteria.

Joe jogged over, boot laces, untied, one eye closed. "What is it? Are you hurt?"

"It wasn't me, I…"

A figure careened down the slope, arms flailing,

stumbling on the uneven ground. Bald Al flapped his arms and wailed in a most unmasculine volume.

"Al," I shouted. "What is it? What's happened?"

Al didn't answer. He kept on screaming as he ran by us. The terror on his face was accentuated by the moonlight which also lent his bald pate a luminous glow.

"Stop, Al," Joe yelled. "Stop running."

Al didn't stop. Impressive speed for a guy with such generous padding.

"He's going to hurt himself," I said.

Joe sighed while he hurriedly tied his boots. Then he took off after Al. It only took two minutes before Joe's lean, muscular legs closed the gap between them. Joe brought Al down in a very neat tackle. I heard the 'oooof' as they hit the dirt.

Big Al was up by then and we both raced over to the fallen men. Al sat up, panting, his face a ghastly white oval. "I.." he panted. "I, was going, to the…"

"The john?" I suggested.

He nodded. "And it was so…."

"Dark?" I was always real good at charades.

He nodded again. "I went in and he beat me over the head. There was another guy outside. I saw him when I ran out. The second guy stabbed me in the back. I barely got away."

Joe aimed a flashlight at Al's shirt Al's shirt before he pulled up the material to check underneath. "There is a small tear in the fabric," he reported. "A few drops of blood but that's about it. Doesn't look like a knife wound."

"I…I broke away fast before he could kill me."

Al looked like he was going to start screaming again so I interjected. "We'll go check it out. You stay together and check on A.J. Make sure he's still where he's supposed to be." I handed a small first aid kit to Big Al. "Can you disinfect and bandage his wound?"

"All right." Al took the supplies and knelt next to his

son. "Stop wiggling, Al," he said as he began his first aid duties.

Joe grabbed a Coleman lantern and the baseball bat which we always took along on overnighters. We'd never used the bat so far, but in the desert it's always a good idea to be prepared. It was no help against bullets, but it might work against a knife. I held a smaller flashlight.

We whispered as we climbed the slope.

"What do you think, Joe?"

"Don't know. Something doesn't add up for sure."

"Maybe those men came back?"

He stepped over a rock. "Why would they be hiding in the Porta Potty? They're not going to find any treasure there. If they were waiting to kill us they'd have had a go at it by now."

I shuddered. "But who stabbed Al then?"

"It wasn't a stab wound. Just a small hole."

My heart pounded against my ribs as we approached the clump of trees. Several yards away from the potty, Joe put his mouth to my ear.

"Stay here." He handed me the Coleman.

"I want to go with you."

"If I yell, you can come running." He readied the bat and tiptoed up to the port a potty. His fingers reached out slowly, grasping the handle.

I held my breath.

He yanked it open.

A dark shape hurtled out. Joe dropped back.

If I hadn't been so oxygen depleted I would have screamed just as loud as Al.

The Mastiff bat whirled up into the sky, his twenty inch wingspan impressive in the moonlight. If I didn't know that bats are really gentle creatures who snack on moths and grasshoppers, I might have been running. Mastiffs can have up to seven inch long bodies so I could imagine how Al got the stuffing scared out of him. Still, he was beautiful as he glided up against the moon wings unfurled to their fullest.

Joe closed the door and peered around. I joined him with the lantern.

"Well I'm sure the bat didn't bite him so how did he get the wound?"

Joe did a slow circle. He picked a scrap of fabric from the needles of a nearby Saguaro. "Here's the knife wielding cactus."

We exchanged a look before we busted out into laughter. To our credit we laughed as quietly as possible, so as not to embarrass our poor bloodied camper. Tears streamed down our faces and we guffawed until we ran out of breath.

When our hilarity dried up we headed back. I decided to let Joe explain the true story to Al. He did, in a most gentle way.

Al laughed weakly. "A bat and a cactus? How embarrassing. This is certainly a vacation I'll never forget." Joe took him back up to the biffy so he could conclude his business before he headed off to his sleeping bag. I gave the man credit. For someone who thought he'd been beaten up and stabbed, he still refused the meager shelter of the tent.

We returned to our respective sleeping quarters and waited for the morning.

I dozed for a few hours, uninterrupted by dreams. Good thing too. It seemed like eons since I'd had a satisfactory sleep period. Except for piggy snores, it stayed quiet.

The next morning A.J. was up with the sun, standing with binoculars ready to witness any dawn U.F.O. landings.

Big Al and Al were rolling up their sleeping bags by the time I had the fire burning.

"We can pack up after lunch guys," I called. "There's another hike we can do this morning after breakfast. It'll take you up to the caves."

Bald Al looked bedraggled. His jowls seemed to droop even more in the morning light and there were bags under his eyes. "We've decided to head back after breakfast. I've got some appointments and Dad is eager to get to town."

Big Al added his agreement. "I've got a deadline to meet."

"Sure. Sure thing." I had gotten their check already so if they wanted to skip out early that was fine by me. I rolled up the biscuit dough into those crescent roll thingies and put them on a pizza stone I'd propped over the fire. Soon the smell of baking bread filled the air. Joe finished packing up the tents and helped me scramble eggs and make coffee. I prepared the bacon as I know the sight of the stuff turns Joe's stomach.

Bacon is gross, I told my rumbling tummy. Bacon is disgusting, I reminded my watering mouth. I am a vegetarian, I informed my hand when it reached for the crispy goodness. The Als helped in my moment of weakness by gobbling up the entire supply of fragrant strips while I poured orange juice for A.J. "Did you see any U.F.O's?"

"Nah." A.J. crammed an entire slice of bacon into his mouth. "But I thought I heard some yelling last night. Or did I dream that?"

Bald Al's cheeks pinked.

"Oh, you never know what you'll hear in the desert." I helped myself to another roll. "It's a place of mystery and wonder."

"Ha. I haven't seen anything wonderful here, only a lot of bugs and rocks. I knew we should have gone to New Mexico. They have lots of sightings there."

"That will be a great place to visit on your next vacation," Joe said.

The two older Als did not look thrilled at the suggestion.

Tito finished the apple I'd given him and curled up against the small of my back. Tito is a master napper. We all have our skills.

The pig didn't even wake up when I packed up the breakfast dishes and doused the fire. I poked him with my toe when we were ready to hit the trail for home. He still lingered behind until I whistled for him.

We drove out of the campsite and I was awash in mixed emotions. On the one side, I was glad to be unloading the Als and more than happy to have a check to deposit. But on the flip side, the closer we got to home the more my anxiety swelled. I couldn't help feeling there was a pile of grief waiting for me at home. And it wasn't going to magically take flight like one of A.J.'s imaginary spacecraft. I had an appointment with the truth.

We'd gone about half the distance when Joe's cell rang. He pulled over and took the call. There is nothing in this world that infuriates Joe more than people who drive while yakking on the phone. I have heard this calm, stoic individual shout at an indecent volume, "Hang up and drive, you nut!" to total strangers. Since I rarely remember to turn on my cell at any given moment, I have been able to avoid his wrath. And with my new policy of pretending my phone didn't exist, I guessed I never would.

Joe's brows drew together as he talked.

"How bad? Where are you?"

My pulse quickened.

He looked at his watch. "Who is driving you? Okay. It will take me a couple hours, but I'll get there. Hold tight." He clicked off the phone and pulled back onto the road

"What is it?"

"Dad fell while he was pruning the lemon tree. If I haven't told him a thousand times to let me do it for him. That guy is as stubborn…"

I redirected. "How badly is he hurt?"

"He says his ankle is only twisted but Roger's driving him out for an x-ray. Roger thinks it's broken because there's a lot of swelling. I've gotta head to the hospital as soon as I drop you off."

"Of course. Poor Mack. Do you want me to come with you?"

"No, you've got enough to do around the sanctuary."

"Are you sure? I can get Lucille to cover."

"We'll probably sit in the emergency room for hours. No sense in both of us being there all night."

"Okay." We lapsed into silence broken only occasionally by Joe muttering something about his father being mule-headed, and A.J. demanding to have the air conditioner turned up or down.

Big Al finally told him to roll down the window and stick his head out. The boy declined.

The three Als, Joe, the pig and I were all relieved when we rolled back into the welcome area. I had an odd fear that the plane would somehow have rematerialized on my property but it was still gone. Only lovely smooth, slightly charred sand greeted us.

Joe gave me a quick kiss. "I'll unpack when I get back. Don't lift the stuff by yourself."

I kissed him back. "Call me when you can," I said, as he headed to his Jeep.

He nodded and took off.

I helped the Als load their gear back in their Pontiac and we shook hands all around. They piled in and off they went.

I breathed in the silence as I meandered over to the enclosures. Everyone was happy to see me. I could tell. Matt's lizard tongue flicked out in an "I missed you terribly" salute and Bob twitched his whiskers which is a bobcat's way of saying, "you are swell.' I gave them a general health check and a cheerful greeting before I let them into their outdoor pens.

J.R. hopped around a bit before settling in next to the baby cottontail. They were creating their own little rodent bond which gave me a lift. Maybe that poor blind rabbit would be okay after all. He was taking tiny hops away from the dark fear that closed around him, learning to trust Buddy to help him along.

I sank down on my knees to watch them through the

fence. Was God trying to teach me through this rabbit? Why not? He'd taught me something with all the other creatures He had delivered into my care. Tito had been an entire education in and of himself. J.R. could be brave and so could I. We would survive.

The sun blazed down from a brilliant blue sky as I headed back. I approached the office door warily. My forehead was still a swirl of sickly rotten banana colors from the last door/cranial meeting. I shoved the key in and turned, keeping my foot firmly pressed against the jamb. Great. I really needed a door phobia on top of my other problems.

The office was in mint condition, meaning it was no messier than I'd left it. I helped myself to an ice cream sandwich to celebrate our safe return from the overnighter. Byron scampered out to watch but I didn't offer him any. Ice cream is not good for squirrels, but Byron did not seem to be aware of that fact. Post ice cream, I eased onto my bed to rest my eyes for five minutes.

I didn't wake up until the office phone rang two hours later.

Joe. I rushed to the phone. A familiar voice spoke into the answering machine.

"Hey, Marty. It's Todd. My ankle's much better now you'll be happy to know. The pictures I took on our night adventure turned out okay, but they don't really have exactly what I'm looking for. I'm going to need to come back again to take more." There was a pause. "Oh and Marty? I'm missing something. A journal. I think it must have fallen out of my backpack. It's probably under the back seat of Joe's car. I'll need to pick that up, too. So call me back and tell me if you found it and when I can come. Today is good, so call me. Bye."

His journal, huh? He neglected to mention the thing belonged to a dead man that he supposedly didn't know from Adam. Sneaky man. I saved the message, figuring it might be some important police evidence type thing. I made a note to return his call right after I won the Olympic Gold Medal for ice dancing.

His call did remind me of an important point. The journal needed to be handed over to the authorities, post haste. I found the ratty notebook and grabbed my keys when I was struck by a thought. Before I left, I dialed the number for Dilly's plumbing. Dilly was still on vacation, but I wrote down the address. It wasn't more than a two hour drive from Ferocious. Joe was gone for a while, at least. Lucille was off planning some sort of wedding extravaganza. Might as well do some detecting on my own. Throw yourself a rope, Marty. It may be the only help you're going to get.

The only problem was, I needed to turn on my cell phone. As much as I hated to do it, Joe might need to contact me. I couldn't let him down.

As I pushed the power button with a clammy finger, I tried hard not to notice the 'one new message' note on the screen.

I had a bad feeling I knew who was trying to reach out and touch me.

DANA MENTINK

Chapter Thirteen

Dilemma.
 Listen to the messages? Or not.
 Might be Joe. Or Mack.
Or not.

I sat in the van with the ignition running. The phone lay like a bomb in my lap. If I didn't make a decision soon, Tito would wake up and hear the van running and I'd have a pig in my lap along with my cell.

I took a deep breath, punched the button and held the phone to my ear.

Ramon's voice was smooth. "Martina, this is not a good way to behave. We're grownups now, you and me. You can't climb up a tree and hide like you did when we were kids. I'll find you, you know it. We have people here, in the southwest. It's merely a matter of time."

I clutched the phone until my fingers ached.

"Be reasonable. Call me back and we can talk. Like old times. Remember when you ran away from kindergarten? Who took you home? Remember? Call me, hermanita. It is the best way, the only way."

He left a number.

No fair bringing up the kindergarten incident. I could feel memory return as clearly as if it had not happened twenty plus years ago. I ran away from the school lunch room because the kids in my class wouldn't sit with me. Their parents told them to stay away.

"Why?" I asked a boy with wild curly hair.

"Your Papa is Patróne," he said, eyes wide. "He is dangerous, and so are you."

I didn't understand what it meant, only that I was shut out. So I ran. I made it as far as the creek before Ramon found me. He dragged a boy behind him. "Here," he said, shoving the kid to his knees at my feet. "This boy will play with you."

The child had a swollen eye and a dribble of blood coming from his nose. The look he gave me was one of sheer terror as if I could vaporize him on the spot. His fear burned into me like an acid. I told Ramon to let him go. I would go back to school.

It wasn't long before Papa gave up on the public school idea and hired tutors to come to the house instead. My isolation from the normal world was complete.

I snapped back to the present.

We have people here. We'll find you.

I didn't doubt that my father's reach extended to Arizona. I knew his drug smuggling endeavors stretched into the states. I figured on Miami, where Papa had a house where we used to spend the summers. Thanks be to God that I was actually born in Miami so my U.S. citizenship was in place. And more thanks to the careless guards who didn't notice my midnight escape on my eighteenth birthday out the second story bathroom window.

I'd been free for nine years, invisible, happy. Since I'd met Joe, the shadows from my past had become fainter, almost surreal. I could almost pretend that I really was Marty

Barr, normal girl with normal life.

Now my carefully built façade was cracking.

I hit the gas harder than necessary as I headed to town, steeling my gut against the fear. He would not take me back. I would not let that happen. "God, please let me figure a way out of this."

I waited for a bolt of clarity, an answer to my dilemma, but nothing came as the miles went by.

I turned the radio up to super blast to drive the dark thoughts from my mind. Simon and Garfunkel. I belted out the words to Cecelia. The temperature was hotter today, but the air that blasted through the open window refreshed me anyway as I sang. I sailed all the way to town on a cloud of hot air and music.

Chief Spotter greeted me in civilian clothes at the front counter of the police station. She looked much more relaxed than the last time I'd seen her except for some noticeable bags under her eyes. She yawned so wide I could see her back molars.

"Chief. How are you? I'm surprised to see you back so soon. How is the baby?"

"Fine, fine, Marty. Baby's at home with Daddy. It's his turn to listen to the wailing. I came here for some peace and quiet and to check up on things. I hear you've had trouble."

I nodded. Gunmen and burglars. It was probably all in a day's work for a police officer. Probably a lot easier to deal with than a crotchety infant. "How is the Spiegel case coming along?"

"Slowly. We can't figure out who owned the plane. All the registration work is faked. We're running prints now but there isn't much to look at with all the fire damage."

I put the journal on the counter. "This was Professor Speigel's, I think."

She stared at me with a look I imagined worked great on wringing confessions out of people.

After a second of drumming her fingers on the counter

she said, "Do I want to know where you got this?"

"We found it in the back of Joe's Jeep when it fell out of Todd's backpack."

"Who's Todd?"

"Todd Chin, he's works at a television studio. He came to take pictures of the sanctuary."

"How did he get the professor's journal?"

I shrugged. Todd would be very busy explaining that to the police that he wouldn't have time to poke his nosey head into my business. "Maybe Deputy Fisk could tell you. He drove him back to Phoenix Saturday night."

The Deputy chose that inopportune moment to come through the door, soda in one hand and a Big Hunk candy bar in the other.

"Hey, Chief," he said. "I didn't expect to see you here."

"So I gathered. Who is this Todd Chin person?"

"A television studio guy." He gestured with the candy bar. "He was on Marty's property when they were shot at. I gave him a ride home. Real closemouthed. Looks so familiar, but I can't place him."

The chief showed him the journal.

Deputy's Fisk's mouth fell open. "How'd he get that?"

"Precisely what I'd like to know, and what you are going to spend the rest of today finding out for me."

He swallowed a mouthful of soda and slam dunked it in the trash. "I'm on it, Chief."

"Good. Now tell me what you found at Speigel's place."

Fisk chewed thoughtfully on the last bit of chocolate. "Not much. He had a small condo in Cactus Flat. It was heavily mortgaged. The electric company had the power turned off two weeks ago for nonpayment. Looks like the university was cutting him loose due to budget cuts and such. The guy didn't own much, just a lot of books on geology and poetry. He liked to paint. The back room was packed with canvas and oil paints. Oh, and he ate a lot of Top Ramen. Fifteen packages in the cupboard. Probably had a time fixing it without any power though."

The chief sighed. "That's not much help. It doesn't explain why he was flying over Marty's property, threw a rock out of the plane, and it doesn't help with why someone would want to shoot him."

She turned to me. "What is it about your property that attracts trouble?"

I swallowed. "Well, er, if I had to guess I'd say, uh. I don't know."

My cell phone rang and I jumped.

They looked at me. "Aren't you going to answer it?" the Chief said.

"Answer it?"

The chief's lip crimped. "Yes, Marty. That's generally what people do when their phone rings."

"Answer it. Right." My finger quivered as I touched the answer button and slowly put the phone to my ear. "Hello?"

"Marty, it's Joe."

I heaved a delighted sigh. "It's Joe," I whispered to the two officers before stepping outside. "How is your father?"

"He's okay. His ankle is broken so they put a cast on, but we've been here overnight waiting for an orthopedist to take a look at it. We'll be at the hospital for a few more hours and then I can take him home. I'm going to stay with Dad tonight and tomorrow to help him get settled. I need to be sure he can get along okay."

"Of course. Tell him I'll bake him a pie."

He laughed. "I'll tell him. Actually, can you do me a favor?"

"Anything."

"Can you bring my bag up to me tomorrow? I want to work on Pumpernickel. He needs some wounds treated."

Pumpernickel was Mack's ancient cat who had a tendency to wreak havoc with the neighborhood felines. "Did Pumpernickel get into trouble again?"

"He thinks he's a mountain lion. It's the root of all his

problems."

"We should introduce him to Tito."

It was good to hear Joe laugh. "I'll swing by your place and get the bag. What time should I bring it to your Dad's?"

"Anytime is a good time to see you."

Awww. "Okay. Give Mack a kiss for me and tell him I'll be there tomorrow with a freshly baked pie."

"Did you remember to have your fire extinguisher serviced this year?"

"Ha, ha. Funny man."

"Is everything okay there? No more signs of an intruder?"

"Nope. Just me and the animals."

"Keep your door locked tonight anyway, will you?"

"Yes, Joe."

"Promise?"

"Promise."

"See you soon, Marty."

"You bet."

I said good-bye to the chief and Fisk and headed out the door. I fought a yawn as I eased into the van. Two o'clock. Just enough time to get a sugar fix on my way to Dilly's Plumbing.

The extra-large Super Chiller Chocolate Milkshake was well worth the two bucks. I sipped slowly to avoid brain freeze. I might have been too late as my mental wheels seemed to be frozen anyway. Why was I driving sixty miles to Dilly's Plumbing? Especially since the guy was away on vacation. I had no logical explanation other than those pickle magnets were stuck to my mind. One on a murdered man's plane, one in the television studio three hours away. Maybe Dilly was a marketing genius and managed to distribute his happy pickles across the great state of Arizona. But why was Todd Chin interested enough to pull Dilly's ad out of my phone book?

About an hour and a half into the drive I stopped for a

potty break and French fry sustenance. I needed some salt to counteract the sugar. The smell of chicken nuggets nearly bowled me over, but I made it back to the van without any meat on my conscience. I would turn into a vegetarian if it killed me. Joe would be proud.

I pulled onto a rundown street when the last French fry ran out. There was a garage on the corner and a tiny market with signs all written in Spanish. Sandwiched mid-block, was Dilly's Plumbing. The windows were dirty and one of the sign letters was missing reducing the place to "Dilly's lumbing." I tried the door, which was locked, so I pressed my face to the glass. The place was a hodgepodge of shelves filled with metal parts and bins filled with tinier metal parts.

A face loomed up at me from the other side of the glass.

I screamed.

The eensy woman on the other side did as well. She clapped a hand to her heart and unlocked the door.

"You scared me," she panted. Her head was about even with my shoulders. She wore a yellow hair band around her unnaturally black hair. "What are you doing staring through the glass like that?"

"Sorry. I was looking for Dilly."

"He's on vacation. I'm his wife, Jean. Can I help you with something?"

"Uh, well actually, I've got a squirrel in my sink." That didn't come out right.

"A squirrel. I see." She peered closely at my pupils. "Are you on something?"

"No, no. The squirrel isn't really why I'm here. I'm not sure what I need. I actually wondered how long Dilly's been in the plumbing business."

"Oh, you need references. Not to worry. Dilly's a lazy toad, but not when it comes to plumbing. He's a genius with plumbing. What do they call them? A savant. He's run this business for twenty years and he's never met a plumbing problem he can't fix."

"Do you help him with the office work?"

"Help him? Ha. That's a good one. I keep the whole place going. Dilly doesn't know a thing about the business end. Still, I don't really mind." She gathered up a pile of papers from the desk. "It's not an easy thing, running a business."

"Does Dilly know a Professor Speigel?"

"Speigel? No. I don't think so. I remember everyone he's ever done work for and that name is new to me. Why?"

"Oh the professor er, dropped in on me and he had one of Dilly's magnets."

Her eyes rounded in satisfaction. "They really do work. I told Dilly those magnets were a good thing. He won't pass them out. Thinks the pickles are silly. They work though, don't they? I even send them out in our Christmas cards. Who doesn't need a magnet?"

"Has he ever thought about television commercials?"

"If you'd ever seen Dilly, you wouldn't ask that. We'd have to hire a double to do the part and then what would people think when the real Dilly showed up?"

"Has he ever met a Todd Chin?"

"Todd Chin. That name sounds familiar." Her eyes rolled. "Oh yes. He called just this week."

"For plumbing help?"

"No. Marketing stuff I think. It was something to do with planes."

"Planes?"

"Yes. He wanted to know if Dilly had been up in a plane. Was he comfortable with flying? Wanted to sell him a flight on one of those planes that pull the banners, I figured. I put the kibosh on that right quick. What do we need to have a flying advertisement when we've got all these lovely magnets? People won't remember a plumber's name because they saw it in the sky for heaven's sake. They only care when they're up to their knees in water. Besides, the whole thing would never work."

"Why not?"

"Dilly is terrified to fly." She glanced at the clock. "So what do you need fixed?"

"Fixed? Oh I don't actually need anything fixed. I was just sort of planning for the future."

Her brows furrowed. "The future?"

"Sure, um, when the squirrel moves out." I edged toward the door. "You never know when you might need a good plumber. Thanks so much. See you later."

I waved as I bolted out the door.

With the van door securely locked, I took a deep breath and reconnoitered.

So Todd was interested in Dilly. And planes. And he had a connection to Professor Speigel, at least enough to get hold of the journal somehow.

I made a list on the back of a napkin before I drove away.

Pickle Magnet, on the plane and in the studio

Prof. Speigel, also on the plane for a brief period.

Dilly the plumber, questioned about flying and the maker of the magnets.

Who was the person who potentially had contact with all of these things?

Todd Chin.

I felt pretty cocky about my mental prowess until I got to the 'why' part.

Why? Why? Why? What did Todd gain by asking Dilly about flying? How had he gotten Professor Speigel's journal? And how in the name of cheese did the magnet get on a plane on its way to crashing?

I could make no sense of the thing. I wished Joe was with me but his father needed to come first right now. I distracted myself by taking on a new challenge. Pie-making. Oh I'd certainly never attempt anything cream filled or meringue topped but really. How hard could it be to make a pie? I'd seen Mack do it a half dozen times, everything from boysenberry to banana cream.

The grocery store offered a number of possibilities. There was the all American pumpkin filling. Cans of cherry, apple and blueberry too. I scoffed inwardly. Mack was too good to be fed canned pie middles. I was going to go for broke. I bought a couple quarts of fresh blueberries and a premade crust. Mack was too good to be fed canned pie filling, but he was also too good to stomach my cast iron pastry. A woman's got to know her limitations, as John Wayne sort of, almost, said.

All was quiet on the desert front when I got back home. It was just me, Byron and my stove. And Tito. He showed up at my heels when he smelled fresh berries. I gave him a handful and left him on the step to enjoy his bounty.

In the name of fairness, I dropped a couple under my sink for Byron, too. Then I washed my hands and donned an apron, ready to face the challenge.

The internet is a handy thing. After a minute of searching, I had at my fingertips no less than two hundred fifty blueberry pie recipes. I picked the shortest one on the first search page. Auntie Meg's Fabulous Blueberry Pie. The name conjured up a comforting image. Auntie Meg was no doubt a plump old lady with a bun who knew her way around a recipe.

What could be better?

I dumped the berries into a saucepan and added sugar and a 'soupcon' of lemon zest. I wasn't clear on how much a 'soupcon' was but I figured Mack would appreciate having his lemons used in my glorious concoction. Then I turned the burner up to high, and clamped on a lid, waiting for my berries to come to a boil so I could lower those babies down to the barest of simmers, as Auntie Meg suggested.

So far, so good. I cracked open a ginger ale to sip while I kept an anxious eye on my purple beauties.

The view out my kitchen window was impressive. Golden land, orange sky fading to amber, cliffs outlined in the distance like proud Indian warriors. Joe's face swam in my head and the perfume of blueberry permeated my nose. I had to talk to him and clear the air so we could really move on in our lives. The conversation lay waiting for me like a coiled snake.

A blurpy noise indicated the berries would soon be ready to snuggle down to a simmer. If only Mack and Joe could be there to witness my culinary triumph. I pictured their faces as I unveiled my masterpiece.

I was filled with a moment of contentment.

Until the door flew open.

Chapter Fourteen

An angry Lucille barreled in. "You won't believe it, Marty. Such a bother. It's just terrible and bad timing to boot."

Ficky followed her. He was draped in multiple shades of crepe paper streamers and, a detail that frightened me, he was carrying a suitcase.

"What's wrong, Lucille?"

She flounced down on a kitchen chair. "Busted water heater."

"Where?"

"At my place, of course. Me and Ficky was looking at the decorations, trying to figure out what would look the best at the bowling alley, when all a sudden, kablam! Water starts pouring outta under the thing and all over the floor. By the time we get the water shut off the place is soggy. Ain't that right, Ficky?"

Ficky nodded solemnly, the streamers around his neck fluttering.

"Uh oh. That's not good."

"No it ain't. Ficky here can fix it of course." She gave him a look of adoration. "He can fix anything, can't you honey? But it'll be tomorrow before he can get a new heater and hook it up. So I ain't got water for tonight."

I waited.

"So I ain't got a place to stay."

"You don't?"

Her cheeks pinked. "Well 'course I can't stay with Ficky. 'Twouldn't be proper afore we are married and all."

"So..." I began to release some of the anxiety that now filled my torso.

She dropped the bomb. "So I figured on staying the night here with you."

Oh man. As much as I loved Lucille, the woman was not the best housemate. We'd bunked together before when her place was being painted and I'd been amazed to find that the lady actually sings in her sleep. I didn't even know that was physiologically possible. I opened my mouth to say no. "Absolutely," I said. "I'll make up the pull out bed for you." Good job, mouth.

Lucille smiled. "You're a good egg, Marty. Didn't I tell you so, Ficky? Marty's a good egg."

Ficky smiled too.

It was a good thing mouth answered instead of gut.

"Now," Lucille said, heaving herself to her feet, "Take a look at these streamers, why don't you?"

Ficky held out his arms, airplane-like, while Lucille pulled rolls of streamers from her pockets. She festooned him with pink, purple, green and all manner of striped streamers until he looked like a float from the Mummer's parade.

She stood back a few paces to admire her handy work. "Give a twirl, honey. Around you go."

Ficky performed a slow three sixty.

Lucille gave equal attention to each streamer. "Hmmmm. I sure like that orange color. Reminds me of

Grandmama's lipstick. What you think, Fick?"

"Real nice," he said.

"'Course that green one, why that's right pretty too, ain't it?"

"Right pretty," he agreed.

"What you think of them stripes?"

He considered them through his thick lenses. "Perky," he said.

She laughed and pinched him gently on the cheek. "You see? My sweet man, he likes them all. So's we need your opinion, Marty. What do you think?"

"They're all nice, Lucille."

"I know, but what you like best? Maybe this purply color? It's just the image of berries in springtime."

Berries.

I whirled to face the stove just as the pot began to vibrate. I grabbed a potholder and shielded my face.

"Look out!" Ficky cried, leaping in front of his bride to be. "She's gonna blow!"

The pot lid flew off in a shower of sticky droplets.

Glops of blueberry lava shot up to the ceiling, the rest slid down the side of the pot, smoking where it hit the hot burner. I fought my way through the berry barrage until I killed the gas and took the pot off the heat.

The trailer was silent, except for the plop of blueberry slime as it dripped from ceiling to floor. Auntie Meg would not be pleased. I turned very slowly.

Ficky stood in front of Lucille, his arms still raised, a splotch of blueberry schmutz on the left lens of his glasses. Lucille peeked out from under his streamer curtained arm.

"Ficky, honey," she said. "Maybe you better be getting along now, precious. Looks like Marty needs a little help making…what was it supposed to be, dear?"

"A blueberry pie," I said through gritted teeth.

"That's right, a blueberry pie. But first we better find the mop."

Lucille sent Ficky off with directions to buy all the colors of streamers when he was in town purchasing a new water heater the next day. She grabbed a bucket and towels and helped me clean the sticky goo.

I felt like a four year old whose balloon popped. "I was making it for Mack," I said, mortified to feel my throat squeezing up. "He broke his ankle and I was going to show him I could bake a pie." A stream of tears began to flow down my face. "I just wanted to make one pie. One lousy pie. Like normal women do, like Auntie Meg does."

Lucille rested a heavy hand on my shoulder. "It's okay there, sugar. Pies can explode on anyone. Ain't nothing at all. We'll go get more berries and whip up another one right quick. It won't take a minute."

I shot a look at my watch. "The store is closed now," I wailed. "It's too late."

Lucille took a hot dog from her pocket and chewed while she thought. "I've got it. I put up some berries last spring. Five jars, I've got left. I'll just hop on my bike and get 'em. Be back in a flash."

I wiped my nose. "You left your Moped here last night?"

"Sure did. Ficky picked me up in his new truck. A Dodge with only twenty five thousand miles on her. Ain't he just slick as a whistle?"

In spite of myself, I smiled to see the admiration painted on her wrinkled face. "Yes, he is."

"So you just set a while and I'll be right back. Plenty of daylight left."

"Lucille?"

She swallowed the last of her hot dog. "Yeah?"

"Thank you," I said.

She picked some meat out of her teeth. "Nothing at all. You got enough butter for the crust?"

"I bought one of those premade ones."

Her brows furrowed. "Marty, if you're gonna learn how to make a pie, you gotta learn the crust, too. Otherwise, you're just flyin' your plane without knowin' how to land." She left, mumbling something about premade trash.

I listened to her Moped thunder down the road. It hit me like a slap. Not knowing how to land. I'd been flying my plane for nine years without any plans to land. Was that because I didn't know how? How to trust people with the truth about me? In Ferocious I had dear, albeit weird friends, fragile animals that depended on me and a man for whom I would lay down my life.

I watched the dust settle as Lucille grew smaller and smaller on the highway.

With God's help, it was time to learn how to land.

Lucille returned armed with four jars of berries and a brick of butter the size of my forearm.

We washed up and set to work. When the berries were simmering with no threat of explosion, she demonstrated the proper way to cut butter into flour. Who knew you could cut butter into pieces the size of 'mother's mole,' as Lucille put it? In no time we morphed that butter and flour into a pliable circle.

Since we had enough for two pies, I was in charge of my own crust. I rolled, I patted, I pinched and I'll be snickered if I didn't get a pie crust plopped in that dish. It wasn't as perfect as Lucille's, of course, there were a few uneven bits and a crack or two, but I thought it was breathtaking. I pricked it with a fork at Lucille's direction and baked in the oven just enough to "give it a tan."

"Didn't your Mama teach you to how to get around in a kitchen?" Lucille said as she crimped the edges of her dough.

"She tried to teach me to make empanadas, but I never wanted to stay in the kitchen that long. She died when I was ten." My heart filled with the same mixture of sadness and longing that it always did when I thought of her.

"Oh. That's a terrible thing, honey." She patted me with a floury hand. "No wonder you explode your berries."

"She taught me a lot though, before she died." I scooped a bunch of glistening purple goodness into my crust. "She taught me about God."

"Well there you go. She done taught you the only important thing then, didn't she? You got her Bible?"

I nodded. It was in the bedside table, unopened for longer than I cared to remember.

"You read it then, honey. It'll bring her back to you."

Lucille filled her own pie and cut a fancy lattice work of strips for the topping. She showed me how to take one piece and spiral it to make a top on the pie.

"Much easier for your first pie. We can work on that fancy dancy stuff later."

We slid the things into the oven and made tea.

It surprised me how fast the time went as we chatted. I found myself enjoying having Lucille there to talk to. In a blink the pies were done, left to cool. The trailer was enveloped in a dizzying cloud of dessert perfume.

I made up the pull out bed for Lucille. She helped tuck in the corners of the sheets with military precision.

"You know Marty, I never knew that about your Mama," she said, her voice soft. "You don't talk much about your kin, do ya?"

I swallowed. "No, Lucille. It's not a pretty story. I…I've got some things I want to tell you, about my family. But, er, I think I should tell Joe first."

"That sounds fair, honey. Joe's your man, like Ficky's my man. You got to square it with your man first off."

After an uncharacteristic silence she said, "We'd better be gettin' them animals in, don't you figure?"

"Yes, I figure."

We walked to the enclosure and stowed the animals for the night. Bob seemed listless. He didn't put up the usual resistance when I herded him into his cage.

"What's the matter, Bob? Life getting you down? Me too, old buddy. Me too."

I checked his water supply and made a note to self to have Joe check him.

A nasty thought wormed around in my head. What would I do if Joe left? Took off when I told him the news? Went back to college and I never saw him again? I'd be missing a lot more than a fine veterinarian. I whispered a prayer as we shuffled back to the office. "God help me make it all right."

In the trailer, Lucille and I breathed deeply of the blueberry fumes.

"Ya know," she said. ""Twould be a tootin' shame if them pies ain't up to snuff. Imagine our men folk eatin' something that wasn't any good. The thought of it gives me the prickle bumps."

"That would be awful," I agreed, my mouth watering.

"Since we made two of 'em and all, maybe we ought to try one out, make sure it's all right."

"It's our duty," I said, getting out two plates. "Shall we have a scoop of vanilla ice cream on top? Just to be sure it will hold up to dairy products?"

"Yes, ma'am," Lucille said. "Can't be too careful about them dairy products."

We settled in around the kitchen table with wedges of still warm pie. The ice cream turned into melty purple puddles where it met the berries.

"Lucille?" I said after the first bite.

"Yeah?"

"Do you think they serve blueberry pie in Heaven?"

"They do if it's this good."

We ate in silence, except for the odd blissful pleasure whine that escaped my mouth on and off. I licked my fork clean. "So this is why people make their own pies."

"Uh huh. I'm thinkin' I'll take the leftover for Ficky and

you take the other whole one for Mack. How does that suit you?"

"Deal."

I cleaned the dishes while Lucille brushed her teeth and wound her hair in sponge rollers. This amused me as the woman's hair always morphed into a frizzy mop by the time she made it to work on her Moped. She emerged from the bathroom in a voluminous polka dotted shift. I was uncertain that her bulk would fit on the small fold out, but she seemed to snuggle down all right.

I was on my way to the bathroom when the phone rang.

"Marty?" Deputy Fisk said.

My pulse quickened. What was I in for this time? "Yes?"

"Ficky told me Lucille is over there. Could you tell her we found her stolen Moped?"

"You did? Where?"

"About ten miles down road from the Desert Star. It was dumped behind some mesquite so we didn't see it at first."

"Did it give you any clues? About the guy who took it?"

"We got one partial print, but it's smudged. We'll see what the lab can make of it. Could you tell Lucille we'll get it back to her tomorrow?"

"She'll be thrilled." I glanced over at the giant blanket covered lump on my pull out. "Did you figure out how Todd Chin wound up with the professor's journal yet?"

"Not yet. We can't find him at the moment. Let us know if he shows up there, will you?"

You bet your Sweet Aunt Petunia's bonnet I'll let you know if he comes here. "Sure, Deputy. Good night."

I turned to the mass of polka dots. "Hey Lucille, good news. They found your Moped."

Growly snores came from the pull out. She'd have to hear the happy details in the morning.

I brushed my teeth and checked the door lock for the third time. I heard the sound of gnawing from under the sink.

"Byron, quit eating the cupboard." The sounds stopped for a minute before he resumed.

I crawled into bed.

Between the snoring and the gnawing, I couldn't sleep. I finally snapped on the tiny lamp and opened Mama's Bible. The pages were worn and dog eared. My fingers glided over the smooth paper, remembering my mother's elegant hands turning the pages as she watched us play.

I asked God again, for the millionth time. Why did she have to die? I knew she couldn't stay where she was. The stress and fear of life in Papa's world made her a prisoner. But why couldn't she have escaped, too? She set up the bank account in Miami under the name Marty Barr so I could have the means to run. She could have run with me. We could have been together. I could have had my mother. The thought was so powerful, it made my head swim.

I wondered again if Mama's accident was a misstep or a purposeful act. She knew so well what it was like to live in fear. Perhaps she couldn't face a lifetime filled with looking over her shoulder and watching every stranger's face who rode by on the highway.

My glance landed on a verse from Psalm 32:7.

You are my hiding place.

I didn't know why Mama died. But I knew she wanted another life for me. A life where I would not be in fear, where I would find peace and a safe place.

Running had given me distance. But it hadn't given me peace. Not completely.

There was only one way I was going to get that.

"Give me strength, Lord. Help me walk into your hiding place and find the peace that waits for me there. I can't lean on myself, I know that now. Thank you for the love that I have found in Ferocious. Even if it all ends tomorrow, I'll always be grateful for that."

I closed my eyes and listened to Lucille's nocturnal song.

"The name of the Lord is a strong tower, the righteous run into it and they are safe," she mumbled.

Byron's gnawing played counterpoint to Lucille's song as I tumbled into sleep.

Chapter Fifteen

My nose woke up first. The smell of buttermilk pancakes filled my nostrils and wandered down to my stomach. Lucille whistled softly as she flipped the spatula on the hot griddle. She was back in her denim overalls with the striped patch on the knee.

I opened one eye. "Are you making breakfast?"

"Yeah," she said. "I was thinking about eatin' the pie, but I know we got to save that for the men folk. I figured on pancakes instead. All right by you?"

"All right," I said, rolling out of bed and heading for a quick shower.

When I made it to the table, she was already down to the last bite on her plate. She served me a stack and refilled hers.

"Whaddya' up to today? Want to help me make wedding favors?"

"I've got to go visit Joe and Mack but maybe when I get back. What are you making for favors?"

"Staplers."

I stopped, the coffee cup arrested on its way to my mouth. "You're making staplers? How do you do that?"

"Well we ain't making 'em. I'm just tying some ribbon up around 'em."

I swallowed a mouthful of fluffy pancake and syrup. "That's very, unique. To give out staplers, I mean. I don't think I've ever heard of that before."

She licked her fork and chewed on some beef jerky from her pocket. "Ficky got them for his business."

Ficky owned a trucking business, but he left most of the management to his brother. I shoveled in more pancake as she continued.

"We figured everyone is gonna need a stapler at one time or t'other, and when they do, they'll see our names and think of our holy day of matrimony. You know, the day me and Fick kinda got attached together. Symbolically stapled, is how Ficky puts it."

"Makes sense. You had them personalized?"

"Sure enough. With the wedding date and everything."

The word date set off an alarm bell. It was Wednesday morning. "Lucille, it's been so crazy here I lost track of the days. Friday is the rehearsal isn't it? That means that next Saturday is…"

She smiled. "You betcha. Me and Ficky's big day."

I dropped my fork with a clatter, overwhelmed by pre wedding hysteria. "What do I need to do? How can I help you? Where do I pick up my overalls? What about the flowers?"

"Simmer down there, girly. You're going to get a pancake clog. All you gotta do is pick up the flowers next Saturday morning and meet me at the church. I decided on yellow daisies. Your overalls are in your closet there and Joe's are at his place."

"What about the cake? Can I pick that up before the ceremony?"

"Arnie's takin' care of all that bein' as how it's tricky to transport the Empire State Building."

"The music?"

"The banjo band's all set to go. They think the bowling alley's got some downright excellent acoustics. They're going to set up in lanes five through seven."

My breathing slowed. "So everything's under control. Good. I sure wouldn't want to let you down, Lucille."

"You won't, sugar. Now I've got to go home and see how Ficky's getting on with the water heater."

"I almost forgot. Deputy Fisk called last night. They found your Moped. He's going to bring it back…" I had a sudden brainstorm. The perfect wedding gift for Lucille materialized in my mind. "They'll bring it back in a few days."

Her eyes rounded. "I'll be. Did he nab the stinker pilot who took it?"

"Not yet. They're still working on that."

Lucille muttered something about justice and smiting as she rinsed the dishes and went outside to straddle her loaner bike. She drove away, overalls flapping in the warm morning air.

Deputy Fisk dropped off Lucille's hijacked Moped as I was loading up the precious blueberry pie in the front seat of the van. I told him about my plan and he agreed it would be a fitting present for the newlyweds. He was still laughing as he drove away.

I retrieved Joe's medical bag from the tent trailer and stowed it in the van.

Tito pranced out after the morning feeding.

"You should stay here."

He circled his pig tail.

"Mack isn't going to want a pig visitor."

He poked his snout into my knee.

"You don't get along with Pumpernickel. Remember our last visit? You spent the entire time hiding under the front porch. It was pitiful."

Now the pig was sniffing at the van door, his swine smile in place.

"Oh all right, but you're riding in the back, far away from my pie." I used a board to roll the Moped into the cargo area.

After a quick stop at Jackie's garage, we were on our way to Mack's place.

Since it was a good two hour drive, I had a chance to practice my confession on Tito.

"Joe, I've got something to tell you. You know how much I love you, at least I hope you do, and nothing will ever change that. My real name is Martina Escobar and my father runs a drug cartel in Mexico."

Tito watched attentively.

"I ran away when I was eighteen and sort of invented a life for myself here in Ferocious."

The pig snorted.

"What's that you say, Joe? Why didn't I tell you? Ummm, because I didn't want to involve you in the mess. I've been in hiding because my father wants to take me back to Mexico. I don't want to have anything to do with him or my brother Ramon."

He flicked an ear.

"How's that, Joe? You totally understand? You know everyone has skeletons in their closets and your feelings haven't changed at all? You love me with a deep and unchangeable love? Thanks Joe. You are the greatest man in the world. I knew it from the first. And have I mentioned I love your hair? I mean, the way is sort of cascades down your back like chocolate syrup. It gives me chills. Really."

Tito hopped off the seat and burrowed under the chair.

"Okay, you're right. That chocolate syrup thing was too much."

Fortunately, the mountain of pancakes I'd eaten filled me up because I didn't get to Mack's place until after one. Joe greeted me with a big hug. The shadows under his eyes showed that it hadn't been a restful night. A layer of stubble carpeted his chin.

Mack lay on the sofa, his ankle encased in a rigid cast. Next to him was a metal walker. He looked tired also, but his face lit up when he saw me. "Marty. You didn't have to come all this way to see me, but I'm glad you did. How about a hug for an old guy?"

"Anything for you, Mack." I kissed his warm cheek and squeezed his shoulders. "I'm sorry, but my pig came along. Is it okay to let him in the yard?"

"Oh fine. Pumpernickel hasn't come out of his hidey hole under my bed so he won't care."

I fetched Joe's bag from the van and brought in my berry magnum opus. "Look what I made."

"You?" His shaggy eyebrows shot up on his forehead. "You made a berry pie by yourself?"

"Yes. Well, mostly anyway. Lucille helped me, but I even rolled out the crust." I beamed. "See? Fluted edges."

"Marty, you are a wonder. We'll have it for dessert. Joe loaded up my fridge with enough food for a decade so you'll stay to dinner I hope."

"I'd love to."

Joe handed me a soda and plopped down on the chair opposite me with a deep sigh. "What a night. We were at the hospital until just after I called you. Dad didn't sleep too well after we finally made it home."

"How could a body get any rest? Every time I rolled over you asked me if I was all right."

"Sorry, Dad. I knew you were in pain." He shot me a look. "He refused to take his pain meds."

"I'm not taking any pills unless I got no choice. And I'm not using that thing either." He kicked the walker with his good leg.

"Then I'm going to have to stay here with you," Joe said, in a tone that indicated it wasn't the first time they'd had the discussion. "If you fall, you'll be in even worse trouble."

"Go into town and get me a cane. I'll be fine." Mack huffed and turned to me. "How's Lucille getting on with the plans?"

"Just fine. She said she'd make you her famous pepper stew so you'll be in good shape for her big day."

"You tell Lucille, I wouldn't miss her wedding for anything."

I laughed. "She'll be happy to hear that."

We talked until Mack couldn't conceal his yawns.

"Marty, why don't you help me fix dinner while Dad has a catnap?"

Joe guided me into the kitchen where I was treated to another hug.

"I missed you Marty. I wanted to come home last night but I was afraid to leave Dad. I'm still not convinced he can stay here by himself. I told him I'm staying one more night at least."

I smoothed the worry creases from his forehead with my fingers. "You're a good son, Joe."

He smiled and began putting together the materials for grilled cheese sandwiches. "You said you wanted to tell me something. What was it?"

Mack stirred in the next room. "Can I have some water?"

"I'll get it," I said. "We can talk after dinner."

Mack was snoring when I put the cup next to the sofa. He looked so sweet lying there, hands folded across his belly. I couldn't resist giving him a kiss on the forehead before I returned to the kitchen.

Joe grilled the sandwiches while I sliced the early tomatoes from Mack's garden and added green salad to the table. In a few minutes, Mack hobbled to his chair, holding on to all available surfaces for support along the way. He said a prayer and we dug in.

When we finished, he asked me to bring him a book

from the coffee table. It was The Collected Works of Samuel Taylor Coleridge.

"I was doing some research about that verse you all found in the professor's diary. It is from the Rime of the Ancient Mariner, like I thought, but the particular passage is about a storm of light above the sea."

"What does that mean?" I said.

"That's what I've been looking into. There's plenty of discussion about this poem." Mack slipped on a small pair of reading glasses. "Some of these intellectual folks think Coleridge wrote it in 1797 when he saw the Leonid meteor shower."

"A meteor shower?" Joe said. "You sure?"

"Well other people credit it to imagination or a hefty dose of narcotics, but this fellow here says Coleridge witnessed the shower caused by the Tempel-Tuttel comet. The thing comes around every 33 years but people have only been able to really see if half a dozen times since Coleridge's day."

I puzzled over the revelation. "I can understand why a geology professor would dig that verse then. Sort of combines both his passions, doesn't it? Was the professor interested in looking for comets when you took him out for the night tour?"

"Not really." Joe yawned. "He looked bored with my wealth of celestial knowledge."

I sighed. "I felt the same way with the Als."

"Has Fisk figured out how Todd got the journal?" Joe asked.

"Not yet. Todd left a message on my machine saying he wanted to come by and pick up 'his' journal and take more photos. Fisk told me to call him if the guy shows up."

Joe frowned. "I don't like the idea of you being alone there with Todd on the loose. There's something weird about him. At the very least, we know he's a liar."

"Don't worry. I've been well chaperoned. Lucille

bunked with me last night and Fisk said he's going to have someone check in every few hours."

"I still don't like it."

"You go home with Marty," Mack said. "I'll be all right here. I don't need a house nanny."

"I am going to take you to your appointment tomorrow. Then I'll go." Joe turned to me. "Do you want to stay the night here? I can sleep in the Jeep and you can have the couch."

My heart fluttered. "You're so sweet, but I'll be fine. The animals need to be fed and Lucille is knee deep in wedding plans. Will you be there for the rehearsal?"

He smiled. "Three o'clock. Ready or not."

Mack yawned. "So how long do I have to wait to get me a slice of that pie?"

"Wait no longer." With a flourish, I sliced my purple beauty and served us all giant wedges.

The pleasure noises warmed my heart.

"This is the best pie I ever tasted," Mack said after two slices.

I actually experienced a momentary swell of tears. "Even though I think that might be stretching things a bit, thank you."

Joe shook his head. "No, he's not stretching. It really is excellent. What's the secret?"

I flashed back to my mother, hair in a thick braid, handing around a platter of cookies. Her voice was low and soft as she murmured, "They're made with love."

So there had been love between my parents. I didn't imagine it.

"The secret is to have Lucille in charge," I said. I shut off the stream of memory and cleaned up the dishes. Mack kissed me goodnight and Joe helped him back to his room.

In a few minutes, Joe and I were snuggling on the couch, blueberries on our breath.

I filled up my lungs and slowly exhaled. "Joe, I've got

to tell you something and I don't think it will wait any longer."

"Okay," he said. "Shoot." He laid his head on my shoulder.

"You know, that I love you, and all. Right?"

He chuckled. "Yes, I do."

"Good. Well I have to tell you that I've been keeping something from you. I'm sorry. It's going to hurt you and I can hardly stand it, but I've got to tell you the truth."

"Go ahead."

I felt my heart slam into my ribs. Now or never. "Joe, my name isn't really Marty Barr."

He was quiet. Probably in shock.

"My last name is Escobar."

Still quiet. Listening attentively.

"My father is a kind of a, well, drug lord, a Patróne. He is wealthy from smuggling and dealing narcotics and I know he's had people killed who crossed him." I held my breath for Joe's response.

Eerie silence. Followed by a soft snore.

"Joe? Are you asleep?" He answered by not answering. I couldn't decide if I was relieved or exasperated. Slowly I eased his head off my shoulder. The lamplight caught his face, a younger version of his fathers.

I pressed my lips to his. "Good night, my Joe. I love you."

I pulled a blanket over his legs and went to find my pig.

Tito came running when I whistled. He had a clump of grass hanging from his nose. I gave him a scratch and bundled him in. It was not even nine o'clock but I struggled to stay awake as I drove. Not good. Joe would have demanded I turn around and sleep at Mack's.

I settled on the next best thing.

Coffee. With plenty of chocolate and cream mixed in to help the caffeine along.

I stopped at a corner store ten minutes before it closed

and scooted in for my java fix. It was a do-it-yourself coffee counter, so I loaded up my beverage with all the goodies, until it threatened to spill over the brim.

As I handed over the money I saw a pile of The Oasis, our local rag newspaper. It isn't much of a newspaper, really. More a vehicle for advertising and local event coverage but whatever news it did contain was old by now.

"Do you want to unload these papers?" I asked the man behind the counter.

He looked startled to hear conversation. "Huh? Oh yeah. They're going to the recycle bin. Take all you want."

I never pass up anything free. Especially a nice hunk of newspaper that would transform into cage liners and a source of delight for burrowing animals. One man's trash is another critter's bedding. I hauled the stack out to the van, glancing at the table of contents.

I was so shocked, I didn't even feel the hot coffee splash onto my feet.

Chapter Sixteen

The title of the front page article read, 'Desert Star is Anything But.' The byline was Al Bento.

Big Al. The mysterious scribbling man.

Right next to the article was a picture of me eating a s'more. The nasty toad must have borrowed his grandson's camera. It goes without saying that it isn't possible to look like an adult while eating a pile of gooey marshmallow and chocolate. The photo captured my mouth open, bangs in my face and smears of chocolate on my chin. Lovely.

I took a deep slug of what was left of my coffee and read on.

'It was supposed to be a family bonding experience but it turned out to be more of an endurance test. The overnight adventure, planned by Marty Barr, owner and operator of the Desert Star Animal Sanctuary, was certainly an adventure, but not in a good way. We arrived just as the wreckage from a downed aircraft was being removed from this supposedly pristine sanctuary. Come to find out, a man was recently murdered the same day the plane crashed. This place was an oasis from civilization? I think not.

How did Big Al find that out?

I drank more coffee and skimmed to the next paragraph.

'The overnighter was far from relaxing. Though the landscape was attractive, it didn't outweigh the shock of coming ankle to fang with a snake, finding a bat in the facilities, or getting speared with cactus spines. Truth be told, the stargazing was excellent, but it didn't capture the attention of the adolescent crowd. The highlight was the food, but really--how many adults like s'mores anyway?'

Gee, I don't know. Like practically ALL of them?

'The next time I pack up for a desert adventure, I'll be sure to sign on with a company that operates large scale operations. No more two bit adventures for me. Grand Canyon anyone?'

Two bit adventure? I threw the paper on the ground. Who in the Sam Hill did Big Al think he was? Enjoying our hospitality, sleeping in our tents, eating our food only to stab me in the back with his pointy pen?

"You nasty, spying, rat fink," I yelled. Tito sat bolt upright and then dove under the seat.

There was only one thing to do. I returned to the store and bought three Mallowbars. I ripped the wrappers off with my teeth and threw them to the floor of the van as I drove.

"What's the matter with that guy?" I fumed, shoving a hunk of mallow medicine into my mouth. "He was lucky to get that close to a bat and snake. That's why people go to the desert, Big Al, you big dope. It's called NATURE."

By the time we got back after midnight, I had a stomach ache and a terrible sugar letdown. The red hot anger was gone, replaced by a whiny sort of 'why me?' feeling. I let Tito out and dragged my sorry carcass back to my trailer. There was a note secured to the door with four Band-aids.

"Don't read The Oasis. You'll have a conniption. Lucille"

I sighed deeply. Been there. Had the conniption and the

Mallowbar chaser.

It was so unfair. Like I hadn't had enough trouble lately. At least the plane crash had been an accident. Probably. The article was a wad of intentional, unadulterated malice.

I showered, took four Tums and sent myself to bed.

Byron's gnawing woke me up late the next morning. I opened a bleary eye. "Ten o'clock?" The old body clock had let me down and the animals weren't going to be happy about it.

Perhaps the whole newspaper smear had been a bad dream. I snuggled back into the pillow to enjoy that happy thought. Everything was fine. People love me and my property. The phone rang and I let the machine pick it up.

"Hey, Marty. Uh, I don't know if you saw my note but you might not want to read the newspaper. It's all junk anyway. Rehearsal's at 4:00. We'll have a barbecue after at my place. What'll Joe eat? Can you barbecue noodles? I'll ask Ficky."

I smiled. Lucille was really a good gal in spite of her meat fetish. Unfortunately, that meant the article was not a nightmare unless Lucille was sucked into my bad dream. I turned on the coffee pot and went to do the chores.

When I returned from feeding the critters there was another message.

"Hcy, yeah, it's Dilly from Dilly's plumbing. I guess you called or visited or something? My wife said you had a squirrel in your sink, but she must have gotten that wrong. Anyway, here's my new cell number. I had to get another phone because I dropped the old one in the lake. Call me and we can talk about your, er, situation." He rattled off a number.

I put down my coffee and dialed immediately.

"Hey, yeah. It's Dilly here."

"Hello Dilly, I'm Marty Barr, I talked to your wife about the pickle magnets. Um, and the squirrel."

"Oh, uh-huh. Say, I read an article about your set up in The Oasis. Bad press, hon. You need some marketing tips all right. I can get the name of that magnet place from my wife. You want that?"

Thank you, Big Al. "No, thanks. I'll manage. I came across your magnet at a television studio and I wondered how it got there. Your wife said you talked to a man named Todd Chin."

"Chin? Oh yeah. He wanted to know something about planes. Did I fly much and all that." Dilly laughed, a wet, wheezy sound. "I told him these feet were meant to stay on the ground. Or in a boat, of course. I caught me the sweetest trout. Must have been an eight pounder. Put up quite a fight, but now it's dinner."

"That's great. So you didn't give Todd any of your magnets."

"Nah. My wife sends them out in greeting cards. That's probably how they got there."

"Why would she send a card to the T.V. studio?"

"'Cause my cousin owns it."

"Your cousin?"

"Yeah. My cousin, Ken Lloyd."

I was speechless for a minute. "You aren't related to a Peter Speigel by any chance, are you?'

"Speigel? Nah. I've got a nephew name of Peter, but his last name is Rogers. LIsten, it's been great chatting but I've gotta run. Call me if you ever need to talk plumbing."

Dilly signed off.

His cousin. Well that explained how the magnet wound up at the studio. Much as I wanted to think Todd Chin had something to do with it, that explanation was pretty easy to accept. But how had the other one gotten stuck on the plane?

Todd "I Left My Journal In Your Jeep" might have an inkling. I wondered if the police had tracked down the mysterious Mr. Chin yet.

I put that out of my head while I went onto more

important matters.

Jell-O.

I'd promised Lucille I'd make some for her rehearsal dinner. Green Jell-O. Ficky's favorite. Good thing he didn't want something tricky like slices of fruit floating in it or anything.

At home the next day, I boiled up the water, dumped packets of green powder in and poured it all into a handy foil pan. While the rubbery stuff did its magic in the fridge, I took care of business, paid some bills, ordered a set of pamphlets, tried to lure Byron out from under the cupboard. Then I cleaned out the van and animal cages being sure to place the Oasis article where it would get what it had coming. That left just enough time to shower, twist my hair into a knob, and slide into a denim skirt with a cucumber green shirt.

A skirt, though of the denim persuasion, was still high falutin' in my neck of the woods. I looked so dolled up I added some small gold hoop earrings, a pair of sandals and slicked my lips with lip gloss. Instant maid of honor.

I pictured Joe rushing off to do the same. Well, minus the jewelry and lip stick. Imagine, Joe and me, all spiffied up, standing together to help Lucille and Ficky tie the knot. The idea put a lump into my throat. I determined that after the ceremonial scrimmage, I was going to have a heart-to-heart with Joe. I'd had a chance to practice on Tito, so it was now or never. I stowed my Jell-O into a cooler and headed to the rehearsal.

The tiny church was stuffed full of people. An air conditioner worked overtime to keep the place cool, but only succeeded in bringing the temperature down to the high seventies. Pastor Farley's forehead was wet with perspiration as he bustled around, herding people into neat lines.

I waved to Lucille. She looked nervous, clutching a sprig of larkspur in her hands. Her cheeks were pink. Ficky nodded at me, then resumed his careful attention to the pastor.

Deputy Fisk, in civilian clothes, walked over. He was standing in for Ficky's best man who had unfortunately broken a hip the month before. "Hello, Martina. Saw that article. Man, that guy sure did a hatchet job on you."

My lip curled. "He sure did."

"And the photo. Almost like he was trying to take a terrible picture on purpose. Your mouth open, chocolate all over your face."

I cleared my throat. "Yes, it was a bad photo."

"And all that business about the snake and the cactus prickles."

I cut him off. "If I had known he was writing a hit piece, I never would have shared my marshmallows. How's the case coming?"

"We've made some headway. The plane belonged to one of those flying clubs outside of Flagstaff. It was stolen a few weeks before it crashed onto your property. The partial print we got identified the pilot as Henry Poleman. He's got a nice long rap sheet, petty theft, assault, that kind of stuff. He was under investigation for smuggling contraband over the Mexican border when he disappeared."

"Contraband?"

"Drugs, most likely. Now that we know who he is, we'll find him. Don't worry."

I opened my mouth for further interrogation when Joe wrapped me in a hug. "Hi, Marty. I didn't think I was going to make it in time."

I hugged back. "How is your father?"

The worry crease appeared again between Joe's eyes. "Better, I think. He slept a little last night. I'm going to call and check on him after the rehearsal." He hesitated. "Uh, Marty? Did you happen to see…"

"The Oasis article?"

"Yeah. Big Al went for the jugular. How are you taking that?"

"Pretty well." I didn't tell him about the Mallowbars. "These things happen in the course of running a business."

His eyebrow arched. "True. That's a very mature attitude on your part."

"Yes, it is. And if I ever see Big Al again, I will be happy to show him the business end of my foot in the seat of his pants."

He laughed. "That's the Marty I know and love."

Thinking about our future conversation, the thought made me shiver.

"Let's all get into our places," Pastor Farley said. He paused when he saw me. "Well, Marty, I read that article in The Oasis. Such a shame."

I held up a hand. "Thank you. Where do you want us?"

He ushered Joe and I to our proper spots next to groom and bride.

Lucille's face was aglow with excitement. "Can ya believe it? Finally the rehearsal. Do I look all right? I got washed and flushed at the salon." She swiped a hand over her billow of hair.

I patted her arm. "You look fabulous. How are you feeling?"

"Right as rain. Ficky seemed a little nervous, but he'll come through. Say, did you get my message?"

"Yes, thank you. I had already read the article by then."

"Oh. Well whaddya' think?"

"It's on the bottom of Bob's cage."

She whacked me on the back so hard I staggered.

"That's my girl."

The pastor led us through walking up, moving over, handing off the marrying folks and retreating in an orderly fashion. We repeated the whole process again just to be sure. By the time he was done, we were all damp with sweat.

"Whew," Lucille said, passing a hand over her forehead. "Who woulda thought it'd be so strenuous to get hitched?"

Ficky fanned her with a handkerchief.

Finally the pastor dismissed us to head over to Lucille's place for dinner.

Lucille lives in a trailer the size of a walk in freezer but it's parked on a pretty good sized piece of yard. The residents of her mobile home park all pitched in to put up shade canopies and card tables on the grass. Someone even filled up a wading pool for the littlest guests and there were bottles of bubbles, and coloring books to keep them happy.

Chief Spotter was there with her band of youngsters. Mr. Spotter held a baby shaped bundle which he jiggled up and down with one hand and drank a root beer with the other. Some of the gang of kids caught sight of the children's area and headed straight for it. The chief took our picture as we entered the yard.

"Hi, Chief. Good to see you."

"You too, Marty. I thought we might be booking you for murder after you read that article in The Oasis."

I hadn't realized that measly newspaper had such an impressive circulation. "I'm over it. Really."

"Uh-huh," the chief said. "That'll be the day."

Lucille and Ficky walked in and everyone cheered.

"Oh you guys," Lucille said with a wave of her hand. "We ain't married yet. Just rehearsed, that's all."

Joe went to the far side of the yard to help stock the coolers with ice.

I filled my plate from the buffet table. Deviled eggs, chips and dips, Lucille's famous enchilada casserole with enough peppers to clear out your sinuses permanently. The dessert table was a marvel of cookies, coconut cake, pies and even doughnut holes courtesy of Arnie.

"Dinner first, Marty," I told myself, a paragon of virtue.

Two of the older Spotter children had already found the dessert table and were filling their pockets with peanut butter cookies. Good thing there was kid-friendly food. The enchilada casserole might just stunt them out of several years' worth of growth.

The fruit salad jogged my memory. Jell-O. I completely forgot about it.

I left my plate and hastened out to the van. Thanks to the scientific wonder of the cooler, my green rubber was still rubbery. On the way back to the party I chided myself. The woman asks you to do one small thing and you almost forget. Some maid of honor. Forget your problems for a while and put your best friend first for a change. I eased the gate open with my foot, happy to see that more guests had arrived to celebrate.

Ficky's cousin Herb was there and Lucille's bowling team, in matching pink shirts swarmed the food table. Hank the tow truck man lounged under an awning. A dark haired man stood with his back to me, talking to Deputy Fisk.

He turned and smiled.

The pan of Jell-O slipped out of my hands and splattered the ground as I looked into the face of my brother Ramon.

Chapter Seventeen

He smiled, the same dimpled grin I remembered from his boyhood. His accent was heavier than I recalled.

He glanced down at the green mess. "I must have surprised you, Martina. I'm sorry."

The bowling team swarmed around me with napkins, picking up blobs of Jell-O off the grass. I tried to breathe. Only small gasps made it into my lungs.

Ramon wore an expensive silk shirt in tasteful muted colors. The browns harmonized well with his mocha skin and dark, cropped hair. "You look good, sister. Much better than your picture in the newspaper," he said. "It didn't capture you at your best."

"What, what are you doing here?" I croaked.

"It's been such a long time since we've seen each other, hasn't it? I came to visit your Desert Star, but found you gone. A friendly man in town told me where I might find you. People are so nice here in the desert, no? They have the gift of hospitality."

Guests gathered around to meet the newcomer. Lucille

and Ficky pumped Ramon's hand.

"Mighty fine to meet you," Lucille said. "'Bout time we were introduced to some of Marty's kin. She's a peach, that Marty. A peach, I tell you. What a way with animals."

Joe brushed flecks of ice from his shirt and joined us. The question was written plainly on his face. "Who is this?"

"Joe…I…."

Ramon cut me off. "I'm her brother."

Joe looked from me to Ramon and back to me. "He's your brother?"

I nodded, a sick feeling welling up in my gut.

Ramon did not extend a hand to Joe. "She didn't tell you she had a brother?"

"No." Joe turned confused eyes to me. "She never mentioned you before."

"Women. They are mysterious at times. One never knows what they will do next. Or where they will turn up."

Ramon's smirk cut through my inertia.

I grabbed Joe's arm and dragged him along. "Come with me. I need to talk to you right now." I felt Ramon's eyes boring into me as I lead the way inside.

Joe peppered me with questions until we made it to Lucille's minuscule kitchen. Then he stopped. Abruptly.

"What is going on Marty? Who is that guy?"

"Joe, I've been trying to tell you something for a while now. There are a few things you need to know and this is a terrible way to say it."

Joe's eyes flashed. "Is he your brother or not?"

I cleared the lump out of my throat. "Yes. He's my brother. He lives in Mexico. That's where I grew up."

"How come this is the first time I've heard of him? You've met my family all the way up to my second cousins."

Sweat rolled down my temples, but I felt chilled to the marrow. "There are big, issues, in my family. I have some, baggage. I've kept it from you for a very good reason."

"Why?"

"Because I've been...in hiding."

He looked like he'd been slapped. "Hiding from what?"

"Joe, maybe you better sit down."

He slammed a hand down on the kitchen counter. "Maybe you better tell me what's going on. The truth, right now, Marty. All of it."

The words tumbled out. "I wanted to tell you sooner. My real name is Martina Escobar. I used the name Marty Barr after I turned eighteen and ran away because I didn't want my father to find me."

His mouth formed a grim line. "Why not?"

I tried to suck in a calming breath but I couldn't get my lungs to cooperate. "My father is Juan Escobar, he's the Patróne of a Mexican drug cartel."

Joe stared without saying a word. The silence was so complete the dripping of the kitchen sink sounded painfully loud.

"I meant to tell you so many times, but I was afraid if the truth got out they'd come for me. And maybe hurt you in the process."

His gaze riveted to mine. "So, for the past eight years, all the time I've known you, you've been lying to me?" The words hissed through the air.

"Joe, please try to understand. I didn't mean to hurt you. I was afraid. For both of us."

"Afraid? And never once, in all those years, did you feel like you could tell me the truth? It was better to pretend to be someone else than trust me?"

"I wanted to tell you. I really wanted to." I reached out to put a hand on his arm, but he jerked it away. "You are everything to me."

"I see. And Ramon? He's in the drug peddling business too, I gather?"

I nodded. "I was afraid to tell you I had a brother."

"I can't believe this, Marty. I thought you were the

person I was meant to be with."

His words tore at my heart. "I am. I am that person, Joe. Only the name is different, not me. I'm Marty, just plain Marty."

There was a hint of moisture in his eyes. "No. You are somebody else. Somebody with a whole other life that I don't know anything about. Someone who took my trust without giving any back."

I couldn't think of anything to say as my Joe slipped further away with every word. "Please Joe…"

"Why is your brother here now?" he demanded.

"He wants to take me back to Mexico, back to my father," I whispered.

"Maybe you should let him." Joe turned cold eyes on me and said words that cut worse than the sharpest blade. "You're a great liar, your father would be proud."

After he stormed out of the trailer, I locked myself in the bathroom. I wanted to cry, scream, anything, but I couldn't. Everything was bound up, numb and cold inside my heart. My Joe. My sweet Joe. What had I done? Why hadn't I trusted him?

A knock on the door made me jump.

"Anybody in there?" Chief Spotter said. "My kid has to go."

"Just a minute." I smoothed my hair and took a deep breath. It didn't help. My reflection in the bathroom mirror showed me a pale faced, red eyed woman who had lost everything. A liar. An Escobar.

I tried to summon a natural tone as I unlocked the door. "Sorry, Chief. Your turn."

She gave me a strange look. "Are you okay, Marty?"

"Sure, sure. I'm going to find some dessert."

"I'm not sure my kids left any, but there may be a stray cookie or two."

I forced a laugh and walked away as fast as I could on rubbery legs.

She bundled the tyke into the bathroom after giving me another searching look as I passed.

I wanted to get in my car and drive off the nearest cliff but I couldn't. It was Lucille's special day and there was the matter of my party-crashing brother. And I had to find Joe. Though my knees were still shaking, I made it back to the party. Ramon sat in a folding chair, one elegant leg crossed over the other, sipping soda. He nodded at me but did not approach.

I didn't see Joe anywhere.

Lucille bustled over. "Glad your brother made it to town. Think he might want to come to the wedding next week? We got plenty of marshmallows. Any kinfolk of yours is welcome. We'll just throw on an extra ham."

"No," I barked, startling her. I moderated my tone. "I don't think he'll be in town that long."

"Oh, okay." She looked at me for a long minute. "He's part of that family trouble you wanted to tell me, ain't he?"

I nodded, unable to speak. Would Lucille cut me out of her life like Joe after she knew?

She took my arm in her strong hand and gave me a squeeze. "All right then. We'll hash it out later. Don't you pay it no never mind now. Ain't never yet heard of a family without a patch of trouble here and there."

One of Ficky's relatives took Lucille under a tree for pictures.

I made idle chitchat with other guests and forced down some punch until I felt my legs threaten to give out. Though I didn't look at my brother, I felt his presence from across the room, as if he was a poisonous spider perched, invisible, above my head. All of my nerves screamed at me. Go find Joe. Make him understand.

After what felt like an eternity, I finally said my goodbyes and left.

Ramon met me at my car. "Who's the Indio?"

I didn't look at him but my body began to shake again.

"What?"

"The Indian guy who took off. Who is he?"

Slowly I turned to face him. "He is none of your business, Ramon. Nothing in my life is your business."

He ignored that. "You know him well, I can see that."

"You have no right to barge into my world and question me. Go away and leave me alone."

His mouth crimped. "For all that's holy, Martina, an Indio?"

"Don't you dare talk about him like that."

"With so many to choose from you pick him? He's not even Mexican."

My self-control vanished. "Neither was Mama," I spat. "If you recall, she was Venezuelan. Now get away from me." I wrenched open the door and half fell into the driver's seat. A cloud of grit rose into the air as I gunned the motor.

There was no use looking in the rearview mirror as I drove home. He would be there sooner or later, always there, right behind me, waiting.

I crashed the door closed and hunkered down in my trailer. The whole nasty mess of my life squeezed in around me like a killer boa constrictor. Joe had always been my rock, the hand to pull me out of the mire when I felt overwhelmed. With him, I had a life, a real life with freedom and forgiveness.

Not anymore. It was all gone. The coldness in Joe's eyes made it clear.

You're a great liar. Your father would be proud.

Maybe he would. I lied by omission. I deceived all the people who cared about me. I'd been so concerned about myself that I hadn't taken the time to consider their feelings. Not enough, anyway. I laid my head on the kitchen table.

Tears rolled down my cheeks, followed by sobs that felt like they were yanked out of me from somewhere down deep. I was lost, spinning in a black grief that took the knees out from under me and dropped me to the floor.

Byron hopped out from under the sink to watch, head cocked, ears erect, wondering if he should run. I wanted to say something soothing, but I couldn't speak. I opened up to grief and let it swallow me whole.

It was an hour before I could summon the strength to get off the floor.

I made it to the kitchen chair, numb.

The thought formed in my head and heart at the same time.

Run, Marty.

Disappear.

Make a new life like you did before.

Re-invent yourself.

I flipped open the computer and clicked on plane reservations.

Destination? Anywhere.

Departure date? Immediate.

Payment type? Cash.

I had a couple hundred dollars in the till. All I needed was a distraction. A phone call to the police. That would do. They'd come out, keep Ramon busy for a while, just long enough for me to head to the nearest airport.

I'd have to write a note to Lucille. I grabbed a piece of paper.

I have to go. I'm so sorry to leave you and the animals. You have been the best friend I could ever ask for and I hope you and Ficky will be happy forever. I've left the deed to this place so sell it if you want and use the money to care for the animals. Or find them good homes, especially J.R.

Thinking about that poor rabbit sent me into rivers of tears again. What would happen to him?

The knock on the door startled me. I closed the laptop and turned the note face down, pulse pounding in my throat.

"Who is it?"

The door opened. My brother came in. He gave the

office a once over before he settled down in a chair.

"How did you get a copy of The Oasis?" I said, happy to note that my voice didn't wobble.

"I knew you were somewhere in the Arizona desert. I've been monitoring the small town newspapers and blogs. It was not hard, the information age, you know." His eyes searched my face. "This doesn't have to be difficult, Martina. Think about what is best for yourself."

"What is best for me? It isn't your right to decide that. You don't even know me anymore. What's best for me is to be left alone to live my life."

"With that Indian?" Ramon sneered. "He didn't seem happy when he left."

I felt a stab of pain in my gut. "No. He probably doesn't ever want to see me again, now that he knows about my family."

Ramon shrugged. "A small loss. He's a nobody living in the middle of nowhere, driving a broken down Jeep."

I stood, my hands balled into fists. "Don't call him that. He is a good, God-fearing man and he doesn't make a living by smuggling drugs and killing people." The hiss of my words was loud in the confines of the trailer.

He leaned back against the cushions. "Martina, Papa does what he does to support his family and all the people of the town. They rely on him, and perhaps they are not so lucky as people in the states. They cannot always choose the lily-white path. They need protection and food and Papa gives them both."

I shook my head. "That's an excuse. You know Papa has had people murdered, Ramon. How can that be okay with you? God lays that out pretty clearly in the commandments."

He shrugged. "It is the small losses that keep the many safe. I am not here to discuss business or religion. Papa wants you to come home."

"Why?" My desperation swelled. "He knows I don't want to be there. Why would he want me back?"

"Because he loves you. Because you are all he has left of Mama."

I felt as though I'd been slapped. He never loved, Mama, I wanted to say. But I knew it wasn't true. He had loved her and he loved me, in his own dysfunctional way. "If you love someone, aren't you supposed to want them to be happy?"

"He knows you'll be happy in time, when you're back home where you belong. Right now, he wants you to be safe."

"I was safe, until you showed up."

A slight smile crossed his face. "You have planes crashing here. You have shooting on your property, and murdered men. That's not safe."

"How do you know all that? Oh never mind. You probably know what I had for dinner last night."

He got up and wandered into my kitchen. "Something with berries, I would guess," he said, pointing to a spot of blue sticky on the ceiling that Lucille and I had missed. He opened the fridge and took out a bottle of water. "Martina, you know that I love you. You are my sister. It is my duty to protect you and I will do that. "

"I'm a grown up. I don't need protecting."

"Your situation would lead me to believe otherwise."

"Does Papa know about everything that has happened here?"

"No. You can tell him when I take you home. He waits to hear from me."

I swallowed. "Think of Mama, Ramon. She wanted me to have my own life, away from Papa's business. You know she died unhappy."

He looked away.

I pressed harder. "You loved her, I know you did. I can still remember us flying kites together, making lizard catchers out of grass. She gave me this life. Please, please Ramon, don't take it away from me."

The afternoon sunlight through the window highlighted

shadows under his eyes that I hadn't seen before. His face softened for a moment. Then he drank the water and tossed the bottle into the trash. "It must be done, Martina. It is the only way. I will give you a few days to finish up your business. Then we will go home."

The door closed behind him.

Through the window I watched him walk in the blazing sunlight, back straight, chin tilted to the sky.

I returned to the laptop with a sick feeling in the pit of my stomach. The cursor blinked at me.

Destination?

I picked a town in a town at random. A tiny dot in the state of Wyoming called Lone Pine.

I hit the submit button.

It was time to pack.

Chapter Eighteen

The phone rang and rang, the dial tone dismal in my ear. "Pick up, Joe. Come on. Just answer the phone. Please."

I was about to leave message number five when Joe's voice filled up the line. He sounded as tired as I felt.

"What do you want, Marty?"

"Joe, please please don't hang up. I have to tell you how sorry I am. I've been a moron."

"I think you covered that in your previous phone messages."

Desperation welled up inside me. "I love you, Joe. I'm sorry I didn't say that enough, but it's true. I'm so sorry I hurt you. If I could do it over again, I would have told you everything right from the start."

Silence.

"Joe? Are you there? Did you hear what I said?"

"Yes. Thanks for calling, Marty. Take care of yourself."

There were no more tears left as I hung up the phone only, a serrated agony in my heart.

Through a blur of tears, I made sure the curtains were closed and unfurled a duffel bag. Jeans, underwear, sweater. Mama's Bible. Some jewelry maybe I'd be able to sell and all the cash I could find. I piled three apples in the duffel bag and stowed two more under the sink in case Lucille didn't get to Byron for a while. A box of Twinkies and two bottles of water and I was packed.

Now to figure out a way to get Deputy Fisk to come over and flush Ramon off my property for a while. I was still working on a plan when Lucille barreled in with a tray full of deviled eggs.

"Ficky musta gone crazy making these eggs. Even after all the folks left I still got three dozen at least. I woulda brought you some of them ribs too, but I didn't on account of your vegetable diet though I still wonder how you have enough strength to get out of bed with no meat in your pipes. It just ain't natural." She thumped the platter on the table and pulled up a chair. "All right. Let me have it."

"What?"

"Your bad family stuff that you were fixin to tell me before your brother showed up. You got grief written all over your face honey, and I know it has to do with Raymond."

"Ramon, but it's not worth the trouble to tell it now."

She scratched her cheek. "You looked like you had a gator in your gizzard when your brother appeared. Ficky thinks he's mob and you've been hiding out in Ferocious on account of you're a relation."

My mouth dropped open. "How did he figure that out?"

She took a paper towel wrapped hunk of bologna out of her pocket and chewed off a piece. "Couple years back Ficky thought maybe he wanted to go into the F.B. I. so he started watching that Most Wanted show. Turns out there's entirely too much violence those poor F.B I. people have to endure, so he decided to stay with the trucking business. It's hard on the backside, but you don't have to collar perps or anything.

It's a relief to me 'cause I want my Ficky around where I can keep him safe."

"Okay," I prompted. "He watched the Most Wanted show?"

"Yup, and he saw an episode about this Escobar family. A clan that smuggled drugs over the border and what not. Bad folks, into bad things. Ficky said you were the spittin' image of Big Daddy Escobar."

That was a miracle on a number of levels as Papa was very careful about letting himself be photographed and I'd always been told I favored my mother. I tuned in again as Lucille continued around her mouthful of bologna.

"And Ficky's brother Stew was a missionary to Mexico and all. Ficky remembered a story he told nine or so years back about a big brouhaha among the villagers regarding a missing girl from the Escobar family. Something about her running away or being snatched or something while she was in the states. Big Daddy sent people into every nook and cranny looking for her, figuring maybe his enemies brought her back to Mexico and took her to some hiding spot in the backcountry. The folks was all astir about it."

I felt a pang. Had my father thought I'd been kidnapped?

"So's Ficky put two and two together and come up with you know, four."

"You and Ficky knew all this time?"

"Nah. Only about the last few years. "Fore then we just pegged you for a real private type. Kinda weird, no offense, but generally good-hearted."

My mind pinwheeled. "Why didn't you ask me about it?"

"We figgered it was your business and you'd tell if you felt like it. Nobody wants to hang their skivvies on the clothesline for all the world to see, now do they? My cousin Stella married a kleptomaniac. She kept that a secret for years. We just thought all them hubcaps was stolen by the neighbor kids every Thanksgiving. If he hadn't been nabbed taking a twenty pound turkey from the Pack and Go store we'd a probably never have known."

I sank down on the chair, stunned. I'd been found out by a woman who subsisted on processed meats and a man who carved giant wedding pelicans. "Are you…mad at me? For not telling you about my family?"

She patted my hand. "No honey, I ain't, but then again, I ain't your sweetheart. Sweethearts don't cotton to lying, no matter if it's a good reason or not."

Tears welled up again. "I've tried to apologize. Joe doesn't want to talk to me."

"Joe's got his pride up in a twist. You gotta admit it's kind of a shock. Ficky figured it out 'cuz he's got a mind like Sherlock Holmes. If it wasn't for those powers o' destruction, we wouldn't have known either. Give it time, Marty. Joe is a reasonable man and he loves you. He will come around."

"I don't have time to wait. Ramon is going to take me home in a few days, whether I like it or not. He'll tie me up if he has to, but I'm going to be in Mexico by weeks end."

"Land sakes. Can he do that?"

I nodded, miserably. "Trust me. He can and he will."

She glanced at the duffel bag. "So you got a decision to make."

A cold vapor seemed to creep through my body, leaving only a dull fatigue behind. "I don't think I have much of a choice. Everything is closing in on me. Oh Lucille, what should I do?"

She finished off the last of the meat, rolling it around in her teeth before she swallowed. The chair scraped the linoleum as she stood. "Honey, I've been thinkin' about all them animals you and me been helping. God gave them four legs so's they can run from their troubles."

Her hand was heavy on my shoulder before she headed for the door. "Seems to me, Marty, you're a couple legs short for that."

I peered through the crack in the curtains the next morning with bleary eyes. I couldn't see Ramon, but his car was still there. Maybe he'd made himself at home in the tent trailer. Best not to risk loading the duffel bag into the van until dark. I still needed to call Deputy Fisk, but there was something that had to be done first. I turned off my computer and hid the duffel under the bed before I locked the office door. Ramon could get in if he wanted too, but he'd have to at least pick the lock first.

As I pulled out onto the highway, his Mercedes slid in behind me. I wasn't surprised. He probably already knew where Joe's father lived. He was like some horrible stalker Santa Claus.

It was still a shock to me that Lucille and Ficky had known for so long. If I had just been able to tell Joe, things might not be where they are. Sure, I would probably still have to disappear one day, but at least Joe would understand why. At the moment, he couldn't understand anything except that I'd lied to him for years. Lied, to my Joe.

Man, could I use another set of legs. Four would just about get me to the border, away from the mess I'd made. Even the late afternoon sun couldn't warm the coldness that was lodged in my gut. The miles crept by and though I turned on the radio, the music didn't penetrate either.

Ramon had the decency to park a distance away when I pulled up at Mack's trailer. He didn't make any signs of following me to the door.

Mack leaned on his cane as he let me in. His ankle was now wrapped in a stiff yellow cast. "Come on in, Marty. I thought you might be stopping by."

"Thanks. How is Pumpernickel?"

"Much improved. Joe is a whiz with animals, but I don't need to tell you that."

My heart squeezed. "No you don't."

Mack got us both a soda from the fridge and we settled in on the worn sofa. "You got a lot on your mind, now."

I nodded. "Did Joe tell you the details?"

He nodded. "I think I got the basic picture."

"Mack, I want to tell you that I'm sorry. You have been nothing but good to me and I feel terrible that I wasn't honest. I thought that's what was best for everyone but now I think maybe it was just easiest for me."

He sighed. "I must admit I was taken by surprise. Imagine keeping that family tree a secret for so long."

"I could have handled things differently."

"Yes, but that's done now."

I massaged my throbbing temples. "Mack, where's Joe? I really need to talk to him. Please tell me."

"I'm not sure he's in the frame of mind to hear you right now."

"I know, but I've got to see him. I need to settle things, face to face before…"

His eyes searched my face. "You going someplace?"

"I don't want to." The rest went unspoken.

Mack rubbed a hand over his wrinkled face. "It isn't going to be good for Joe to have it end like this. He told me not to interfere, but I'm going to pull the father card here. He's at the church, helping them fix the roof. I think you can catch him if you get right over there."

"Thanks, Mack." I got up and put my soda can in the recycle bin. "Can I ask you something?"

"Shoot."

"When you had kids, did you… change at all?"

He frowned. "What do you mean?"

"Did you make different choices when you had children looking up to you?"

His sigh was gentle. "I still made plenty of bad decisions, I'm afraid. The Lord helped Joe turn out okay anyway. He gets the credit."

"That's the part I don't get, Mack. Papa goes to church

and says prayers and sings hymns. But he murders and smuggles drugs and extorts money from innocent people. That didn't change even when Ramon and I came along. How can those two things go together?"

"I don't think they do, Marty." He shook his head, looking at the ceiling. "These are the times when I wish my wife was here. She'd know how to say it. All I can tell you is, God loves His people. He doesn't always approve of their actions, but he waits patiently for them to turn to him. Fully. With their whole hearts and minds. Your father is still living by his own rules, making God fit into his plans."

"I wish, I wish he could have changed. For us, and my mother."

Mack's smile was gentle. "That's between your father down here," he pointed downward, "and your Father up there."

"And you can't pick your family.'"

"No ma'am, you can't."

If only I could have. I gave Mack a hug. "Thank you for letting me in."

"You're always welcome here, Marty."

My eyes filled with hot tears. "Is there anything I can get for you?"

"Got another blueberry pie on you?"

I laughed. "I'm afraid not."

He patted the roll around his stomach. "Just as well, I guess."

Mack led me to the door. We stood on the porch, surrounded by buttery sunlight.

"You know," Mack said. "I've been reading that poem again, The Rime of the Ancient Mariner. It's a mighty long bit to slog through, I'll tell you. But that part that you kids found, in the journal, it made me remember." He walked to the kitchen and opened a drawer. "Joe's mother and I went to Utah once upon a time and we bought this. Probably paid twice what it's worth, being ignorant tourists."

He dropped a small rock into my palm.

"What is it?"

"A meteorite. A little chunk of a planet, sent down to earth."

I hefted the jagged pebble. "It's heavy."

"Mostly iron, they told us. Funny, isn't it? How such a small thing can be so heavy?"

I fingered the rough surface. I never thought my heart could be so heavy either. I handed it back.

"It set me to wondering."

"Wondering about what?"

"Why do you think God made stars, and comets and constellations and such?"

"I don't know, Mack. Why do you think?"

"Because He wanted to remind us to look up."

Ramon remained on my tail as I drove over to the church. I tried to rehearse what I should say, but I couldn't think of a thing. I probably should have brought Tito along.

My phone rang. It was my shadow calling.

"I am hungry, Martina. Why don't you come with me to get some dinner? There has to be some decent food somewhere in this town of yours."

"No."

"Why not?"

"Because you don't share a meal with someone who is going to kidnap you."

He laughed. "I see you have not lost your flair for the dramatic. Taking a person back home is not kidnapping."

"It is if they don't want to go. Go away, Ramon."

"Not likely, hermanita."

I hung up.

The phone rang again, jangling my very last nerve.

"Listen here," I shouted. "Why can't you leave me alone? I don't want to talk to you or listen to you and there will be igloos in the desert before I share a dinner with you.

Go away, go away, go away!"

There was an alarmed silence on the other end of the phone. "Er, Marty? It's Jackie from the garage. Sorry for, uh bugging you and all. I was calling to tell you I finished Lucille's Moped. You can pick it up any time. Or I can hold onto it. Whatever you want is okay."

He could probably feel my burning cheeks through the phone. "Oh, sorry Jackie. I thought you were someone else. I'll stop by the garage on my way home tonight. Okay?"

"Sure, sure. Uh, did you say something about igloos?"

"Ummm, yeah, but never mind that. I'll see you in a few hours."

"Whatever you say. Bye."

If there was anyone left in this town that didn't think I was a complete nutcase, or a big fat liar, I'd love to meet them. My brain continued to spin like a hamster in an exercise ball. I'd leave the money for Lucille's Moped at the garage before I caught the flight on Sunday afternoon.

Ramon's car followed me into the church parking lot. Several people were packing up their tools and washing their hands with the hose. My palms felt clammy and my breath grew shallow as I searched for Joe among the workers.

Pastor Enrique in jeans and a ripped tee shirt came over to my car. "Well hello, Marty. So good to see you. Looking for Joe?"

"Yes. Is he here?"

"Sure. He's been working since sun up. Let's see if I can find him." He shaded his eyes against the glare of the setting sun. "There he is. Right by the flower bed, talking to that dark haired man. I don't know his name."

I peered closer. That man. I knew him well.

Joe was knee deep in conversation with none other than Todd Chin.

Chapter Nineteen

My knees trembled as I approached. Was it the fear that Joe would freeze me out? Or the alarm at finding him with Todd?

They both stopped talking at my approach. Joe looked at me and quickly returned his attention to the toolbox he was packing. Todd pasted on an easy smile.

"Hey there, Marty. I've been looking all over for you. I came back for my journal."

"Your journal? Don't you mean Professor Speigel's journal?"

He paused. "Well it's kind of mine by default. I found it."

"You found it where?"

"At the television studio."

I blinked. How did the journal get there? Never mind. It was probably a lie anyway. "It's evidence in a murder case. You should have given it to the police."

"You're right. I'll take it over there. Where is it?"

"Ask Deputy Fisk. He had it last I heard and he was

looking for you."

If Todd was surprised, he didn't show it. "Okay." His glance went over my shoulder. I turned to find him staring at Ramon's car. "Who's that guy in the Mercedes?"

My first instinct was to lie. Instead I held up my chin. "That's my brother, Ramon."

His eyes widened as he looked from me to the car. "Your brother? When did he get into town?"

"Yesterday."

"Is he here on business?"

"I don't know. Why don't you ask him?"

Todd's stare never left my brother. "I will. Excuse me."

He walked toward the Mercedes. When he was within three yards, my brother took off, tires crunching as he headed out onto the highway. Without a word, Todd hopped onto his motorcycle and zoomed after him.

Finally something was working in my favor. Much as I didn't like Todd and his shifty ways, at least he would keep my brother busy for a while. I hoped, for his sake, he didn't catch Ramon.

I watched Joe for a minute. His broad back was dusty, sweaty. There was a sprinkle of sawdust twined in his braid.

"Looks like you put in a full day's work."

"Yeah," he said.

"I want to talk."

"Me too."

My pulse quickened. "You do?"

He straightened, brushing his hands on his jeans. "I'm thinking about starting college again in the fall. If I get another loan and work in the city I should be able to swing it. I thought you'd better know so you can find yourself another tour guide."

I felt something tear in my heart. The words came out in a whisper. "You are so much more to me than a tour guide."

"That's what I thought until recently." He shoved his hands into his jean pockets.

"Can't you understand in some tiny way why I did what I did?"

He breathed out slowly before he answered. "Yes, I can. I can understand why you are here in Ferocious. I understand that you don't want to be involved with your family. I get all that."

"But?"

"But, I don't understand why you didn't trust me enough to tell me. We've shared our lives for the past eight years, Marty. It hurts that you have so little faith in me after all that time."

"I do trust you, Joe. I didn't want either of us to get hurt."

"So what was your long range plan? Were you going to lie to me forever? Or just disappear one day and leave me wondering?"

"I'm no good at planning, Joe. I was trying to tell you, but things just kept getting in the way."

His eyes were sad. "Too little, too late."

Too late.

The words echoed in my ears. Too late for me and my Joe. "I should have told you. I made a mistake, a huge, enormous, gigantic mistake."

He sighed. "Yeah, you did, but the problem is deeper than that."

"What do you mean?"

"You aren't hiding from your father, Marty. You're hiding from your feelings."

My jaw tightened. "What?"

"I think you didn't tell me about yourself because way down inside, you're ashamed."

"What are you talking about?"

"You're ashamed that your father is a criminal and you love him anyway."

Heat rushed into my gut. "And just what do you know about it, Joe? Your dad is a wonderful man. Your mother was a saint. What do you know about my father?"

"Not a thing, but I know you."

"Well maybe you don't. I was hiding here because I don't want to go home and live on a compound in Mexico, marry a gangster friend of my father's and watch my children grown up with a Patróne grandpa who dangles them on one knee while he sends his men out to make their playmates fathers disappear. If you can't understand that, Joe Hala, then maybe I don't really know you." I ran back to the van and slammed the door, taking off in a shower of gravel.

I didn't even glance in the rearview mirror until I hit the highway. When I finally brushed the tears from my face, I noticed only a few cars. No motorcycle, but a Mercedes keeping a steady distance behind me.

"Okay, Ramon. Maybe you're right. Maybe I'd be better off in Mexico living with a bunch of thugs." My angry breath made steamy spots on the window. Hiding from myself? How come I hadn't realized how sanctimonious Joe could be? What did he know, with his Beaver Cleaver family?

"At this very moment," I snarled to no one, "I would KILL for a chicken nugget."

Accck. That did sound sort of thuggish. As I rattled along, my plans grew clearer. I'd let go of the lot of them; Joe, Ramon, Papa. "Lone Pine, here I come."

You're ashamed.

"Well what kind of Christian wouldn't be ashamed about having a bad man for a father?"

Ashamed of loving him.

Loving him?

I shifted on the worn seat.

Did I love him? No. Absolutely not. Who could love a murderer? Who could love a hypocritical lawbreaker? The answer came out of nowhere.

God.

The One who sent His precious son. He loved all kinds

of sinners. He not only loved them but He forgave them when they asked.

But He was Lord and I wasn't. I was just....who? A mobster's daughter? A small town girl? A woman on the run?

My knuckles whitened on the steering wheel. "God help me," I breathed. "I'm a mess and I've botched the life my mother tried to give to me. What do I do?"

I felt no comfort. In a fog I raced along, almost missing the road to Jackie's Garage. The sun set as I turned in, painting the ground in gray shadows.

I looked at my watch. Nine o'clock. Ramon would no doubt wonder why I needed a mechanic so late. A reckless feeling coursed through my body. Let him wonder.

The single window on the run down building was dimly illuminated. Maybe Jackie had waited for me.

I hoped so.

I'd made a mess of everything, but I at least wanted to give Lucille her wedding present before I left it all behind. She deserved so much more from me, but this was all I had to offer. I climbed out, feeling like each leg was weighted down with lead.

"Jackie?" I called as I knocked. The loud noise silenced the chorus of crickets. "Jackie? It's Marty. I'm here for the Moped. Are you in there?"

Only quiet. I leaned my head against the door jamb. "This is just the perfect end to this day." Then I noticed a slip of paper under the dirt encrusted door mat.

Marty, I had to go home. Bowling night. Moped out back. Slip money under door. Jackie

With a surge of relief I stuffed a check under the door and trotted around the side of the building, skirting flattened tires and piles of metal parts. I let myself in through the rusted gate. The moon made the car shrapnel glitter against the dark ground. A rat scampered along the junk, keeping pace with me.

Lucille's Moped was parked against the building. Though it was hard to fully appreciate Jackie's work in the moonlight, I smiled in spite of myself. She would love it. At least I'd done something right.

I stuck out my toe to put up the kickstand when I heard the shot.

It slammed through the quiet.

A gunshot from the front of the garage.

I froze until the need to flee took over. Frantically, I scanned the dark, fenced yard. There was nowhere to go.

I dove behind a tower of tires and dialed my cell.

"Somebody's shooting," I whispered as loud as I dared.

"Where are you?" Joe demanded.

"Jackie's garage. I'm scared."

"Stay out of sight. I'm on my way."

I disconnected and dialed the police who dispatched a car as I explained as loudly as I dared.

Silence filled in the space around me. The smell of old rubber and gasoline choked me and my legs cramped in their squatting position. I strained to pick up any noises, but the thump of my heart was too loud.

Was it Ramon? I knew he carried a gun but who would he be shooting at in the front of the garage?

Another thought dawned on me, causing my stomach to contract even further. What if Ramon was the victim? The Escobars had plenty of enemies, the cost of doing a dangerous business.

I squeezed my eyes against the tears. Ramon was bad, like my father. Bad men attracted violence like a porch light brings moths.

But he was my brother. And I loved him. God help me, I loved a mobster and his father, too. Tears went unchecked down my face.

You are my hiding place.

The psalm danced in my brain. I'd been hiding for the wrong reasons, and in the wrong place. "Lord, forgive me.

Forgive me. Forgive me."

The minutes ticked away in an eerie slow motion. I heard the slight scuffing of feet.

I held my breath, a clammy film of sweat on my face.

Closer.

The sound of heavy footsteps.

Rounding the corner.

The whine of the metal gate latch being lifted.

Closer.

A scream formed way down low in my stomach.

The feet stopped, yards from my hiding place. Was that the man's breathing? Or mine?

A police siren cut through the darkness. The feet turned quickly and headed back toward the gate.

In a minute, there were many feet, running towards me and away at the same time.

"Marty," Joe half whispered, half yelled. "Where are you?"

I launched myself out of my hiding place and barreled into his arms so hard I knocked him over. We both went down in a pile.

My body shook, blubbery sounds coming out of my mouth as Joe struggled to get us upright. "Someone was coming. For me. Oh Joe, I was so scared. There was a shot."

He helped me to my feet and smoothed my hair. "It's okay. You're safe now. Deputy Fisk saw the guy take off. He ran after him. It's okay."

I clutched him in another death hug. "Joe, you were right. I'm sorry. I shouldn't have called you but there was shooting and…" I broke off and looked at his face. "Was anybody hurt?"

Joe looked away. "Marty…"

"Tell me."

He met my eyes, his face like a piece of carved sandstone in the moon light.

My knees began to shake. "Who?"

"You need to sit down. You're trembling all over."

"Joe," I said, my words steady and slow, "tell me who was shot?"

The whine of an ambulance grew louder as it neared, cutting off with a squawk as the motor stopped in front of the garage.

Without another word, I ran for the gate, faster than I'd ever run in my life.

Chapter Twenty

A man was on the ground, paramedics buzzing over him. They'd cut away his shirt, exposing skin. And blood. Lots of blood that soaked down to his pants and into the white bandages piled in a heap on his chest.

I willed my feet closer.

The medics held his neck straight while they strapped on a collar.

I closed the gap and looked into the face of Todd Chin.

His eyes were closed, mouth slack.

"You need to move away," the nearest medic said, shouldering me aside.

"How…" I cleared my throat and tried again. "How badly is he hurt?"

"Can't tell for sure. Seems like the bullet missed his heart, but he's lost a lot of blood."

Joe caught up and pulled me away. "Did you leave the van doors open?"

"Huh?"

"The van. Did you leave it open when you got out?"

I couldn't make sense of the question as I watched them extend the stretcher legs and wheel Todd into the ambulance. "I don't think so. No. No, I closed the van."

Deputy Fisk returned, panting. He talked into the radio clipped to his shoulder. "Marty. Are you okay?"

I nodded.

"You'd better take a look at this," Joe said, pointing to the van. Fisk and Joe looked into the interior, illuminated by Fisk's flashlight. I heaved myself up and joined them. It was a mess. I wasn't anywhere near Joe's clean car standards, but I knew I hadn't left it like that. Papers from the open glove box were strewn all over. The first aid kit was ripped open and my backpack with extra clothes and water had been dumped.

"What happened?" I mumbled.

Fisk rubbed his forehead. "The guy just had to go be a Lone Ranger. Just because we're small town, he thinks we can't manage an investigation. That really chaps my hide."

Joe spoke for both of us. "What are you talking about?"

Fisk jerked a thumb at the departing ambulance. "Chin. I knew I recognized that guy from somewhere. Finally figured it out two days ago so I went to see him." He shook his head. "If he'd let me in on his plans, we could have provided backup. Would that have crowded his limelight too much? I've been through the police academy. Well, I hope his pride was worth getting shot over."

Joe tried again. "Pride about what?"

Fisk sighed. "The guy is CBP."

"A what?"

"He works for Customs and Border Patrol. He's a Border Patrol Agent."

Todd was law enforcement? I groaned. And here I thought the guy was a criminal. Keen detective work, Marty. "So he's a cop. That figures, with all the questions he's been asking. He was looking for a way to get to my father."

Fisk blinked. "No. It's got nothing to do with you unless

you or your father has been smuggling aliens."

"Aliens?" I pictured Al Jr. and his Roswell fixation. "That's been a hot topic lately. Why would Todd think I've been smuggling aliens?"

"He was investigating the T.V. station owner, Ken Lloyd. He thought he could connect him to a ring that smuggled in Mexican illegals and dropped them by plane in the desert. The professor showed up at the T.V. studio and he figured the guy might be involved somehow, too. Todd even took his journal." Fisk snorted. "The only thing that guy was into besides debt was rocks. I know. We've been in on that much of the investigation at least, and it's been a by the book effort I can tell you."

I tried to sort through the mental muddle in my head. "Todd thought the Professor was involved in smuggling illegal aliens? Why?"

Fisk shrugged. "Speigel and Ken Lloyd were roomies in college. Speigel turned up a few times at the station and on Lloyd's phone records."

"Why does he think they're using the Desert Star as a drop point?" Joe said.

"Because of the sketches in Speigel's journal and the plane crash. It's clear that somebody's interested in your property for some reason."

"Did Todd get any proof that Lloyd was smuggling people in?"

"Nothing that would stick. The guy's probably dirty, but it's back to square one now, thanks to Chin's hot dogging."

The paramedics loaded Todd into the ambulance and took off with sirens blasting. "Is he going to be okay?"

Fisk sighed. "I don't know. He should have let us in on the thing."

We lapsed into silence. Joe took my hand and squeezed it between his.

The deputy squinted. "There's another part here. Chin was investigating Marty so that's probably why he followed her here. I doubt that he messed up the van. That's not good undercover work."

"Maybe he was in a hurry," I said.

"Could be, but there's another problem with that theory," Fisk said. "Todd Chin did not shoot himself."

The awful truth of that was too much. My knees buckled and I slid to the ground.

Time passed in a blur. Joe helped me to a bench while Deputy Fisk and another officer dusted for prints in the van. A man in coveralls took pictures of the whole place and another rolled a measuring wheel around and jotted notes.

Someone miraculously produced hot coffee for everyone. I drank it, but it didn't warm my insides. At last we were allowed to go home but the van had to stay. I did convince the deputy to let me take Lucille's Moped which we somehow crammed into the back of Joe's Jeep.

Joe opened the door for me. "Come on, Marty. I'll drive you home."

We slid in and buckled up. Though the night was clear and starlit, everything seemed enveloped in a fog. Joe's words came from far away.

"Are you all right?"

"No." I could feel his gaze on me. "Why did you come? I mean, you made it clear things were over between us. Why did you come?"

"For the same reason you chose to call me." He sucked in a deep breath and then exhaled. "Because I love you. My pride was hurt and it still is. But I can't ignore the fact that I love you, whether you're a Barr or an Escobar."

I went all blubbery. "I love you, too." I threw my arms around the parts of him I could reach. He squeezed me in a tight hug.

When my sobbing let up, I wiped my eyes with the tissue he gave me. "But can you trust me again?"

He was quiet for a minute. "It's going to take some time."

That hurt. But it was fair enough.

"Do you think…we could get back to what we had before?"

He cocked his head. "I'm not sure. Let's try it and see."

I nodded, blinking back tears. "Macaroni is no good without cheese."

"What?"

"Never mind." I had another chance with Joe. My Joe.

Joe fired up the heater as the night cooled down.

I looked out the side view mirror. No car followed us. Dread swept through my joy. There was one thing standing in the way of my second chance with Joe. Ramon.

And if I wasn't mistaken, Ramon had blood on his hands.

The blood of a border patrol agent.

Joe must have read my mind. "So, uh, do you think your brother is…still in town?"

"I'm sure of it."

"Wouldn't make too much sense for him to stick around. This is going to draw a lot of attention from law enforcement types."

I rolled down the window to let in a rush of cool air. The scent of night blooming cactus brought back a memory. "When Ramon was sixteen he had a bunch of dogs, one was named Chico. Kind of a grumpy retriever, but purebred, beautiful. A guy driving an R.V. came through one time and admired the dog. The next day Chico and the R.V. were gone."

"What did your brother do?"

"He tracked the guy for three days." I shivered. "He got his dog back."

"Do I want to know what happened to the R.V. driver?"

"No."

"I see."

The moon slipped from behind a cloud. A vast expanse of stars glittered above us.

"Joe?"

"Yeah?"

"I think maybe you were right."

He waited.

"About me, er, loving my father and brother and all. Papa is bad, real bad, and I shouldn't love him, but I do. And Ramon, well maybe he was the one who shot Todd and I hate that, but even so…" The words trailed off.

He put a warm hand over mine. "Jesus loved all people, especially the bad ones. There's no shame in that."

A tear fell down my face onto my jeans. "I know I'll have to go back and face Papa. Someday. But I don't want to now. I want to stay here and build a life." With you. With you, Joe.

There was a tremor in his voice. "I'm so glad to hear that. If you want to stay here, I will help you in any way I can."

"Ramon won't give up."

"He'll have to."

"You don't know Ramon."

Joe's jaw tightened. "And he doesn't know me."

It struck me for the first time that they were a lot alike. Stubborn, passionate, proud. Under different circumstances they might have been friends. I sighed.

He continued to check the rearview every few minutes. "Would you feel safer staying at my place?"

"I don't want to put you in any more danger than I already have."

He squeezed my hand. "I can take care of myself."

My fingers felt cold under his. "I'll bet that's what Todd said."

We finally reached a compromise. I would stay in the office and Joe would hang out in the tent trailer again. I still had prickles of alarm. Ramon would come. He wouldn't accept my decision. He might see Joe as a roadblock to be dispensed with like the R.V. driver.

I fretted all the way back to the Desert Star. Ramon's car wasn't there. As we headed into the trailer, Tito crawled out from under the porch, oblivious to the dangerous people that seemed to pop in on a regular basis.

"Hi, pig pig," I said, giving him a scratch.

"Hi, Marty," he said. "I'm glad you're staying. It wouldn't feel like home without you. You are family, even if you don't have a snout."

Okay. He didn't actually say that, but I could read it in his eyes.

He grunted and pressed his nose to my shin.

"Did you miss me little guy? Let me see if I can find you some celery."

I unlocked the door and me, Joe and Tito piled in.

It was kind of crowded because there was another person already sitting in my best chair.

"Hello, Marty. Where have you been? It's quite late."

I closed my mouth. "I should be asking you that question, Ramon."

Ramon slid his eyes toward Joe. "Would you excuse us? I need to speak with my sister."

Joe kept his eyes glued to Ramon as he sauntered to the couch and sat. "Think of me as wallpaper."

There was a dangerous glitter in Ramon's eyes. "Marty," he said, not taking his gaze off of Joe, "the situation has gotten out of hand."

"What has?"

"Him." He bobbed his chin at Joe. "El Indio."

"Stop calling him that. His name is Joe."

"You weren't meant to be matched with an Indian. They're drunks and losers."

Joe stiffened. "Funny. I've heard the same about Mexicans."

Ramon half rose.

"Would anyone like a soda?" I said in a panicked falsetto.

Ramon sank back on the chair, his back rigid, eyes narrowed. "Who are you, Geronimo? Why do you think you're good enough for my sister?"

"I've got chocolate milk," I babbled, "juice, water."

Joe leaned forward, fists on his knees. "Because I'm honest, I work hard, and I love Marty."

"There are men back home who could say the same. Many of them with great wealth who would consider it an honor to have the hand of Martina Escobar."

"I'm my own man," Joe added. "I answer to no one but myself. I don't have to grovel at the feet of any drug pushing mob boss for approval."

"Or orange fizz," I shouted as they both shot to their feet. "It's very refreshing!"

They stood, inches apart, face to defiant face.

"I've killed men for less than that," Ramon hissed. "Maybe I will kill you too."

Joe didn't flinch. "You could try, man. But you better get it right the first time."

I stopped breathing as I watched them, terror balled up in my stomach. They would kill each other right here in front of me and I was helpless to prevent it.

Finally, after an endless silence, Ramon smiled, the barest slice of a grin. "You are a man of courage. Stupid, perhaps, but not without courage." He stepped back very slowly and returned to his chair, never taking his eyes off Joe.

Joe too, sank back down on the couch, shoulders still taut, lips pulled into a thin line.

I rummaged around the kitchen, pouring drinks in cups and tossing some celery stalks to Tito. The cups nearly slipped through my fingers as I shoved one at Joe and Ramon. They looked suspiciously at their beverages.

"What is it?" Joe said.

I looked at my slapdash cocktail. "It's apple juice and orange fizz. Or chocolate milk and lemonade. I'm not sure."

Both men put their cups down without a sip. At least they'd left off plotting murder for a moment.

"Martina," my brother began, "we will need to leave soon. The police will come now. Many of them. It's best that we go."

"I'm not going, Ramon. That's number one. The second thing is you need to tell me the truth. What happened with Todd Chin?"

His brows furrowed. "Who?"

"Don't give me that 'who' business, Ramon. Todd Chin, the Border Patrol agent that you shot tonight at the garage."

His face was expressionless. "I didn't know his name. I recognized him when he talked with you at the church. He's arrested several of our people, after it took such effort to get them into the states in the first place." Ramon shook his head. "A waste of time."

"So you recognized him? You knew he was an agent?"

"Yes. That's why I left the church. He tailed me for quite a while. Not a bad driver. I didn't expect such tenacity. I finally lost him though it took several hours." His black eyes gave away nothing. "I wasn't aware that he'd been shot. Is he dead?"

"No." I was torn. I didn't want to believe Ramon shot Todd, but I knew he was capable of it. Very capable. "You didn't shoot him?"

"No. It was not me."

"How do we know you're telling the truth?" Joe demanded.

Ramon raised an eyebrow slightly. "You don't. But I did not shoot him. Killing government agents is a messy business. It attracts attention, and that is not good for business."

The cold way he said it chilled me.

"He's probably telling the truth," Joe said, "much as I find it hard to believe. Your van was searched and he wouldn't have any reason to do that."

My mind was running like a cat chasing a yarn ball. "But if you didn't shoot him, then who did?"

"That would be me," Henry Poleman, the plane-crashing stinker pilot said, bursting through the door with a gun in his hand.

Chapter Twenty One

Ramon and Joe made it to their feet, but Henry waved them back down with the barrel of the gun. His stomach pushed against the front of his stained blue tee shirt and bulged out over his belt. The bruise on his face was gone but he looked gaunt, exhausted. "Sit down. Nobody do anything stupid."

Ramon spoke softly. "This is a mistake, friend."

"I don't think so." He pointed the gun in my direction. "She's got something that belongs to me. I want it. I've been through plenty of trouble to get it back too, so don't give me a hard time because I'd just as soon kill you two as look at you."

"Still, it would be better for you to put that gun away," Ramon said.

"You shut up," Henry yelled. "I had enough from you, smart boy."

He trained the gun in my direction again. "We got to talk, girly."

Somehow, the weapon in his hand didn't seem to instill

the fear reaction in me. Maybe it was the fact that I'd had a very long and tiring day, but my mouth seemed to speak up without consulting my brain. "Listen here, Henry Poleman, if that really is your name. I don't have anything of yours. If you're looking for the plane, the cops have it and it wasn't yours anyway from what Deputy Fisk tells me. The rock that nearly brained me is at the station, too and Professor's journal was with a border patrol agent until you had to go and shoot him. Was that really necessary? What did you accomplish by that attempted murder?"

Henry looked confused. "I was following you."

"Decided to join in the parade, huh?" Miss Sarcastic Mouth said.

"I was following you to get my papers back. I already checked your office and I couldn't find them."

"Ransacked, not checked, ransacked. I still have the bruise on my forehead."

"Yeah, anyway, I was looking through your van when the guy stopped me. I panicked and shot him."

"You shot at us too, didn't you? That night out on the bluff," Joe said.

"You were poking into our business."

"Our business?" I said. "Who is working with you and what are you looking for on my property? Are you smuggling people over the border by way of the Desert Star?"

His eyes narrowed. "Never mind that. I'm not here to have tea and chit chat. I want those papers."

"What papers?" I said. "I don't have any of your papers."

He stepped toward me. Joe and Ramon tensed.

"Stop playing dumb. The Professor's papers. You took them out of the plane after I stole the Moped."

"I didn't take anything out of that plane."

He pointed the gun at my head. "I know the professor wrote it down before I shot him. You must have taken it after we crashed."

I swallowed. Now the fear was having its way. "Why did you crash anyway? I know it wasn't engine trouble."

"The idiot professor grabbed for the gun and we struggled. It went off a few times before I killed and lost control of the plane."

"Why were you flying over my property in the first place?" Out of the corner of my eye, I saw Ramon reach slowly behind him.

"Shut your trap. I'm the one doing the talking. I want the papers and I want them now." He stepped toward me and tightened his grip on the gun.

Ramon's hand was coming back around his body, inch by painstaking inch.

"All right," I said, feeling sweat run down my backbone. "I'll get the papers. They're in the other room hidden in a bag of rice."

I turned toward the kitchen. Henry followed my progress for one second too long.

Joe launched himself from the sofa with the explosive energy of a mountain lion.

He landed on top of Henry and they rolled. The gun went off as they crashed into the kitchen table. A bullet drilled into the cabinet. Ramon pulled his own gun and pointed it at the two men.

"Don't shoot," I screamed at my brother. "You'll hit Joe."

Somewhere in the middle of the wrestling, the gun went off again with a deafening bang. A bullet shattered the kitchen window. Ramon and I ducked. Tito made a beeline for underneath the bed, almost knocking me over in the process.

Another bullet whistled over my head.

Henry kneed Joe in the stomach and shot out the open door, throwing a chair behind him to slow my brother who was after him in a flash.

I ran to Joe. "Are you okay?"

He nodded, trying to suck in a breath.

In a few minutes my brother returned, breathing hard. "He got away. I saw his car and I know which way he headed. I'm going after him."

Joe groaned.

Ramon looked at him, head cocked. His smile was bigger this time. Without a word he ran out the door after Henry.

Though my own knees felt like overcooked noodles, I helped Joe to a chair. His gasps grew easier. I wrapped my arms around him from behind our hearts hammering away. "You are crazy. You could have been killed. What were you thinking?"

"Seemed like the thing to do at the time."

I kissed the top of his head. "I love you, Joe, you big crazy dope."

"You need to work on your pet names for me. Most people just go with Honey or Sweetie Pie."

"I'm glad you didn't let Ramon shoot," Joe said. "He'd have probably killed both of us."

"Oh, I'm not so sure. He's a crack marksman."

Joe shook his head. "Henry better hope he's luckier than the R.V. driver."

I shuddered. "What do we do now?"

"We call the cops and wait."

"Wait for what?"

"For Ramon to come back or the cops to show, whichever comes first."

"Okay. But if we're going to do sustained waiting, I'm going to need some shoring up."

I made two bowls of mac and cheese while Joe called the station and filled them in. They dispatched a unit. I wondered who would find Henry first...my brother or Deputy Fisk.

We ate mac and cheese and sipped bubbly water. I

skidded a banana under the bed to soothe Tito. He munched away, but wouldn't come out even when I whistled. Poor pig. He was going to need therapy.

"I can relate to his feelings," I said. "I just want to crawl under the nearest piece of furniture and stay there until the world goes away."

He raised an eyebrow. "The whole world?"

"Except for you."

We sat on the couch in a post carbohydrate haze.

Tito snored. And my eyelids felt heavy. Something else weighed on me too. "Joe, do you think Todd is going to make it?"

"I don't know. I hope so."

"I feel so guilty. He was following me and being a general pain in the caboose, but when Henry started to rifle through my van, Todd intervened. If I hadn't stopped at the garage, he wouldn't have been shot."

"It's not your fault that he didn't ask for backup. You had no idea."

"I know. It just seems weird, to be sitting here, safe and cozy while he's in the hospital fighting for his life. I wish there was something we could do."

Joe took my hands in his. "There is," he said, closing his eyes. "Lord we ask you to lay your healing hands on Todd. We know that your grace and mercy are so much more than we could ever imagine. Please help him be at peace, and free of pain. We ask in your most holy name. Amen."

Joe took my mother's Bible from off the bedside table and opened it to Isaiah, the book we'd begun to study together before the plane landed and our lives went kablooey.

I leaned my head against his shoulder as he read, letting the warmth of him seep into me.

"Trust in the Lord forever, for in God the Lord we have an everlasting rock. Isaiah 26:4."

"I love that part," I said.

We snuggled down together and held hands. I felt the worries slip away as sleep took over. My eyes had almost closed when a streak of movement, caught my eye.

Byron poked his head out from under the cabinet. Through my half opened lid, I watched him do his squirrel stealth walk. He scurried over to the kitchen on his teeny claws and snagged a stray paper napkin from the floor before he jetted back to safety.

Byron must have quite the nest going on in there. Joe was right, I really did need to get that squirrel to relocate before his nest outgrew the cupboard. It made me smile, though, picturing him sitting there atop a giant bundle of paper.

Paper.

I sat bolt upright so fast I woke Joe.

"What?" he said. He looked around the room wildly. "Are they back? What happened?"

"Paper," I said.

"Paper what?"

"When the rock fell out of the sky, it was wrapped in pieces of paper. I put it on my desk during the chaos."

He blinked and rubbed his eyes. "Am I supposed to be having a light bulb moment here?"

"I handed the rock and the paper over to the police, but I wonder if something didn't leave this trailer."

"I give up. What?"

"I think Byron took some of the paper and squirreled it away, if you will."

"Good one. So you think whatever paper Henry is looking for is in Byron's nest?"

"Yes, I do."

"That's crazy, you know."

"Yes it is."

"It's like a bad detective novel."

"Yup, only they don't put squirrels in detective novels.

Hercule Poirot would never share page space with a rodent."

He sighed. "I guess that leaves only one question. Who's going to roust the squirrel? You or me?"

It was a size thing. Joe's wide shoulders were just not made for under cabinet exploration. I put on a pair of leather work gloves and shimmied into the hole. The space was deeper than I thought and pitch black. I was in up to my waist before my flashlight beam picked up the glare of rodent eyes.

"Hi there, boy. No need to panic. I was in the neighborhood and I thought I'd stop by. How's everything in Squirrelsville? The acorn supply holding up? Neighbors treating you well?"

He stiffened, his tail splayed out.

"Uh, Joe?"

"Yeah?"

"What do I do if he panics?"

"Suggest he try some deep breathing exercises."

"Thanks. You're a real help."

"Anytime."

Byron drew back into the puffy nest of papers. I reached out a gloved hand at snail speed.

"Just relax there, Byron. I'm not getting personal." I hooked one finger around the nearest paper shred. "I only need a peek under your sheets."

That did it.

The movement of his cozy bed caused Byron to commence the freaking out process.

At first he darted back and forth bashing into the side walls. When that didn't work he leaped over my head and ran down my back. My squealing did nothing to calm him. When he realized my posterior was plugging up the opening, he ran back up and sailed over my head again.

"Sit still, Byron and let me get out of here," I yelled. He continued to zing into walls and trample up and down my back. I snatched the nest and wriggled my caboose out of the cabinet. At one point, Byron actually got stuck between my bottom and the cupboard frame until I squeezed myself small enough that he popped out into the kitchen.

When I finished my freedom wriggle I emerged to find Joe laughing so hard tears ran down his face.

I brushed off my jeans with dignity. "I'm glad you're amused, Mr. Hala."

He wiped his eyes. "Sorry, but you should have seen what that looked like from my end."

"It was a hoot from my side too, let me tell you. You haven't lived until you've had a squirrel doing laps on your back."

I carried the wad to the kitchen table and we tried to make sense of the jumble, carefully separating the shreds into different colored piles. Fortunately, Byron is a very tidy squirrel so he didn't leave any unwanted punctuation on the papers.

"Would you look at this." I held up a ratty pink paper. "A phone bill. I knew I got one, but I couldn't find it anywhere. You're paying those late fees, Byron," I called into the kitchen.

"Unless they take acorn payments, you're on your own with that." Joe smoothed another paper napkin and a grocery receipt. "You got a good deal on mac and cheese back in November."

"Aha. Look at this." I held a torn newspaper. "I think it's the one that was wrapped around the rock, but there's only half. Where's the other piece?"

We scrounged through the pile. Joe found the missing section and we patched it together on the table.

"I don't see any writing," I said, peering at the faded newspaper text.

"Me neither."

I fished out a magnifying glass and we pored over the page until my eyes began to cross. I felt suddenly foolish. "Nothing. Not one message anywhere. I guess I was wrong."

"It was sure a clever idea though." He toyed with the ragged paper. "Wait a minute. Look at this. He took the magnifying glass from my hand and held it over the bottom corner. Then he handed it to me.

I could just barely make out some faint pencil scratches. "Numbers and a letter here and there. Can you read them?"

He squinted, pressing his finger to the paper. "Some of it has been chewed on but I think I can make it out. Write this down for me." He began to dictate. I wrote it on the back of a recipe for split pea soup. When he was done, I read the numbers back. "One, one, one, dot thingy, four seven period six teeny slash w, three four, dot thingy, eight five teeny slash n." I sat back in satisfaction. "Okay. Now what does that mean? Is it a safe combination or something?"

"No." Joe frowned. "But if we assume the dot thingy stands for degrees and the teeny slash for minutes, I'd say the answer is pretty clear, even if it does have tooth marks."

"The answer? Well what is it? What does that jumble of numbers mean?"

"One hundred eleven degrees forty seven minutes west. Thirty four degrees eight five minutes north."

I goggled. "So it's a longitude and latitude?"

"Yes, ma'am." Joe went over to the map of the Desert Star tacked on the wall. "And I would say, Professor Speigel wrote down the directions to a spot right about here." He jabbed a finger to a tiny ridge.

I closed my gaping mouth. "But directions to what? Nice as it is, I've got to admit the Desert Star is a basically a big blob of desert. I haven't explored every bit of it, of course, but I'd have noticed if there was the entrance to a diamond mine there or something. "What is the treasure on this property that people are willing to kill for?"

Joe grabbed his backpack from the chair and opened the door, gesturing for me to follow. "That, my dear Martina Isabella Barr Escobar, is what we are going to find out."

Chapter Twenty Two

We made it to the bottom of the steps before Ramon drove up. His hair was ruffled, but that was the only sign that he'd been in pursuit of the pilot.

"Did you find Henry?" I asked, biting my lip.

"No, but I will. I know where he's headed."

"How do you know that?" Joe asked.

"Mexicans can track too, Geronimo." He looked at me. "We need to go home, Martina. The police will be coming to investigate their agent's shooting. It is best to leave now."

I steadied my quivering stomach. "Ramon, I am not going back to Mexico. My life is here and I like it that way."

He frowned. "You are in trouble here. Henry Poleman, plane wrecks. You cannot stay."

"Just listen, Ramon. Joe and I figured out what they're after, or, at least where they're after. We're going right now to check. And you said yourself you're going to find Poleman eventually."

"The more attention for you here, the more likely our

enemies will find you. They would find it the perfect opportunity for leverage against Papa."

"We're close to solving this mess," I said. "I know it. I can feel it."

He turned away. "It will be dawn soon. Pack your things."

I heaved a sigh. It was like talking to a parrot. "Ramon…"

We all turned toward the sound of an approaching siren.

"That's probably Fisk. He said he would come as soon as he could." Joe turned to Ramon with a wicked grin. "I'm sure you'd like to meet Deputy Fisk. He's probably eager to meet you, especially since the whole Todd Chin incident."

Ramon leveled a hostile glance at Joe. "It would not be an opportune time." He headed toward his car. "I will be back to get you, Martina. Soon. Make no mistake about it."

He drove the opposite direction of the approaching police car.

Deputy Fisk stepped out. "Who was that?"

"My brother."

"Yeah? The one from Lucille's shower? Where's he from?"

I swallowed. No more lies. "Mexico. He is trying to persuade me to go visit my father."

"Oh." The officer patted his pockets and produced a notebook. "Okay, let's have the current situation. I've got Petey looking for Poleman now. What did he want when he busted in on you?"

"Some of the professor's papers."

"What papers?"

We gave him the Reader's Digest version and handed over the tattered scraps.

"We think it's a longitude and latitude," Joe said.

Fisk blinked. "You do? For a point on this property?"

He looked as surprised as I had when Joe enlightened me. "Yeah. We were just on our way to check it out when you arrived."

The radio on Fisk's shoulder's crackled. He listened to the excited voice and answered. "I've gotta go. Frank thinks he's got Poleman holed up at the creek."

He headed off into the pre-dawn gray.

Joe pulled some water out of the fridge and loaded up his backpack.

"I'm gonna grab my jacket before we go." I pulled on a windbreaker and stuffed the bedding back under the sink. "Sorry about the mess, Byron. You go ahead and remake your bed. You'll have it ship shape in no time."

I stuffed some granola bars in my pocket because you never want to find yourself in the desert without food and the mac and cheese was wearing off. As I pulled my hand out, something fell to the floor. I picked it up.

A lightning bolt sizzled through my brain. Isaiah 26:4. It had to be, it all made sense. But why? That was the missing piece.

The Jeep engine rumbled to life. I grabbed my laptop and hurried out to meet Joe.

Tito squeezed through my legs and into the Jeep before I could stop him.

"Do you mind a pig passenger?"

He shrugged. "I've had worse."

We were on our way. It was a few minutes before four. The air was cool, delicious, the smell of the damp ground strong.

I looked at the man behind the wheel. The growing light silhouetted his brown face in a gleam of silver. He was strong and gentle at the same time, like the sheer rock walls that sheltered the birds in their rocky crevices. He was the man I was meant to be with, I was sure, the reason God brought me here to start again. Thanks God, for giving me the strength to tell the truth.

"Why the computer?"

The screen glowed as I powered it up. "You aren't

going to believe this, but I think I know what the treasure is."

His eyes widened. "Really? What is it?"

My cell phone rang. I hoped it wasn't Ramon telling me he'd caught up with Henry. With only a mild tremor, I answered it.

"He drives like Speed Racer," Lucille yelled into the phone.

"What?"

"Your brother, Raymond."

"Ramon. Where is he?"

"I just saw him racing after some guy in his car down by the wash." She whistled. "Some drivin. Maybe he'd give me a couple of pointers for when I get my wheels back. He can turn on a dime. What a sight."

I suppressed a shudder. "Did he, er, catch the man he was chasing?"

"Not yet, but he's goin' to at that rate." She breathed noisily into the phone. "I wanted to ask you something."

"What?"

"I know you might need to uh, leave town and all on account of your family situation but, er, I was kinda wonderin' if maybe should move up the weddin' date so's you could be there and all. I know preacher could do the ceremony anytime, now that we've practiced and all. We could see about switching the bowling alley for maybe today or something."

My eyes filled. That crazy, bizarre woman. My dearest friend. "Lucille, I will be at your wedding on Saturday if I have to crawl all the way from Mexico on my hands and knees. I promise." I thought I heard a sniff.

"Good then. That's just fine. It would be a shame, you know, to waste those overalls and everything. And the ham. I've got twenty pounds of the stuff. Okay. I'll tell Ficky. He'll be pleased as peas."

We signed off.

I brushed away a tear.

Joe navigated around a pothole the size of Tito. "Was that Lucille?"

"Uh huh. She was going to move the wedding up so I could be there before…"

He looked at me. "Are you thinking about it? Running I mean?"

I thought about J.R, the blind rabbit who put all his trust in me because he had no one else. I could be his life line and his protector because God first showed me that He was mine. "Not anymore." I gave him a watery smile. "I'm going to stand my ground this time and trust Him like I should have been doing all along."

His grin lit up the morning gloom. A gleam of moisture danced in his eyes. "Well all right then. So what are we going to do about your brother?"

"I don't know. Once he's decided on something, he'll never give up."

"Then we've got to convince him to decide on something else, don't we?"

"That might be like convincing a tiger to go vegetarian."

"It's worked for you, hasn't it? For a whole three months?"

I laughed. "You bet."

We jounced over a rock as the road steepened.

"All right, spill it Marty. The suspense is killing me. What are we going to find at the end of this desert rainbow?"

"Let me check something out first." I got ready to Google. It took only a few minutes of surfing before I had my answer. It was all so simple and so unbelievable. I almost laughed out loud.

"Joe?"

"Yes?"

"Here's a riddle for you. What kind of alien is worth its weight in gold?"

"Oh boy. I give up, but I'll bet Allen, Jr. would know."

"I'll give you another hint. Isaiah 26:4."

Joe screwed up his face in thought. "For in God the Lord we have an everlasting rock."

I took the small stone from my pocket. "An everlasting rock. Remember when A.J. threw this at the van? I couldn't imagine how such a tiny rock made such a big dent. Remember?"

"Yeah, you were ready to throttle him, but what's that got to do with anything?"

"It's because this rock is made of iron. That's why it's so heavy. Professor Speigel took along the pickle magnet when he went into the desert with Henry Poleman because that's one of the quickest ways to test."

"Test for what?"

"Iron content."

"I still don't get it."

We pulled up at an overcropping of rock that looked down onto a flat, sandy plateau. The rising sun illuminated the ground, picking up an occasional scrubby bush and playing against the dark rocks that littered the space at irregular intervals. Joe and I grabbed binoculars and Tito hopped out to enjoy the fresh air. We followed, taking in the view.

"Magnets stick to iron and iron is one of the primary elements in meteorites. Martian meteorites to be exact." I pointed to the black rocks below.

His eyes darted back and forth in little arcs. "Those things? Those rocks are meteorites from Mars?"

I nodded.

"So Professor Speigel was into meteorites? That's why he copied that Coleridge poem in his journal."

"Uh huh. But he was a geologist first. He must have known what he was looking at when you took him on the overnight tour."

"That would explain why he wasn't interested in star gazing."

"He saw treasure on the ground, all over." I handed the tiny rock to Joe.

He laughed. "So I guess A.J. really did find an alien from outer spac, but I'm still not clear on the why part. I mean, meteorites are of scientific interest and all that, but are they really all that valuable? Worth dying for?"

"Last year three Martian meteorites went for over two million dollars at an auction."

Joe's mouth fell open. "What? That's unbelievable."

I giggled. "They're the ultimate limited edition collector's items."

The voice came from behind us. "Why are you standing here looking at nothing?"

I screamed and whirled around to face Ramon, hands clutched to my heart. "You scared me. How did you find us?"

"It wasn't hard. I followed the trail of dust." He joined us looking down on the ground below. "What did you find?"

"Meteorites."

Ramon blinked. "And why is this important?"

"They're worth their weight in gold," Joe said.

My brother still looked unimpressed.

"They're easiest to spot in sandy landscapes." I swept a hand across the landscape. "The Desert Star has a bona fide meteorite field right under our noses."

Ramon snorted. "And for this you have planes crashing and people shooting? For rocks?"

"It looks that way," I said.

"At least you can't get high on meteorites," Joe said. "Much healthier than other things people kill for."

Ramon's lips thinned into a line.

"So," I said hastily, "Did you catch Henry Poleman?"

"Actually…" Ramon's answer was lost in the sound of a gunshot.

Joe fell, knocked backward by the impact. A spot of blood blossomed on his shirt front.

I screamed and ran to him.

Ramon was in the process of drawing his own gun when Ken Lloyd, the T.V. station owner, stepped from behind a massive tangle of cactus.

"Easy, amigo. Keep your hands where I can see them."

"Joe." My voice was hardly audible. "Joe, Joe. Answer me." I saw the round hole in his shirt and the blood oozing, inky dark against the fabric. His eyes were closed.

"Why did you do that?" I shrieked at Ken. "Are you crazy?"

His round face was passive, the huge mustache drooped over his lips. "I'm here to take the meteorites. I've been through enough to find them."

I took off my windbreaker and pressed it against Joe's side. "You didn't find them. Professor Speigel did. He told you about it, didn't he? And you cooked up a plan to take them for yourself."

"Some plan. How'd I know the idiot would throw the coordinates out of the plane before Henry could kill him?"

Anger burned hot in my gut. "Imagine. Someone with a will to live." I felt my hand grow wet with Joe's blood. "You need to let us go. I've got to get him to the hospital right now, before he bleeds to death."

"You're all staying here. I think you'll even help me load up some of these meteorites in my truck. They're heavy buggers."

"Why would we do that?" Ramon said his smooth voice not quite concealing the steel underneath.

Ken pointed the gun at Joe. "Because if you don't, I'll put a bullet in his brain."

Ramon lifted his chin. "And if we do, you put a bullet in all of us anyway."

Ken smiled. "Seems to me you don't have much choice then. Life is precious, ain't it? You'll do it, for the slim chance at survival. Anything to keep yourselves alive for a few more minutes. Who knows? I might even let you go."

From my kneeling position next to Joe, I noticed Tito under the Jeep directly behind Ken. I shot Ramon a look.

His face remained impassive but I could see that he'd gotten the message. He knew I was up to something.

I hoped the something wouldn't wind up getting us all killed.

I edged around behind Joe so I could get a good eyeful.

"We can find some other agreement, I'm sure," Ramon said. "I have certain connections, friends who would help."

"Yeah? Well unless you've got two million bucks in your pocket I don't think your connections are worth my time."

"Two million is pocket change," Ramon said.

Ken laughed. "It's enough for me, smart mouth. Now get moving. You look like manual labor is right up your alley, amigo."

Ramon stiffened, but he moved in the direction Ken pointed.

It was time. Before Ken moved away from the Jeep. It had to be now.

I whistled as loud as I could. "Tito, come here boy. Come."

Tito shot out of under the Jeep, running toward me on exuberant piggy hooves. He smacked into Ken on his frantic dash, jostling the gun in his hand.

Ramon was on Ken in a minute. He dove head first into the man's stomach. Three vicious punches and Ken was down. Ramon pressed a gun to his temple. "Would you like to talk about bullets now, my friend?"

The anger made his face ugly.

Ken's faced was flushed and sweaty. He was pinned face down in the dirt.

"Stop," I whispered. "Don't."

"He doesn't deserve mercy," Ramon hissed.

"That's not for us to decide. Please, Ramon. Don't."

Slowly he straightened. "As you wish, Martina. You are

a soft-hearted woman like Mama. What do you want done with him then?"

"There's rope in the back of the Jeep. Tie him up and we'll, uh, strap him to the passenger seat."

His eyebrows shot up.

"I'm gonna drive while you apply pressure to Joe's wound. You'll have to ride in the back."

"This is crazy."

"Just do it, Ramon," I shrieked. "Please."

I ran to the Jeep and threw him the rope. "Hurry. You've got to help me get Joe into the car. He's losing a lot of blood." I looked at the streaks of blood on my arms and shirt.

Ramon stayed frozen for a moment in his position on Ken's back. He sighed heavily and bound the downed man's hands behind him.

Ken's face was mottled with dirt and rage as Ramon hauled him to his feet.

"I'll kill you. I'll kill you all."

Ramon whispered something into Ken's ear. Whatever it was, Ken's face turned beet red and he started to sputter like a teakettle.

I handed Ramon a pair of clean socks from my backpack. He shoved them into Ken's mouth before he tied him to the passenger seat.

My fingers shook as I ripped open the first aid kit and pressed a bandage against Joe's bloody side. His eyes fluttered open.

"It's okay, Joe. It's okay. We're getting you the hospital. Stay awake, honey. Keep your eyes open and talk to me."

After a moment, his eyes closed again.

Ramon and I struggled to heave Joe's six foot frame into the tiny backseat of the Jeep. We finally settled on propping him up with Ramon next to him, holding the bandage in place.

Ramon shook his head. "All this trouble for an Indian."

I was alarmed to see the blood already seeping through the bandage and in between Ramon's fingers where he pressed them to Joe's side. I started the engine. Tito scampered into my line of sight, his hooves making tiny dust whirls on the ground. I'd forgotten all about him.

The back of the Jeep was full and I couldn't drive with a pig crammed under the steering wheel. I would never leave him so far away from home base. There was only one choice left.

"Here boy," I whistled, reached across Ken's knees and opened the door. Tito launched himself into the car, landing squarely on his lap. Ken recoiled, yelling something through the sock.

"Be quiet," I snapped. "He'll have digestion issues if you upset him and you don't want that in your lap."

Ken drew back as far as he could against the seat while Tito made himself at home, doing a little circle before he settled in.

I slammed the Jeep into gear and took off down the slope as fast as I dared. The car jounced and shuddered.

The wind slapped at my face as I pushed the car over seventy. Time seemed to stand still except for the crazy thump of my heart. Though I wanted to look in the rearview, I was too afraid to see the dark shadow staining the front of Joe's shirt. All this time. All this time I worried about the danger from my family of lawbreakers and it turned out Joe was shot by someone stealing rocks. I would have laughed if I hadn't been so terrified.

"Martina," Ramon shouted. "How much farther? His breathing is not good."

My fingers turned to ice on the steering wheel. "Five minutes. Put another bandage over the top of that one and press. Hang in there Joe."

Please, God. Please.

Chapter Twenty Three

We squealed into the parking area in front of the hospital. I ran inside.
"Somebody, please help. A man's been shot." Two startled hospital employees ran after me to the Jeep.

The doctor and nurse gave my front seat passenger an odd look as they helped Ramon pull Joe from the car and onto a stretcher.

"Does that guy with the pig on his lap need medical attention?" the nurse said, nodding at Ken, before they wheeled Joe inside.

"No. He's in mint condition," I snapped. "My brother is going to stay with him."

I tossed the keys to Ramon and told him to make sure nobody took Ken as I ran through the sliding doors and searched for Joe.

He was gone.

I was left standing in the waiting room, empty except for the nurse behind a massive counter that bristled with files and phones.

"Here honey," she said, handing me a bag with a hospital tee shirt. "Go change in there. You can clean up a little."

"I'm not going anywhere. I'm waiting right here." I swallowed the tears that threatened to choke me.

Her voice was gentle but firm. "It will take a while for the doctor to help your friend." She pointed to my shirt. "Won't be good for him to wake up and see you looking like that."

I perused my shirt front. It was filthy and spattered with blood. Streaks of rust covered my arms and hands. "Thank you," I said meekly and went into the bathroom to change. My face was pale in the mirror, through the streaks of dust and the smear of blood on my cheek. Joe's blood. The whole thing was one unfathomable nightmare.

Cold water on my face revived me a bit but didn't dampen the fear. I stuffed the ruined shirt into the trashcan.

Ramon was there when I emerged. The same nurse must have found him because he was also wearing a tee shirt and his hands and face were clean.

He fisted his hands on his hips. "What do you want me to do with the fat man? He's attracting attention."

"The fat...oh rats. I forgot about him." I pulled out my cell phone. After three rings I got Chief Spotter. "Hello, Chief? I can fill you in later but I'm at the hospital and Joe's been hurt. Ken Lloyd shot him. He was stealing meteorites,"

I waited for her to finish her barrage of questions. "I can't talk right now but Ken is tied up in the Jeep and..." I covered the mouthpiece. "Ken is still alive, isn't he?"

Ramon smiled. "Yes. And I even reparked in the shade to as a kindness to the pig, not the man."

"Uh, yes, Chief Spotter. He's in the hospital parking lot in an, er, shady spot. I've gotta go. Can you bring Lucille with you because Tito's in the car with Ken. I promise I'll explain everything later." I disconnected before she could start her second interrogation.

Ramon sat down on a green upholstered chair to watch me pace. He checked his watch, probably gauging the amount of time he could stay before the cops showed up.

"I can't believe this," I muttered. "How could I miss a bunch of meteors on my own property? Some naturalist, I am."

He shrugged. "Who can tell one rock from another?"

A vision of Joe lying on the ground bleeding overwhelmed me for a moment. "He's gonna pull through. He's got to. Oh man, I should call his father." The thought of telling Hank what had happened made my eyes fill.

Ramon stood and put a hand on my shoulder. His voice was quiet, almost a whisper. "Do you want me to call him for you?"

The warmth of his touch steadied me. "No. Thanks, but he should hear it from me."

I gripped the phone in my hands just as the doctor came out.

His face was serious, pallid against the green of his scrubs.

I stood on barely stable legs. "How…how is Joe?"

"The bullet passed through cleanly. He's lost a lot of blood, but I think he'll mend just fine, barring any infection and that kind of thing. You can see him after we get him patched up."

I couldn't even say thank you. Fountains of tears ran down my face and I collapsed into a chair. A nurse kindly brought a box of Kleenex, and put it next to me without a word.

I pressed my hands together around a wad of tissue. "Thank you, sweet Lord. Thank you Father, for saving my Joe. Thank you, thank you, thank you." It wasn't the most eloquent prayer ever, but it was all my most heartfelt emotions rolled into one sentence.

"You really love this Indian." Ramon's expression was slightly puzzled, slightly amused.

I honked into the tissue again. "Yes, I do. I love him more than anyone in the whole world, Ramon. He's my soul mate."

He looked at me for a minute without a word. Then he let out a long breath. "Papa will not understand."

My heart thumped as I dared to hope. "I'll explain it to Papa. I'll come, I promise, of my own free will, but not right now. When things are calmer, I give you my word."

His gaze wandered to the window. "It is crazy, to live in this place."

"It's not so bad when you get used to it."

He cleared his throat. "We'll be watching, Martina. Always."

I swallowed. "I know." I threw my arms around him and squeezed. He hugged me back, lapful of Kleenex and all. "Thank you, Ramon. I love you."

He coughed and patted me. "You're an odd little bird, hermanita, and you've picked a strange place to make your nest."

I laughed, feeling my heart fill and swell, light as a butterfly on a spring breeze. Someone approached down the tile corridor. "Hi, Chief. Did you find Ken Lloyd?"

"Yes. Fisk is taking him into custody and Lucille's got the pig. How's Joe?"

"He's going to be okay."

Her smile was relieved. "That's good. Chin is going to pull through also, but I intend to have a few words with him as soon as he's up for it. Good news all around." She eyed me carefully. "How did you tie Lloyd up and get Joe here all by yourself?"

"Oh I didn't. My brother Ramon helped me. He's…." I turned to find an empty chair beside me. "He's kinda shy."

She sat down next to me. "Uh huh. Go ahead and give me the details. Why was this Ken guy interested in your property again? I thought I heard you say meteorites but I must have been mistaken."

I eased back in my chair, still bobbing along on a current of joy. "You won't believe it, but it all has to do with some aliens from Mars."

The wedding day marshmallows turned out to be a great idea, until the temperature topped ninety. Then they began to melt when the guests tossed them at the happy couple. It didn't phase Lucille one bit. She trampled right through the sticky mess, with a beaming Ficky on her arm, waving and shouting hellos at the bystanders. The other guests tried to avoid the goo, but they wound up with it smeared all over their shoes anyway.

I maneuvered Joe's wheel chair around the sticky globs. He'd insisted on performing his wedding duties standing up, but the exertion had tired him to the point where he'd agreed to be chauffeured.

Pastor Farley let Dino out to clean up some of the fluff. I promised to come after the reception and do the remainder after I dropped Joe back at home to rest.

Lucille and Ficky made it out to the sidewalk where my wedding gift was waiting. Her mouth dropped open at the sight of her repainted Moped, complete with sizzling orange tiger stripes, gleaming like fire in the sunlight.

"Lands sakes. Lands sakes." She danced around it, dragging Ficky along. "Get a load of that. This is the nicest present anyone could ever be askin' for. Look at those stripes, Ficky. Just look at them."

I kissed the top of Joe's head. I didn't tell her, but I'd been given a much better present. She and Ficky put on their matching tiger helmets and sputtered off to the bowling alley.

We followed in the Jeep.

Joe eased into the seat, tired but smiling. "You know we look like a couple of Ooompa Loompas in these white overalls."

"Be grateful she didn't pick green. How are you

feeling?"

"Okay. Sore, but I'm managing. Dad says we're a couple of walking wounded."

"At least you're walking."

He nodded. "Yeah, but we both argue about who should be caring for whom."

I laughed.

He cleared his throat. "Marty, I've been thinking about college."

I'd put that nasty thought out of my mind. "You have?"

"Yeah. I need to finish my degree. I've looked into it and I think if I do an intense six months I can be done by Christmas."

I swallowed. "So, you'll be leaving then?"

"I'm going to do all the classes I can online. The rest I'll do at the state college. I'll home on weekends, every chance I get." He squeezed my hand. "Can you live with that?"

"As long as I know you're coming back, I can live with anything."

We pulled up at the bowling alley. A row of sticky marshmallow shoes was lined up along the steps with a hand written sign that said, "Leave yer shoes out here."

A lively banjo tune filled the space. Streamers of all colors hung from the ball returns and shoe rental counter. Daisy centerpieces dotted the tables. True to his word, Arnie had managed a cake that was the image of the Empire State Building. Lucille's bowling team, again dressed in matching pink shirts, snapped pictures of the mountain of frosted layers.

Lucille and Ficky were arm in arm, a blur of overalls and mile wide grins. Lucille waved at me from across the room.

It was hot inside and someone had given up on the air conditioner and thrown open all the windows.

"Let's dance," Joe said, struggling to pull himself out of the chair.

"I think you should rest. The doctor didn't say anything

about dancing."

"There's plenty of time for resting later."

We walked to the arcade area which doubled as the dance floor. Chief Spotter's oldest kids were there, feeding coins into the pinball machines. I felt someone touch my shoulder.

My brother wore a silk suit, his hair freshly trimmed, tie smooth against his pale shirt. He smiled and kissed me on the cheek.

"Ramon. I wondered where you were. I haven't seen you in days. I've kind of missed your car in my rear view mirror."

"I've been touring the area."

"And staying away from the cops," Joe put in.

He chuckled. "They seem to be content, having caught this Henry person who shot their cop."

"And killed professor Speigel," I added. "Not to mention having Ken Lloyd in custody. Chief Spotter is grateful for your help in catching him, Ramon. I'm sure she'd like to thank you," I teased.

"Perhaps another time." There was a sparkle in his eye. "These meteorites, what will you do with them?"

"I'm not sure, but most likely they'll stay where God put them." I laughed. "Imagine what our guests will say when they can tour an authentic meteor field? Think of the people it will attract."

Joe chuckled. "That might even impress Big Al."

I snorted. "I doubt anything would make an impression on him."

Ramon looked at his watch.

"Are you late for an appointment?" Joe said.

Ramon eyed him with a trace of a smile. "I'm going home today. I came to say good bye to my sister."

Joe grinned. "Have a safe trip."

They inched closer to each other.

Ramon raised his chin, his voice level and soft. "If I

hear that any harm has come to Martina, I will find you, Geronimo."

Joe's eyes were hard. "If harm comes to Martina, you won't have to. I'll find you first."

They stared at each other for a moment. Then Ramon looked at me and winked. "Until we see each other again, sister."

I led Joe to the dancing area and he wrapped me in a warm embrace. When I looked again, Ramon was gone.

I couldn't believe all the trouble was behind me. Well, almost behind me. Ramon wasn't kidding when he said they'd be watching. The eyes of my father and brother would always be on me. I snuggled my head under Joe's chin with a sigh, breathing in the scent of his musky aftershave.

I thought about the everlasting rocks, sent from Heaven, down to the desert. Joe kissed me, and I knew he'd been sent from Heaven, too. For me.

We swayed to a plucky banjo tune.

I closed my eyes and let the music wash over me as it drifted through the open window, into the Ferocious sky.

THE END

You might enjoy Desert Desperate. Enjoy the first chapter.

Chapter One

The Arizona desert is lovely in August.
    If you're a cactus.
    If you're not green and prickly it's like standing in the bottom of a volcano hoping your SPF 15 will do the trick. You can run, you can hide, but there's no escape from the vast, unforgiving sandbox. As I hung up the phone with my Aunt Stella, I wondered again what would possess her to settle in such an inhospitable location. Probably the same thought process that prompted her to call me every year on precisely the same date, August nineteenth -- National Potato Day. I didn't even know spuds had their own holiday, but it seemed to impress my aunt. Every nineteenth day of August she and my uncle had a baked potato feast and called me to fill me in on the action. She's an odd sort of spud, Aunt Stella, but I love her anyway. Sometimes I'd call her up and we'd pray together, even if it wasn't a vegetable holiday.

It was hard to wrap my mind around my aunt's potato details as I clicked off the cell phone. My thoughts were steeped in a much cooler climate; the foggy world of San

Francisco. I was planning a wedding: my wedding. Well not just mine, it included my soul mate Doug too, of course.

It was going to be a lovely outdoor affair at a winery in the Napa Valley. The flowers: white roses and lily of the valley. The music: a tasteful combination of harp and string quartet. The food: smoked salmon pate and lobster in puff pastry among other items. And those little square sandwich thingies. What are they called? Canapes, with brie and basil. The dress: a Vera Wang; fitted bodice inset with pearls and a flared shantung silk skirt that was a perfect compliment to my olive skin and black hair.

I could practically feel the soft swish of the fabric around my body as I twirled gracefully. The buzz of an office phone cut through my reverie. I pulled my mind away from these glorious details to focus on the matter at hand.

I was ushered into a tidy office and the editor of Rock Your World read from my resume. She clasped my hand in a bone crushing grip. "Well Miss Greevey, I'm glad to meet you."

"Please call me Simone."

She regarded me over the rims of her electric blue reading glasses. "Simone then. You're coming in on the ground floor of something special. We are an E-zine unlike any other, the first in the San Francisco area. Real cutting edge stuff. We've got readers as far away as New York and Montreal." Audrey wrenched the cap off her sparkling water. "Where did you get that bag?"

The conversational segue nearly gave me whiplash. "My bag? Nordstrom's Sigrid Olsen."

"Cute, it goes well with the shoes. Anyway, we're a Christian medium, but we want to appeal to twenty somethings, not the white haired old ladies who still wear hats and gloves to church."

Audrey, I surmised, hovered somewhere in the middle part of her fifties but old didn't seem to be part of her personal mental picture. She was whip thin, with a helmet of close cut black hair. I bet she ate vegetable protein patties and wheatgrass for breakfast. She looked fit enough to snap me like a toothpick.

"Do you have a boyfriend?" she said.

"What? Uh, yes, a fiancé actually."

"What's he like?"

"He's great. He's a chiropractor."

"Too bad."

"I beg your pardon?"

"My nephew is looking for a girl, but he's a shoe salesman. No contest for a chiropractor." She gulped some water.

"Ah."

"I introduced him to Donna but she's already got a structural engineer."

I wasn't sure whether to offer condolences or the number of a dating service.

Audrey scribbled a note on a steno pad, crossing the t's with vigor. "Like I was saying, the market is ready to recognize that Christian people can be hip too. The younger generation is not the placid, hymn singing fogies their parents were. They wear thong underwear and listen to rock music, just like their non-Christian counterparts."

I tried to picture Audrey in a thong. It caused distress to my synapses so I let it drop. "What exactly will I be responsible for?"

She flipped her bob of hair and slammed back the remainder of the water. "That's it, a to-the- point gal. That's what we need. A young person who isn't afraid to ask questions. You'll start as copy editor in the Leisure Life section. There's some blogging involved too. Alfie runs the department now but he's retiring. Prostate trouble."

"Oh, how sad."

"By the end of summer I want you on board and running things in that section. What do you think? Can you handle it?"

I tried not to leap out of the chair and do a happy dance. Six years of college and two degrees later and I was finally going to be an editor. I took a cleansing breath. Be professional, Simone. Professional. "Definitely."

"Excellent."

She whisked me down the hall to show me my office.

Okay, the gloomy space did look an awful lot like a room used for hanging meat or developing film, but it was mine. I felt around for a chair and put down my bag. "Thank you, Ms. Stanner. I really appreciate this opportunity."

Audrey was speaking into a cell phone. "Yes, I want to arrange a mud bath. Is that mud filtered everyday?" She covered the mouthpiece. "I'll send Donna in to get you started." Before she cleared the threshold she called to me. "By the way, you are a Christian, aren't you?"

***

Donna was also a twenty something with good skin. She had hair the color of apricots and all the subtlety of a buzz saw. I liked her immediately.

"Hey there. I'm Donna. Praise God we've got you on board. I'm developing a squint from doing all this extra work. Men think I'm winking at them." She flopped down on top of my purse, then extracted the flattened bag. "Oops, sorry about that. Hope I didn't squish anything."

I didn't mention my new pair of sunglasses which had probably been reduced to a fetching set of monocles. "I'm Simone, good to meet you. I heard Alfie is having health problems. Have you been helping him out?"

"Helping Alfie?" She snorted. "Alfie phones in from the golf course once in a while with directions. Other than that, I am Alfie."

"I thought he had a prostate problem."

Donna laughed, setting her freckles dancing. "He doesn't seem to think it's as much a problem as his doctors do. It gets him out of the weekly staff meetings though. I'm so glad to have another gal my age around here. Finally someone to hang out with. Do you like the theater? I've got an extra ticket to see My Fair Lady next week."

"That sounds perfect. Count me in."

"Good." She looked at my left hand. "Are you married?"

"Engaged. His name is Doug."

She grinned. "That's great. I'm still just cruising the singles scene but my boyfriend is really tops. Maybe we can double date or something. What does your fiancé do?"

"He's a chiropractor."

"Oh man. I could use a good back cracker after scrunching over the computer all day. I look like Quasimodo by quitting time. Does Doug like the Forty Niners?"

"With a passion."

"Excellent. Our men will get along famously."

A tiny beep sounded on Donna's watch. "Is it eleven-thirty already? I've got to go. We can chat some more this afternoon. Anyway, here's a computer you can use for the Bloggin' With Brandi deal. We've got a laptop around here somewhere for you to use."

"Who is Brandi?"

She blinked at me. "Didn't Audrey tell you? You are."

"I am?"

"Well, I have been for the past six months but I'm passing the keyboard to you. Congratulations. I never really got into the whole dual identity thing. I keep signing the thing Donna instead of Brandi. Anyway, just update the blog weekly, you can introduce a new topic then if you want. Have you blogged before?"

"Sure, but just with friends." The phrase sounded ridiculous once it passed my lips.

Donna smiled. "Then you're well qualified to do this. Basically, you're just an ear to listen and a spiritual guide when necessary. It's not usually anything too taxing. We average about two hundred hits a week but we're hoping to increase those numbers. Ask me or Audrey if you get anything you can't handle."

I wondered if I was qualified for the spiritual guide part. Fashion tips yes, counseling, not so much. I'd have to call up Aunt Stella if I ran into anything too sticky. She always seemed to have the right soul soothing verse right at her finger tips. Donna's last sentence sunk in. "Did you say Audrey gives people advice?"

"Actually, she's only chimed in once. She told someone to put on their big girl pants and deal with it. Come to think of it, maybe just ask me if you need help." She consulted her watch again. "I gotta go. I have a lunch date with a friend. Do you want to come? There's a place down the street with unbelievable falafels. I'll buy."

I looked around at the small space, cluttered with files and papers. Even in the gloom it was hard to miss the overflowing trashcan and the spilled container of paperclips on the desk. "No thanks. I really should get settled in here."

I was Simone Greevey, professional editor type person and soon to be chiropractor's wife.

It was time to get cracking.

***

Three months and six days later, my life was turned upside-down in Sunday school. Isn't that just the way things go? Who would think you could experience catastrophe in a church room filled with miniature chairs and dozens of safety scissors?

That particular Sunday I was in good spirits in spite of my teaching assignment. I'm not in tune with the natural vibrations of children, so I avoided Sunday school duty like people skirt mysterious fluids on a bathroom floor. But desperation is apparently visited on the clergy as well as civilian people and the pastor's wife pleaded with me until I agreed to one day of service in the preschool room.

She beamed at me, tucking a flyaway strand of hair back into her braid. "Don't worry about a thing. All you have to do is sing a song, read a story and serve snack. It will be an hour, tops. If worse comes to worse, get out the Play-doh. The kids are dolls; you'll love them to pieces."

Having seen some of the little darlings running around the church sanctuary, I was not confident in this assessment, but I figured they couldn't get too crazy in the space of sixty minutes. All I had to do was watch them play and try to slip in a little Biblical gem in between snack and story. No problem.

When the fateful day arrived, I showed up full of God's grace and a bucket of Play-doh under each arm. All seven children filed in and sat in a circle on the carpet. I had to admit, they did exude certain cuteness, especially the girl with the pink pinafore and the fancy hair dealie bobbers. My confidence swelled. Simone Greevey, preschool teacher extraordinaire.

"Hello boys and girls." I consulted my notes. "Today we are going to talk about David and Goliath. Does anyone know that story?"

Ralph Sarnecky, the boy with plump cheeks and a missing front tooth spoke up. "Oh yeah. Everyone knows that story. We heard it a zillion times. It's the one about David, this wimpy kid who kills this big ugly giant with a rock." He pantomimed smashing a skull with his fist.

"Yes, that's right." I read the script from my booklet. "David was a young boy who was called by God to do great things."

Jon Jon shouted, "Yeah, yeah. But what if he didn't use a rock? What if he used a light saber?" He leaped to his feet, wielding an imaginary weapon around the circle.

Two boys and a girl jumped up to join him. "Cool!" a curly haired kid shrieked. "I want a Lifesaver too."

"Not Lifesaver, light saber, dummy," Jon Jon said.

"Hold on there kids," I began. I was pretty sure the people in charge wouldn't condone the use of light sabers in church. My eyes landed on a helpful poster on the wall. "We should use our inside voices and gentle hands."

A tiny blonde girl stuck three fingers in her mouth and began to cry. I gave her a pat on the head. "It's okay. Don't cry, honey."

"I want my Mommy," she wailed in a range that made the windows vibrate.

Jon Jon whirled to slay another hapless classmate. One of his elbows caught me in the ribs. "Jon Jon, that's enough. Everyone sit on the carpet." I might as well have had a cone of silence on my head for all the good it did me. The class was attempting mutiny. If I didn't act quickly, I'd be tied up and forced to walk the plank.

"How about a song?" I scrabbled through the annals of my mind to come up with some sort of happy tune. Mac the Knife? No. The one about the ants and the rubber tree plant? I couldn't remember the words. Ah ha. Brainstorm.

"Just sit right back and you'll hear a tale, a tale of a fateful trip."

Their little mouths fell open.

"That started from this tropic port, aboard this tiny ship."

"I never heard that one before," Ralph said.

"I have," said pinafore girl. "It's about a shipwreck."

"Cool! A shipwreck!" Jon Jon shouted. He began to make loud storm noises and careen his ship from side to side.

"The mate was a mighty sailing man, the skipper brave and sure," I hollered.

Ralph jumped up and down. "I love ships. I'll be the pirate. Look out. I'm going to chop you with my sword."

I stopped singing. "Hold on. There were no pirates on Gilligan's island."

"What did they have there?" a chubby girl asked.

"Uh, well, coconuts, little grass huts and the odd visitor."

Jon Jon crashed his vessel into my chair. "Well if they had visitors, how come no one rescued 'em?"

"I, uh, I don't know."

They resumed their mayhem.

Kids crawled under the tables, seeking cover from Ralph's cannon fire. One kicked over a tower of blocks sending them flying. A bunch of girls began to tickle each other until there was a pile of giggling small people in front of my feet. Even pink pinafore girl joined in the brouhaha. She didn't look so angelic when she put her classmate in a headlock, yelling "arrggghh!" all the while.

"Boys and girls, let's sit on our bottoms and listen to the story. Look at this great picture of David." I thrust the book out for them to see.

They were under whelmed.

"I've got a wedgie," Jon Jon said, pulling at the seat of his pants.

"We'll you're going to have to take care of that yourself," I told him firmly.

The chaos continued.

After several useless verbal corrections I gave up. I announced in as loud a shout as I could manage, "Snack time!"

As if by magic, the children lay down their invisible weaponry and put away their tickly fingers. The pile of children untangled itself and stood up. Then the pirates materialized at the snack table and folded their hands. It was nothing short of a miracle.

"Heavenly Father..." I began until I noticed Jon Jon kick Eddie under the table. "Thanks for the snack, Amen."

"That was short." Eddie rubbed his shin.

"God appreciates brevity." I handed out the napkins.

"What's for snack?"

I held up the bag of fishy crackers.

"Goldfish again?" Ralph wrinkled his nose. "I'm sick of goldfish."

"Me too," Sarah, the sniffly girl, said. "They taste yucky. I want something else."

The scent of rebellion swirled in the air and made my stomach muscles tighten. I could see the plans forming for another pirate sortie. "What do you like for snack?"

There was a moment of silence while they considered the question. I eyeballed the cubbies in search of better grub.

Jon Jon screwed up his face in thought. "Twinkies and ice cream. And Skittles. That would be good."

There was a loud chorus of agreement.

The thought of these children hopped up on Skittles sent a shiver down my spine. "Goldfish crackers are the only thing I can find."

Seven pairs of eyes looked mournfully up at me from their tiny chairs. In desperation, I rummaged through my purse. The search yielded just enough to satisfy my charges. When they were all settled in with a handful of goldfish, one cherry Lifesaver and a minty breath strip apiece, I looked up to find Doug in the doorway.

"Doug." I hugged him like a dieting woman holds onto her last chocolate bar. "Thank goodness you're here. They're almost done with the Lifesavers. Do you know any good preschool songs? What about that one with the ant and the plant?" Doug used to play cello in his college days so I was hopeful he could come up with something. He was a sporadic church goer and definitely not a frequent visitor to the early service but I was too frazzled to wonder why he was there.

"Hey, Sisi." He ran a hand through his sandy hair and surveyed the munching children. "I never pictured you teaching Sunday school."

"Me neither." I consulted the wall clock. "But I've only got thirty minutes to go. So far there hasn't been any bloodshed so I'm doing great."

"I can see that." He took a deep breath. "Uh, Sisi...I wanted to come by and talk to you. I thought I'd catch you after the service."

"We're going to see each other this afternoon, remember?"

"I really can't make that appointment." He smiled, but there was a hint of hesitation on his thin face.

"I'm out of juice." Ralph waved his cup in the air. "Hello? Can I get a refill here?"

I poured him another Dixie cup full. "Doug," I said, handing my fiancé a bag of goldfish to distribute, "the wedding is in two months. We have to choose a disk jockey now or it will be too late. You don't want to wind up with your uncle's banjo band, do you? It was enough listening to them at your last family reunion." Doug had a tendency to try to wiggle out of wedding planning. I had to bribe him with Giants tickets to get him to commit to Raspberry Swirl for a wedding cake flavor.

"Yeah, I know. That's sort of what I need to talk to you about."

I practiced some relaxation breathing. "Can we talk about this after Sunday school is over?"

He poured more goldfish into Sarah's open palm. "I think I'd better tell you while I have the nerve. The problem is, I actually have this other thing going on."

I tried to smother my irritation. "Come on Doug. What other thing? What other thing is more important than our wedding?"

"Before I tell you, I just want to say I'll always love you, Simone."

I experienced a momentary flutter of concern. "What is it? Are you sick? Did you get bad news from the doctor or something?"

He paused for a long moment, twiddled with his glasses and scratched his eyebrow. "No, nothing like that. It's sort of ...another girl."

The room fell silent. Even the chewing stopped.

I felt my eyes grow to ping pong ball size. "What? What did you just say?"

Doug didn't answer. His mouth opened and closed but nothing came out. He crinkled the goldfish bag between his fingers.

Blood stampeded through my temples. I was sure I hadn't heard him properly. "For a minute there I thought you said something about another girl."

Jon Jon nodded soberly. "That's what he said all right."

"Here kids." My voice hissed out between clenched jaws. "Play with the Play-doh." I dumped the bucket and accompanying accoutrement on the table. Goldfish scattered everywhere. The kids made no move to touch the colorful clay.

"May I see you over here, Doug?" I grabbed his sleeve and pulled him to the farthest corner which was a mere three feet away. "This isn't a great time to joke around. Especially not in front of a bunch of kids. It's not funny."

"Sisi, I'm not joking." His eyes gleamed with moisture. "I don't want to hurt you, really I don't. I will always love and respect you, but I can't marry you. Not anymore. I'm doing us both a favor."

I waited for the part when he would make sense of his crazy utterance. No doubt he had just been to the dentist and his system was still offline due to the effects of Novocain. Or he had eaten too many doughnuts and the carbs had pickled his brain. "What do you mean you can't marry me?"

He spoke to his shoes. "I sort of met someone. She came to my office for an adjustment. She's a teacher for the hearing impaired and she loves backpacking, too." He looked up. "Isn't that great?"

Great was not the adjective I would have applied to the situation. Disbelief clouded my mind. The scene was right out of a bad movie. Doug had met someone else? That was just not possible. We were supposed to be choosing wedding music. "You met someone?" I echoed.

He smiled wistfully, blue eyes sparkling. "I tried to ignore the feelings for a long time, Sisi, I really did. I kept it strictly professional, but then I happened to notice on her chart it was her birthday so I took her out for lunch. Just a friendly lunch, but one thing kind of led to the next and now we're a couple. She's a lot like you Simone: funny, intelligent, good looking."

Lunch? Backpacking? Couple? All I needed was a pinch to snap out of this nightmare. With extreme effort, I kept my Sunday school smile plastered over my gritted teeth. "We have been busy planning a wedding, Doug. You know, matrimony? 'Til death do us part? Cake and presents? Does any of this ring a bell with you?"

"No, *you've* been busy planning a wedding. I hardly had anything to do with it. I should have said something earlier, but you were so into the whole thing, I didn't think you'd even hear me."

I felt as though he'd slapped me. "You sure as shootin' didn't pipe up with this information earlier. You could have mentioned another girl say, before we chose the cake or the lobster in puff pastry. I'm pretty sure I would have heard you then." My whisper edged closer to a bellow.

He looked at the floor again. "You're right. I meant to,

Sisi, but I didn't want to hurt you. Rachel insisted that I tell you before we hired a disk jockey."

Rachel, huh? Well wasn't she a thoughtful little maid?

"Thank you for being so considerate of my feelings, and don't call me Sisi anymore." I tried to reduce my volume a few octaves. It was pointless as the whole group of children hung on our every word. To my dismay, my voice faltered. "I thought we were soul mates. I was ready to share my life with you. I thought ...I thought God brought us together."

His mouth opened and then closed. "I don't know what to say except I'm really sorry."

The sight of his puppy dog expression made me furious. "How could you be such an..." I eyed my rapt pupils, "a-s-s..." I spelled.

"I know what that says!" Jon Jon shrieked with glee.

"A-s-s-t-e-r-o-i-d," I finished in a rush.

Jon Jon chewed a goldfish thoughtfully. "Why did you call him an asteroid, Miss Greevey? That only has one "s" anyway," he added, helpfully.

Just my luck to have a child prodigy in class. I clasped my hands together so tightly my nails dug into the palms.

Doug gave me a worried look. "What are you doing?"

I fixed venomous eyes on him. "I am praying that I don't kill you in front of these children." The words came out loud enough to be heard down the hall. I considered grabbing the Play-doh cutter and gutting him like a fish. It might take a while, but it would be satisfying.

"Are you gonna kill him?" Ralph squealed. "Cool! Just like David did to Goliath. Maybe we can find a rock." He began to search under the tables.

"Look, Sisi, I know that right now you think I'm a..." Doug looked furtively at the little snackers, "b-a-s..."

Jon Jon's eyes rolled upwards as he sounded out the letters. I pointed savagely at the boy.

"k-e-t-b-a-l-l," he covered, " but I think that ultimately this is the best thing for both of us."

"What did he spell?" Sarah whispered to Jon Jon.

"Basketball."

"Why does she think he's a basketball?" Sarah asked.

"Doug," I said, sweet as Splenda, "I think you're right. This has got to be the best thing that has happened to me because I have been saved from marrying the biggest asteroid I have ever met. I don't want to lay eyes on you, hear your name, see your car, run across your phone number or even smell that wretched excuse for cologne you wear ever again."

"Hey now." Doug frowned. "What's wrong with my cologne? Rachel says it's earthy."

"It smells like Pine Sol," I hissed.

I don't remember exactly how the Play-doh got into my hand, but the parents arrived to find their children sitting open-mouthed, watching the Sunday school teacher pelt her ex fiancé with purple clay. I believe I was shouting at the time, words which should probably not be uttered in a Sunday school classroom.

I do recall the phrase, "You are a first class basketball!" leaving my lips at a totally inappropriate volume.

Seven sets of parents hurriedly ushered their tots out the door. The pastor suggested that there was an opening in the coffee and doughnut ministry.

As Jon Jon passed by, he stopped. "Are you going to teach next week? That was the best time I ever had in Sunday school."

I gave him the last Lifesaver and walked out of the

church.

Read the rest here

Or you might enjoy Trouble Up Finny's Nose. Enjoy the first chapter.

Prologue

The view from up Finny's Nose was amazing, breathtaking even. According to the guidebooks, it offered an "uninterrupted panoramic of the majestic Pacific Ocean and its pristine coastline."

Frederick Finny admired the coastline for a different reason. While aiming for a secluded nook in which to unload his Canadian rum for the parched victims of Prohibition, he ran aground in the treacherous California riptide. The only hope of escape for his vessel was to empty hundreds of barrels of premium liquor into the ocean.

After every precious drop was dribbled into salty oblivion, the vessel remained stubbornly wedged. The ship was lost, but Finny old-timers elevated to legend the exploits of a gaggle of drunken crabs that wove their way to the beach and marched in dizzy circles for hours.

Finny slogged ashore and made the best of his misfortune, changing careers from rum smuggling to beekeeping, eventually settling at the top of the steep bluff that looked, for all the world, like a tremendous nose.

In the afternoon sun, through squinted eyes, the town of Finny was straight out of a postcard. The residents and buildings alike seemed to age gently into a condition just shy of shabby with enough quaintness sprinkled throughout to make the town a charming little stop for tourists looking for that perfect coastal escape. Not the overnight, weekend getaway, but more along the lines of a lazy morning stop on the way to the larger towns like Carmel and Monterey—places less shabby and more chic.

On this day, except for the peeling paint on the Finny

Hotel and the dead man propped on his head in the Central Park fountain, the town was definitely postcard material.

Alva Hernandez walked his entire route along the foggy main street before he finally stopped to chat with the upside-down man in the fountain. Eventually, he put down his remaining newspapers and whacked on one of the protruding muddy boots. Scratching his grizzled hair, Alva removed his teeth, inserted a lemon drop, and sat down to await further developments.

Chapter One

"Oh no!"

She slammed on the brakes and skidded to a stop inches from the squad car. "I get a parking ticket for an expired meter, and this guy can park his cruiser practically in the middle of. . ." Her words trailed off as she noticed the cowboy boot sticking out from under the open car door. "Ohhh. This is not good." Ignoring the pinging of the keys-in-the-ignition warning, she slid out of the car.

The cop was facedown in the gravel, one arm stretched toward the radio, which rested just out of his reach in the dust.

"Are you all right?"

Really smart question, Ben. *People commonly lie facedown on the road if they are fit and perky. Especially cops.* Trembling, she knelt down and patted his shoulder.

"Ummmm. . .sir? Officer? Can you hear me?" She patted some more. With shaking fingers she felt for a pulse under the prickly brown hair just below his throat, recoiling at the stickiness left on her fingertips.

"Ohhh boy. Calm down. Think what to do. Get your cell. . .no!" The phone sat on her kitchen table, recharging. "Think! People used to do charitable deeds before cell phones. Okay. Radio."

As she fumbled in the gravel for the receiver, a mustard-colored sedan pulled out of the copse of trees and began backing up. Stopping about fifteen yards from where she *crouched, three men got out.*

She felt her body go cold as she struggled to breathe. Frantically, she pounded the prone figure on the back. "Please wake up, Mr. Officer. I think this is what you would call a situation."

She squeezed the button on the radio. In a cracking sotto voce tone she quavered, "Help me, please! I am Benjamina Pena. I am with, er, a really big cop, and he's unconscious. There are three nasty-looking men on Old Highway One just past the breakwater. I think they're gonna kill us. Ten-four, uh, over and out, oh no!"

Praying her message had been received by someone— a truck driver, crop duster, anyone—she peeked over the top of the driver's side door. The three men had slowed to a stop a few cautious yards from the car, peering into the windshield and under the front license plate.

"Hey, lady. What you doin' to that cop? He ain't no business of yours."

Desperately, she fumbled with the fastener on his gun belt. "Yeah? Well, I don't reckon he's any business of yours, either." That sounded pretty close to the John Wayne movies she'd seen.

They laughed. One said, "She has a streak of somethin', eh? We goin' to have fun with you."

With a jerk, the catch finally gave way. She yanked the gun out and stood up so quickly it made her dizzy.

"Okay. Now you listen up, you troglodytes. Any one of you comes a step closer and I'll drop you right where you stand."

That brought them up short. After a second of shocked silence, they relaxed. "A trogla-what?" said the skinniest one.

The tallest one with the bandanna tied like a sausage casing around his head interrupted the laughter. "Well, well. Ain't she a tough girly. I guess we got ourselves here a Jane Wayne."

Their eyes widened as she released the safety on the semiautomatic.

Aiming at what she took to be their midsections, midway between the bandannas and underwear poking out of oversized pants, she croaked, "I don't know what your problem is with this cop, but I will shoot you if you take one more step."

Later she tried to recall if they had actually stepped or just realigned their slouching, but somehow she pulled the trigger. The recoil knocked her over, slamming her shoulders into the gravel.

Lying on her back, shoving the hair out of her eyes, she watched the thin man grab his ear and howl in pain. The others hoisted him by the pants and hauled him up the road to their car. They roared away in a shower of loose gravel.

Benjamina watched the dust settle.

She flopped back onto the gravel. "I can't believe I just did that."

Ruth rolled the papers into a tube, clutching them to her breast. "What is this?" she stammered. "What is going on here?" The story, this novel, whatever it was, had hit her blindside. Phillip was supposed to be writing memoirs or something, a collection of stories from the life of a country vet. What in the world was this thing?

She had discovered the small pile of papers in the file drawer, next to the information on her funeral plot. The bizarre surprise threw her completely off balance, compelling her to read and reread before tearing the file cabinet to pieces looking for more. By the time she returned to what was left of her senses, she had missed her morning hair appointment by an hour.

By now, Felice was boarding a plane to Fiji. Ruth felt like crying.

It was not just a matter of vanity. Ruth was not, nor ever

had been in her forty-seven years of living, a beautiful woman. Nevertheless, she refused to be wandering around town looking like Miss Havisham. When Phillip was alive, he made a point of taking her to lunch after her monthly salon appointments.

"You look like a million bucks," he would say. Her cheeks would warm every time.

Rescheduling with another hairdresser was simply out of the question. Ruth would die with numerous sins on her conscience, but committing infidelity to her long-time hairdresser was not one of them. She would just have to endure the three weeks until Felice returned.

The striking of the clock made her start. She felt guilty, as if she had been caught reading a teenager's diary. "Oh, for goodness' sake," she muttered. "It's not like he'll catch me reading it."

Phillip had been gone for almost two years, and she still expected to see him around every corner like the Ghost of Christmas Past.

She stuffed the papers back into the crammed file drawer and sat in the chair, listening to nothing. There was only a faint rustling from her flock of handicapped seagulls and terns outside and the ticking of the clock inside to break the silence. Ruth looked around the space she had lived in for twenty years and wondered why the furnishings seemed strange to her, as if she were an insect that had just flown through the window to reconnoiter. She folded her hands to pray. "Dear God," she began. After a minute more of silence, she gave voice to the thought that grieved her most. "Where are You?" There was no answer, only that endless tick.

She looked down to see what she had put on in the middle of the night when she mistook it for morning. Faded denim stretch pants and a ragged crocheted sweater the color of a rusty scouring pad. Now that it really was Monday morning, she felt as though she hadn't slept at all the night before. She sat as the silence squeezed in on her with the inexorable pressure of a glacier, until she couldn't stand it any longer. After a quick check of her backyard gaggle, she set off.

The cold morning air left her breathless as she crested the bridge of Finny's Nose. She figured it was an enterprising sweatshirt manufacturer who spread the rumor that California was one warm sandy beach from Canada to Mexico. Though the drive along the rugged coastal cliffs bordering Highway 1 provided spectacular views of secluded beaches, the sun had to wait until the fog evaporated to make an appearance. She had sold many a photo of this amazing scenery to travel magazines. It was quaint, poetic even, and colder than a well-digger's toes. All in all, it was the kind of sleepy little town that fine postcards are made of. The kind of place that, at one time, spoke to Ruth's soul. As she plodded along, her mind replayed scenes from her late husband's. . .novel.

Lost in her own thoughts, she murmured a hello to Alva Hernandez seated on the edge of the Central Park fountain and passed by. Then it hit her. A quick double take dispelled the notion that she was hallucinating. There was definitely a pair of ragged boots protruding from behind Alva's shoulder. A few moments of closer examination convinced her that she wouldn't need her rusty CPR skills.

"Alva. Are you. . .all right?" she asked.

"Yep," he said around a mouthful of yellow candy.

"Oh. Good." She fiddled with the zipper on her jacket. "You know there is a man in the fountain, don't you?"

"Sure do." He stuck a finger deep between check and gum to dislodge a sticky ball.

"Well, he—he doesn't seem to be all right," she proposed gently.

"Nope. Ain't moved a bit. Never seen anyone hold their breath that long."

Marveling at the sheer ludicrousness of the situation, she suggested to Alva that perhaps they should have a go at removing the upside-down man from the lazily bubbling water.

"Sure thing. I'll get the starboard side," Alva said cheerfully.

It was as if she were watching from outside herself as they each grabbed a handful of the slippery figure. The man was heavy and uncooperatively stiff. Fighting the bile rising in her throat, Ruth clasped the slick boots, and with Alva tugging vigorously on the man's overalls, the pair hauled the body onto the grass.

The dead face seemed surprised to be looking up into the two live ones. He was cold and slimy, like celery left too long in the vegetable crisper. Ruth leaned back on her heels, nauseous, and then noticed several people hastily making their way over to the damp trio. A few chilled tourists clapped their hands over their mouths in astonishment. The slippery dead man was definitely not part of their mental postcards.

"Ewwww," cried a woman in an *I Went up Finny's Nose* sweatshirt. "Is he really dead?"

"Yep," said Alva. "Pretty much."

By this time, Bubby Dean had emerged from the nearby High Water Pub and ducked his head back inside to call for help. The small crowd grew. Two middle-aged women stood with their hands fluttering over their mouths. A well-dressed man with a speckled bald head talked on a cell phone.

Ruth sat down on the edge of the fountain, suddenly overwhelmed by the outrageous events of the day. The novel. The man in the fountain. Felice in Fiji.

Alva patted her head and said gently, "It's okay, chickie. I got somethin' here for you." He fished around in his pocket and handed her a sucker. It looked as if it had been licked a few times and rewrapped.

The police arrived to find a huddle of tourists, a sticky old man asking bystanders for change, and a middle-aged Ruth Budge, laughing until the tears ran down her chin.

Read the rest here

Books by Dana Mentink

Trouble Up Finny's Nose (2008)
Fog Over Finny's Nose (2008)
Treasure Under Finny's Nose (2008)
California Capers (2008)
Killer Cargo (December 2008)
Flashover (January 2009)
Race to Rescue (September 2009)
Endless Night (January 2010)
Betrayal in the Badlands (October 2010)
Turbulence (February 2011)
Buried Truth (August 2011)
Escape the Badlands (upcoming)

* * * * *

About Dana Mentink

Dana Mentink lives in California where the weather is golden and the cheese is divine. She has published more than eight books with Harlequin's Steeple Hill imprint. Dana is an American Christian Fiction Writers Book of the Year finalist for romantic suspense and an award winner in the Pacific Northwest Writers Literary Contest. Her recent romantic suspense, *Betrayal in the Badlands*, is a Romantic Times Reviewer's Choice Nominee.

Dana loves to hear from her readers. Feel free to visit her website at www.danamentink.com or her Facebook Reader Page.

www.ingramcontent.com/pod-product-compliance
Lightning Source LLC
LaVergne TN
LVHW012053070526
838201LV00083B/4242